ELIZABETH WHITE
KATHLEEN FULLER
SUSAN M. WARREN

*Romance fiction from*
Tyndale House Publishers, Inc., Wheaton, Illinois
*www.heartquest.com*

Visit Tyndale's exciting Web site at www.tyndale.com

Check out the latest about HeartQuest Books at www.heartquest.com



Edited by Lorie Popp

Designed by Zandrah Maguigad

*Will and a Way* is published in association with the literary agency of Alive Communications, Inc., 7680 Goddard Street, Suite 200, Colorado Springs, CO 80920.



---

**Library of Congress Cataloging-in-Publication Data**

White, Elizabeth, date.
Chance encounters of the heart / Elizabeth White, Kathleen Fuller, Susan Warren.
p. cm.
ISBN 0-8423-3574-9
1. Christian fiction, American. 2. Love stories, American. I. Fuller, Kathleen. II. Warren, Susan. III. Title.
PS648.C43 W48 2002
813'.085083823—dc21 2002009702

---

Printed in the United States of America

08 07 06 05 04 03 02
9 8 7 6 5 4 3 2 1

## PRAISE FOR ELIZABETH WHITE'S BOOKS

"I couldn't put it down. It was a wonderful story, and I can't wait for your next book."

› **Debby Lowe, Alabama** ›

"Wonderful; the message of the redeeming love of the Lord was so true."

› **Julie Kingery, Illinois** ›

"I loved it! I will definitely recommend it. Keep up the good work!"

› **Pam Gentry, Indiana** ›

"I really enjoyed it. I hope you write more."

› **Shelley Williams, Pennsylvania** ›

*romance the way it's meant to be*

HeartQuest brings you romantic fiction
with a foundation of biblical truth.
Adventure, mystery, intrigue, and suspense
mingle in these heartwarming stories of
men and women of faith striving to build
a love that will last a lifetime.

May HeartQuest books sweep you
into the arms of God, who longs for you
and pursues you always.

# CONTENTS

*To Ryan*
*May you be persistent in pursuing and obeying God.*

*Many thanks to Kathryn Olson, Sheri Cobb South, and Flora Thompson, who read early versions of this story and provided valuable input. I'd also like to thank Austin and Pam White for hosting our trip to Boulder. You live in a magnificent state, and the airline strike wasn't your fault.*

# Will and a Way

ELIZABETH WHITE

# CHAPTER ONE

WILLIAM Barton Fletcher III stood to be fired, disinherited, and grounded all in one fell swoop if he didn't get a flight out of Denver by six this afternoon.

He stood in line at the check-in counter, alternately praying and sneezing because the kid in front of him had evidently bathed in Tommy Hilfiger cologne. Unheeded, Will's cell phone screeched the "Hungarian Rhapsody" from his shirt pocket. He didn't answer it because he knew exactly who was on the other end.

*Lord, assuming the airline industry is under your control, please help me out with a seat on this plane.* It was the only plane left that would get him to Dallas in time to hook up with the last flight of the day to Jackson, Mississippi. Will's presence was required in nearby Yazoo City, where he lived and worked, by tomorrow morning.

He sneezed again, wishing desperately for a tissue.

Granddad always carried a neatly pressed handkerchief in the inside pocket of his jacket. You wouldn't catch him surreptitiously wiping his nose on his sleeve.

"Bless you," said a soft, slightly husky, feminine voice behind him, mellow with lingering southern vowels. "Would you please answer that thing or turn it off? I really don't think I can take it anymore."

Will had to look down to find a very small person dressed in an ankle-length black skirt and a white knit top, with a red cardigan knotted about her shoulders. Plain and neat, except for a blinding mop of strawberry blonde hair and a pair of enormous tip-tilted brown eyes.

*Bless me indeed,* Will thought, bemused. Then the young woman's tea-colored eyes narrowed, and her full mouth went ajar as she took in his Snoopy as Joe Cool tie. It was a collector's item of which he was quite proud.

Or maybe she was looking at the source of the noise.

He fished the phone out of his pocket so that it played its tune even louder. "It's my dad," he said, as if she cared.

Her red-gold brows crinkled. To his astonishment, she took the phone out of his hand and hit the Talk button with her thumb. "Hi, Mr. Fletcher," she said. "Will can't come to the phone, but I'd be happy to take a message."

"Who is this?" Zoë heard in a drawl as thick as Mississippi Delta mud. "Where's William?"

"Oh, he's standing right here," she assured Will Fletcher's father. "I'm screening his calls."

Smiling up at Will's bewildered face, she could all but see his brain clicking as he tried to place her. She knew he wouldn't. Too many years gone by, too many changes.

*Miranda should see him now.*

Zoë herself might not have been sure it was him, except for the tie. He'd worn it one night when he picked Miranda up at their dorm for a frat dance. Zoë had peeked over the stair rail and watched her bubbly, curly-haired roommate leave on the arm of the only guy Zoë knew with the self- assurance to wear a cartoon-character tie to a formal dance.

"Who is this?" repeated William Fletcher Two. Zoë wondered what gene had flipped to give Will his sense of humor. "Young lady, would you please put my son on the phone?"

Will grinned, white teeth framed by his dark, neatly trimmed, imperial beard—new since college. He shook his head and opened his hand as if to say, *Knock yourself out.*

*I'm flirting,* Zoë realized in surprise. *My goodness, how times do change.* She looked around. The two of them were nowhere near the front of the line, which had moved six inches in the last ten minutes. She'd be fortunate to reach Dallas before tomorrow morning.

"This is Zoë," she said sweetly. "Will wants to know if it's important."

Silence hummed on the other end of the line. "Of course it's important," blustered William Fletcher. "Tell him—never mind, I'll call again in five minutes. He'd better not get on that plane without talking to me first."

An indignant click sounded in Zoë's ear. She flipped the mouthpiece shut and pursed her lips. *What now?*

"You know you just blew off the Sultan of Western Civilization," Will said. "I may not get my allowance for the next six months." He squinted one bright blue-gray eye. "Okay, where do I know you from?"

Zoë's heart bounced, but she put on a nonchalant smile. She should have kept her mouth shut. "It was—"

"Wait, don't tell me." He put up a hand. "Were you a cheerleader at USM?"

"No, but you're warm." A cheerleader? *Yeah, right.*

"Zoë. Zoë," he muttered. "So you did go to USM?"

He continued to stare into her eyes, until Zoë felt as if her soul had been unzipped. She wanted to close her eyes against the blazing warmth of his gaze but instead felt herself helplessly drawn in. *Oh my, no wonder Miranda . . .*

"I'd remember that hair." He reached up and fingered a lock near her ear.

Zoë stepped back, face hot.

Will snapped his fingers. "That's it—you've colored your hair."

"I've always been a redhead," she mumbled. "Never mind. I'm sorry I interfered with your call." She handed Will his phone and turned, hitching her purse onto her shoulder.

"Oh no you don't." Will moved to face her, stooping to her eye level. "The only Zoë I can think of from USM was Miranda Gonzales's—" he straightened abruptly—"roommate! It's Zoë Hancock!"

Zoë stood blushing under his baffled but smiling examination. Down over her now-trim figure, up again to the outrageous fire of her hair, which she had recently returned to its natural hue.

*Bless him for not saying, "You've lost weight."* Not major poundage, but at her petite height enough to dramatically change the shape of her face. *I've got cheekbones now,* she reassured herself every time she looked in a mirror.

Will's smile grew, but it was warm rather than wolfish. "Well, Zoë, what are you doing in Denver? Where are you off to? Have you seen Miranda lately?"

She started with the last question. "Not in a long time. I'm going to Jackson, which is where I live." Explaining about her job was too complicated for casual conversation with this all-but-stranger. "Hey, the line moved."

Will nudged his carry-on case backward with his heel. "You were going to be an English teacher, right?"

Zoë remembered sitting at a cafeteria table with Miranda and Will one Sunday morning before church. Miranda had been bleary-eyed and yawning, but Will was apparently one of those people who subsisted on a couple hours sleep and gallons of coffee. He'd quizzed her unmercifully that morning, evidently unaware that Zoë had been dying a thousand deaths.

"Yes, but I'm certified K–12. I'm a tutor."

Will's expressive dark brows lifted. "Public school?"

"No, I teach entertainers' children."

Will blinked. "Who'd'a thought?"

She changed the subject. "I heard Miranda married Tony Mullins."

"Yeah, the high school boyfriend won out. Mullins was square as an ice cube. What a waste."

Eyeing Will's wavy, stylishly shaggy hair, the rumpled denim shirt, and skewed tie studded with Cub Scout pins, Zoë had to grin.

"What about you?" asked Will. "Found Mr. Right yet?"

She shook her head. "Since the entertainment industry isn't exactly a bastion of marital fidelity, I pretty much keep to myself."

For some reason, Will looked skeptical. Zoë wanted to turn the question back on him, but the teenager standing behind Zoë reached around her to poke Will. "Hey, dude, the line's moving again."

*Just as well,* Zoë thought. What good would it do to catch up with a man she most likely would never lay eyes on again? Still, she had to admit she was curious. She knew he'd majored in communications, despite his parents' pressure to join the family law practice. Zoë couldn't imagine Will as a lawyer. Eight years ago he'd been more interested in girls and beer and music than academics.

On the other hand, Will's grandfather, the original William Barton Fletcher, was a United States senator from Mississippi. It occurred to her that Will would make a great politician too. Zoë listened as Will carried on a mostly incomprehensible conversation with the teenage boy. Apparently Will hadn't lost the ability to talk the paint off the walls.

Since Will was otherwise occupied, Zoë moved to the check-in counter and presented her ticket to the agent. "I'm flying standby. What are my chances?"

The harried woman swept a hand over the crowd of exhausted travelers clogging the waiting area. "Honey, you should have been here two hours ago."

"I know, but I couldn't find a rental car out of Boulder, and there was a mix-up with my hotel bill. . . ." The woman's eyes had glazed over. Zoë realized she was just going to have to wait. "Okay. But you'll call me if a seat becomes available?"

"You're on the list," the agent assured her. "We'll call you after everyone else boards."

"Thank you," Zoë said forlornly and stepped aside so Will could take her place.

Boarding pass in his briefcase, Will looked around for Zöe. The look on her face as she'd walked away from the check-in counter worried him.

During the short span of his thirty-one years, Will had barely been responsible for himself, much less anyone else, but it suddenly occurred to him that some practice in that field would be in order. The idea of Sir William of Yazoo looking out for his fellow Mississippian both appealed to his sense of humor and brought a certain swelling to his chest.

*Ah.* There she was, seated on the floor by the window, feet modestly tucked to the side so that her long skirt covered her legs. Predictably, she had a book in her hand.

As he stepped over piles of suitcases, stray children, and a carrier containing a hairy little creature that might or might not have been a dog, Will tried to guess what Zoë would be reading. As a teaching professional, she'd probably be working her way through the more obscure works of Tolstoy or Thomas Wolfe. Or improving her teaching skills with some deadly boring book on classroom discipline.

He crouched in front of her and bent sideways to read the title of Zoë's book. "*Hearts in Space*?"

Zoë looked up, obviously startled, her cheeks afire. "Will! I thought you were gone." She flipped the paperback shut.

"Where would I go?" He reached for the book. "What are you reading?"

"Just a novel." She moved it out of his reach.

"Come on; let's see," he coaxed. "I like to read too."

"It's science fiction," she said defensively, handing him the lurid purple-and-silver book.

"Have you read *Out of the Silent Planet*?" he asked, scanning the back-cover blurb.

"No." At her sheepish tone, he looked up. "I'm not a hard-core sci-fi fan. I like a romance thread."

Intrigued, he handed the book back and sat down on the floor beside her, folding his long legs to make himself comfortable. "So tell me what movie they're filming in Colorado."

"You must really be bored."

So she didn't willingly share private details. Which made Will more determined to get her to talk. "I'm interested."

She sighed. "I wasn't here for a movie. I'm interviewing for a new job."

"What, traveling and meeting famous rich people isn't exciting enough for you?"

"Will, I spend most of my days in a trailer with children who'd rather be with their parents or other kids. Some of the locations are so godforsaken that it's almost impossible to be active in a church. Rich and famous people have troubles just like everybody else, just more dramatic ones." Zoë bit her lip, looking rather appalled that she'd said so much. Then she blurted, "I'm sick of it."

There was a wealth of personal experience buried in that statement. Will decided it was his duty to exhume it. Before he could start, his phone went off again. He reluctantly pulled it out of his pocket. "Hi, Dad." At Zoë's uh-oh look, he winked.

"William, are you on the plane?"

"No, sir. Not yet. Everything's behind schedule."

"I need the tape of that Jeglenski deposition first thing in the morning."

"I know. If something happens I'll FedEx it to you."

"If *what* happens?" Will's father's voice took on ominous overtones. "William, you will not get sidetracked by mountain climbing or rock concerts or any other absurd distraction."

Will thought guiltily of his conversation with Roxanne Gonzales earlier that morning. He supposed technically the Galloway brothers could be considered a distraction.

Luckily his father continued before Will could

mention his first real clients. "Which reminds me," said the Sultan, "who is this Zoë who answered your phone?"

Will glanced at Zoë, who had politely looked away. "You haven't met her," he said. *But I hope you will.* The thought crackled like static into the generally uncomplicated airwaves of Will's brain. He hadn't brought anyone home since Miranda.

Or maybe the static was the agent's voice over the loudspeaker. "Any passenger willing to give up his ticket will receive a two-hundred-dollar airfare voucher. If you wish to take advantage of this offer, please report to the counter immediately."

Will heard his father in his ear again. "Sassy little thing." William II snorted. "Behave yourself, Willy, and get home with that deposition tape tomorrow or you'll be clerking for the DA again."

"Okay, Dad. I'll talk to you when I get to Jackson." Will palmed the phone, looking at Zoë and weighing the consequences.

"Are you really a lawyer?" She looked skeptical.

"Uh-huh," he said absently. Getting demoted might just be the best thing that ever happened to him. Besides, Granddad said chivalry always paid off in the long run. "Watch my stuff. I'll be right back."

Knowing he was committing yet another in a long line of what his mother called "Will-isms," he ignored Zoë's questioning look and headed for the agent's counter.

The woman glanced at him in surprise. "Can I help you?"

"Yes, ma'am. I want to give up my ticket. Can I pick who I want to give it to?"

"No." She gave him an amused look. "What difference does it make to you?"

"See that pretty redhead over there by the window?"

He waved at Zoë, who responded with a confused smile. "I want her to have my ticket."

The agent smiled and shook her head. "Would it make you feel better to know that the next person on the list is a woman whose grandchild is undergoing surgery in the morning?"

Will's heart sank. He was going to have to be chivalrous with no immediate reward in sight.

"Sure," he sighed. "That makes everything just peachy."

"You gave up your seat?" Zoë could tell by Will's expression that there was something odd going on. "I thought you had to deliver a deposition."

"How did you know?" Will's dark brows lifted.

"Your father has a rather—" she searched for a euphemism and found none—"stentorian voice."

"Ideal for carrying across courtrooms and cell phones. Come on, let's go scope out our options for breakin' out of this joint."

"Will, that was the last flight for today. We're here for the night." Judging by the number of travelers stranded at the gate, they might be here for another day or two.

Will slung an arm around Zoë's shoulders. "Chin up, doll," he said in an exaggerated Humphrey Bogart voice. "Stick with me and I'll fly ya to Rio."

"I'd rather go home," Zoë said, but allowed herself to be towed toward the ticket counter.

# CHAPTER TWO

"ARE you sure the fastest way to Mississippi is through California?" Zoë resisted the urge to reread the ticket she'd just stuffed into her purse. It most definitely said "Denver to San Jose."

She and Will stood in line at the food-court cash register, where Will had ordered Chinese rice and vegetables smothered in a brownish green sauce that made Zoë nauseous just looking at it. Juggling her purse, suitcase, grilled-chicken sandwich, fries, and diet Coke, she followed him to the center of the noisy, crowded room. There wasn't an empty table in sight.

Will gave her the self-assured look she was beginning to recognize as dangerous. "The ticket agent said the direct flights to Dallas tomorrow are loaded to the gills. Overbooked, in fact. The best way to get there is to fly to a less crowded airport tonight and leave from there first thing in the morning."

"Yeah, but California? Couldn't we have just gone through Colorado Springs?"

"You're really going to make me do it, aren't you?" Will said severely.

"Do what?"

"Sing 'Do You Know the Way to San Jose.' "

"A fate worse than death." She wrinkled her nose at him. "Never mind; just find us a place to sit down."

Will thickened his drawl to the consistency of Mrs. Buttersworth's syrup and talked two silver-haired matrons into sharing one corner of their table. Zoë found herself squished between a trash container and Will's solid left shoulder.

Will looked entirely too pleased with himself. "Serendipity's a wonderful thing, isn't it?" He stole one of Zoë's fries. "I mean, what are the odds of us running into one another again after all these years?"

"Pretty good, apparently." Zoë looked around for some salt. "What astonishes me is that the Wild Man actually went all the way through law school without setting it on fire."

Will shook his head. "There are people who still call me that."

"Hard to believe," Zoë murmured. "So tell me how it happened."

He grinned, enthusiastically stirring the stuff on his plate. "Eh, my friend, 'tis a long and remarkable tale of rebellion, retribution, and ultimate restoration."

Among other things, Will had a fine talent for rolling his *R*s.

Zoë checked her watch. "Well, since we'll be here for at least another three hours, a long and remarkable tale sounds like just what we need."

"Okay, you asked for it. I suppose it starts with Dear

Old Dad." Will grimaced. "My father must've inherited every legalistic gene on the family tree. Remember the old Beatles song?" He brought a plastic fork to his mouth for a microphone and crooned, " 'You say yes, I say no, you say stop, and I say go, go, go.' "

Zoë laughed. What was he going to do next? "I can tell your dad's the no-nonsense, my-way-or-the-highway type."

"You nailed it." Will shrugged. "Soon as I got to college I picked the highway. It's a wonder I didn't drown myself in beer. Remember when Miranda nearly killed herself on that window ledge? I was there."

Zoë nodded and briefly closed her eyes. That had been one of the most horrifying nights of her life.

Will's expression was sober now. "Shook me up a little, but not enough to change anything."

"Thankfully, it changed Miranda." She tipped her head. "I noticed you disappeared after that."

"Yeah." Will didn't look proud of himself. "Eventually I got kicked off the cheerleader squad." Will had been the school mascot, the Golden Eagle. "I was convinced I was immortal. Quit school and went on the road with some fraternity buddies. I was going to be the next Phil Collins."

Zoë tried to picture Will rocking out behind a drum set. "What band?"

"Southern Pie. The best-kept secret on the local festival tour." He chuckled. "We all nearly starved to death before I went crawling home to ask for forgiveness and tuition."

Zoë wistfully thought of her father, whom she barely knew. "I bet your dad was standing in the road waiting for you."

"Yep. With lecture prepared and law school application in hand after I finished college."

Zoë heard the slight edge underneath Will's humor.

Her own experience gave her some understanding of his resentment. Will had run away, but at least he had returned broken. And it impressed her that Will had no reservations about sharing past stumbles in his life.

*Lord Jesus, he's looking at me like I've never been looked at before.* His eyes were the color of a clear winter sky. It was both exciting and unnerving to realize that Will was bound to expect reciprocal confidences. They would be seated side by side during the flight to San Jose and then the remainder of the night in the airport.

*Why me, Lord?*

Ultimately, it didn't matter. Tomorrow they'd go separate ways, and she'd most likely never see him again. But she was, she had to admit, a sucker for a good story.

"So did you actually like law school?"

"Well—" Will scratched his nose—"it wouldn't have been my first choice, but I could kind of see myself putting on a show in a courtroom, so I went along with it."

"Okay, we've covered the rebellion and retribution. What about restoration?"

"What a memory for alliteration," Will said with obvious admiration. "This is where it gets good." He stopped and gave her another one of those penetrating looks. "You used to be a Jesus Freak. Still?"

"Well, I . . ." Challenged, Zoë lifted her chin. "I certainly am."

"I thought so," Will said, considerably warming Zoë's heart. "In that case, you'll understand. God was in charge of my life, though I sure didn't know it at the time. Law school turned every belief I'd ever had inside out. Even with the discipline that was required for classes, I was still wild on the inside."

He waved his fork, obviously unable to talk without his hands. "But I met a professor who lived an example of godliness that nobody could shake, rattle, or roll. And believe me, there were a bunch of us who tried." Will smiled. "During my last term, I wound up on my knees in Dr. Williams's office, giving my heart to Jesus. Best day of my life."

Zoë swallowed a lump in her throat. "Thanks for telling me that."

*He's a believer, Lord.* It explained the clarity in Will's gaze, the steadiness beneath the almost palpable energy that still surrounded him.

*I wish we weren't going separate ways tomorrow.* The thought popped into her head before she could swat it away.

"Hey, look at the time," she said, checking her watch again. "We'd better get to the security-check line. We don't want to miss that plane to California!"

Will led the way to their seats on the plane to San Jose. Neither he nor Zoë had had to check any luggage, for which Will was profoundly grateful. Dealing with a luggage mishap would have added insult to injury.

Their seats were halfway back on the left side of the small jet. Will hefted his case into the overhead bin and reached back to help Zoë, who straggled several steps behind him. In the artificial cabin light, her skin looked almost translucent, her brown eyes dark with weariness.

He wished he could send her home on a magic carpet, but the best he could do was stow her suitcase for her and ask, "Would you rather have the aisle or the window?"

In spite of her fatigue, her mouth tipped in a tired smile. "Window, please. For some reason it makes me feel safer."

That was a pleasant surprise. Will liked to be able to stretch his long legs into the aisle. He let Zoë get settled, then plopped down beside her and turned off both reading lights. He hailed a flight attendant. "Could we have a blanket and a couple of pillows?"

Zoë huddled under the blanket Will handed her. The plane began to taxi and the overhead cabin lights went off, leaving Will and Zoë in a dark, comfortable little cocoon of privacy. Will tucked the blanket behind Zoë's shoulder, and she closed her eyes and laid her head back against the seat.

As his eyes adjusted to the dark, Will could make out the soft, rounded lines of her chin and jaw. A peculiar ache of tenderness burgeoned inside his chest. *Lord, this is proceeding a lot faster than I'd anticipated.*

"Zoë," he said softly.

"Hmm?"

"Are you asleep?"

"Not yet." She sounded drowsy but amused. "Are you?"

"I guess not. You never told me what kind of job you were interviewing for."

"Another teaching job. A boarding school in the Rockies. The position opened when a teacher quit unexpectedly."

"Bet you have good references," Will fished.

"Will—" there was definitely a smile in Zoë's voice—"I'm not telling you who I worked for. I just don't do that."

"Restraint is an admirable quality," Will conceded, "if a rather irritating one."

Zoë laughed. "I can tell you this, though. I'm positive the Lord is leading me away from the show-business industry."

"Why?"

"Let's just say I've been disillusioned."

"Disillusioned how?" Will strained to see Zoë's expression in the dim light.

She hesitated. "It's just that I want my life to count for something. Something specifically for the Lord." Her words came in a rush. "People around me think I'm a freak because I don't sleep with every handsome man who asks. Because I read my Bible and go to church whenever I can. And I'm labeled *intolerant.*"

"Zoë, you've got to hang in there," Will said, eager to encourage. "People in the entertainment industry need Jesus; they need us to point them to him. In fact, that's why I'm in the process of changing careers myself."

"Changing careers? But you made it sound like the best thing that ever happened to you was going back to your family and finishing law school."

"It was. It was the Lord's way of yanking me back onto the path. But I can understand your discouragement. You know what I spend most of my time doing?"

"Well, no . . ."

"Sneezing my head off in a dusty law library while I research some obscure case that might or might not apply to whatever suit my dad or some other grossly overpaid attorney is arbitrating. Or flying to Turkey Foot Fork, Arkansas, to depose some scumbag who witnessed some other scumbag siphon funds off a third scumbag's company. Or—"

"I get the picture," Zoë said. "Not exactly the glamorous lifestyle portrayed on *The Practice.*"

"Hardly."

"Okay, Counselor, tell me about your new and improved career path."

"I'm going to start a Christian entertainment agency."

"An entertainment agency," Zoë repeated carefully. "Oh, Will." *Lord, I finally meet a Christian guy who's not married or boring or eighty years old. Now I find out he's after the whole fame-and-fortune thing.*

Her expression must have revealed her disappointment, but he misinterpreted it. "What's the matter? Don't you think I can do it?"

"It's not that at all. I'm just wondering why you'd leave a stable, respectable job—even if it might be a tad boring—to go into a profession where success demands a whole lot of unsavory characteristics."

"Such as?"

"Well, like flattering insecure artists. Pushing said artists on companies who'll only use them as long as they're making big bucks. Holding out hope of fame and money to people who probably ought to be pursuing a normal nine-to-five job."

Will whistled through his teeth. "I'm sensing some personal animosity here. You want to go into a little more detail?"

She could steer the conversation any way she chose at this point. Give a vague, generic reply. Turn the question into a joke. Tell Will Fletcher to mind his own business. After all, Zoë never talked about her past, any more than she discussed the entertainers she'd worked for. *Everybody* had something hurtful that helped shape who they were, and she'd gotten past dwelling on hers, letting it control her.

But there was something genuinely compassionate in the way he'd turned to her, with warmth in his voice. It was balm to a sore heart spot that until now she hadn't even known was there.

Zoë took a deep breath. "Okay, I'll try. I grew up in Nashville. I've seen the music industry from the inside, and the reality is no prettier than your description of law practice." She paused but could tell that Will wasn't satisfied. "Both my parents were musicians. They never married, and I lived with my mother. Nashville was sort of a home base in between tramping around the South in an old Winnebago camper."

"Unbelievable."

"Yeah." Zoë grimaced. "Picture me playing with my dolls behind the bar in a honky-tonk while my mom is wailing on some little two-by-four stage."

"How in the world did you graduate from high school?"

"Part of the time she'd leave me with my grandmother. I read a lot. Took my math book and worked problems on my own. When I got old enough for high school, my grandma insisted I stay with her permanently. That was fine with me. By that time Reeda June was fed up with my, quote, 'preaching' at her."

"So your grandma—"

"Led me to the Lord. Kept me from going insane."

Will blew out a breath. "I can't believe you waded right into teaching showbiz kids. Seems like you'd go for a more normal school."

Zoë laid her head back against the seat, considering her words. It had never before seemed necessary to explain all this to anyone, outside her journal and one youth pastor who had helped her through the worst of it. "Will, the Lord had brought me so far, and it seemed that some good ought to come out of all that weirdness. Too, it was like opening up a closet where bad things had been before—just to make sure they're truly all gone."

Only it hadn't exactly worked that way. Her life had

gotten more confused and hectic. Now she looked forward to getting out.

She could feel Will's attention, strong and openly curious. "Okay," he said after a moment, "but I'm still not sure what that's got to do with my wanting to do entertainment law."

"There's more." This was so humiliating, but she was going to tell him anyway. "After my father left us, Reeda June—"

"That's your mother, right?"

"Yes. Anyway, she used to hang around the edges of backstage parties, sort of like a groupie. But she really wanted to be a singer. She would've done anything to . . . well, you can imagine. Long story short, this agent scammed her, promising the moon, and left us high and dry. If Grandma hadn't bailed us out—" Zoë shuddered. "Listen, I know I'm not going to convince you to change your mind about what you want to do. I just hope you'll pray about it very carefully before you jump into something you don't know anything about."

"Zoë, I can't argue with your experience. But remember I did dance around the edges of musical success for nearly a year. I'm going in with my eyes open. And you're smart enough to know that all agents aren't con artists."

"I suppose," she said, unconvinced. "I'm pretty tired. Why don't we try to sleep while the plane's in the air?"

She wasn't up to arguing anymore, and she probably ought to mind her own business. *Lord, I don't have any right to lecture Will. But I pray you'll give him direction in his choices. I care what happens to him.*

From beneath her lashes, Zoë watched Will turn on his reading light and pull a thin, black leather Bible from his briefcase. She couldn't see what passage he was reading, but she noticed the Bible had been banged around, written on, the pages creased. Will slid down in his seat, shoving his long legs out into the aisle.

Zoë frankly didn't know what to do with Will Fletcher.

So she pretended to sleep.

# CHAPTER THREE

"ZOË, the plane's landing." Will gently shook her shoulder.

"What?" She pushed her hair behind her ear and rubbed her eyes, smearing mascara everywhere.

"We're in San Jose," he told her. "See the lights?"

"Oh yeah. San Jose." She gave him an unfocused look, then turned her head to peer past the wing of the plane.

"Wish you could see it in the daytime. It's a really pretty city."

"I bet." She yawned. "What time is it?"

Will grinned. "My body clock is pretty messed up, but I think it's eleven o'clock California time."

"You're kidding." She flopped back against the seat and closed her eyes. "Wake me up when we're on the ground."

"Okay." While Zoë had been sleeping, Will was thinking and praying about their earlier conversation. He couldn't help wondering what else was in her "closetful of bad things." He felt her move restlessly now and took it as an invitation to talk. "What were you dreaming about?"

The cabin lights flickered on, and Will could see the spasm of embarrassment that crossed Zoë's face. "Was I talking in my sleep?"

He nodded. "Who's leaving you?" he asked gently.

She began to fold the blanket. "I guess I was dreaming about the last time I saw my father."

"When was that?"

"Oh, a long time ago. I think I was seven or eight." Zoë pulled out a small mirror and grimaced. "Yuck! I look like a raccoon!" She began to repair the damaged makeup.

"I bet you remember exactly where you were," he said and watched her bite her lip. *Okay, God, I'm being nosy, but it's for a good cause.* He touched her hand. "Zoë—"

She sighed, but to his relief didn't pull away. "I was up in a tree, playing with my dolls. I wanted to say good-bye, but he never looked up."

Will watched her purse her mouth and use the tip of her pinkie to smear on some clear, sparkly lip gloss. "Why didn't he come back when you called him?"

"He didn't hear me." Zoë put away the fragrant little pot of lip gloss and faced Will. Her eyes were sad but dry. "I was screaming on the inside, but nothing came out. My father was so stoned he just left us and never came back."

On top of everything else, her father had been a stoner, and she'd grown up without him. Will somehow knew that Zoë had just told him something nobody else knew. It made him feel privileged and thrilled and a little frightened. He silently held her gaze for a moment. "So that's why you wanted to be the kind of teacher you are? To be a piece of security for some of them?"

"Maybe. But as it turned out, I'm the one who has to keep saying good-bye." She hugged her purse to her chest. "Shouldn't we be on the ground?"

As if in response to her question, the plane began a rapid descent, the city lights smeared into a maze of runways, and the landing gear hit the tarmac.

Though he realized he was headed places with Zoë that he'd never intended to go when he'd given up his ticket home, Will told himself he wouldn't pass up the chance to get to know her better. *Thanks, Lord,* he prayed. *I won't be looking back either.*

Zoë stumbled through the jetway several steps behind Will. She barely managed to keep his broad shoulders in sight because he'd taken off like a six-year-old en route to Toys "R" Us. Then she wondered why she was chasing after him with such determination. After all, she was a big girl. She could make it on her own.

She slowed down. Someone banged into her from behind, muttered, "Sorry," and moved past. She stood, letting the flow of deplaning passengers rush by on either side.

*Lord, I'm so tired. I'm in San Jose, California, in the middle of the night, and I have to go home to start another teaching contract. When do I get to settle down?*

She hefted her purse, got a better grip on her suitcase, and trudged on.

Will waited for her inside the gate, frowning. He fell into step beside her. "You okay?"

"Just feeling a little wilted." She looked up at him.

"Thank you, but you don't have to baby-sit. I can get home on my own."

His animated face lit in a smile. "By clicking your ruby slippers together?"

She rolled her eyes. "Not unless you're Glinda the Good. What are we going to do with ourselves until six in the morning?"

"Are you hungry?"

"No, mostly just tired. I know we just spent two hours sitting down, but my knees are about to buckle."

"Okay, then we find a place to curl up until morning."

Will approached an airline agent clearing her computer for the night, spent a few minutes in lively conversation, then returned carrying a couple of blankets and pillows. "She said we'll have to spend the night in the lobby. They're closing down all the gates until the first morning flights."

The lights above them were already going out, so they made their way down a few connecting concourses lined with closed-down snack bars, gift shops, and bookstores. Zoë was embarrassed to hear her stomach rumble, giving the lie to her earlier claim.

Will grinned at her. "Tic Tac?" He stuck his hand in his pants pocket and pulled out a rattling little box of mints.

"Thanks," she said. "You won't vote me off the island, will you?"

Will and Zoë stepped onto a steep escalator that brought them to the airport lobby. Spacious and brightly lit, it was tiled in beautiful shades of adobe brown, turquoise, and rust. And it had the temperature of a meat locker. Zoë suddenly longed for earmuffs and a fur-lined parka.

She assessed the situation. The lobby was deserted except for a few stragglers like Will and herself. Borrowed pillow and blanket tucked under one arm, Zoë lugged her case toward an unoccupied bench next to a middle-aged couple. They would be quieter than the preteens in the corner, who were squabbling over a video game while their parents slept.

Zoë looked down at the bench that was to be her bed for the rest of the night. Somehow its polished black surface mocked her, bouncing back a warped reflection with wild hair sticking out in every direction, a caricature of a halo. Shivering, she shoved her gear under the bench and lay down. Since her feet stuck out from under the blanket, she decided to leave her shoes on.

Thirty seconds later she sat up straight.

"What's the matter?" Will, who had commandeered the neighboring bench, paused in the act of opening his briefcase. The knot of his tie was askew, his sleeves rolled up to the elbow. His beard looked smudged because of new growth at his jawline, and he'd left his loafers where they dropped. He had a hole in the heel of one black-and-blue-checked sock.

Zoë noticed all these details because—well, she didn't know exactly why she noticed. How could he be so bright-eyed and alert in the middle of the night, after a day like today?

"I know I've got worrying down to a fine art," she said, "but if I go to sleep, somebody might steal my stuff."

Will glanced around, and Zoë followed his gaze. The older couple were sound asleep and the family of four had curled up in their corner like puppies in a cardboard box. Even the video game was silent.

"I don't think anybody will bother it." A twinkle in his blue eyes, Will rubbed his jaw. "But if it'll make you feel better, I'll watch it while you sleep."

"Are you sure?"

"I'm not tired," he assured her. "I'll wake you up if I get sleepy, and you can have a turn at sentry duty."

"You're laughing at me."

He opened his eyes wide and innocent. "Serious as a heart attack. Scout's honor." He raised two fingers in a peace sign. "I'll work on my deposition. Make both you and my dad happy."

"Well, all right." She lay back down and scrunched her eyes shut to block out the fluorescent lights, then tipped her head back and said, "Thank you."

"You're welcome. Sweet dreams, Dorothy."

Zoë woke up from a dream that a *Star Wars* X-Wing was zooming toward her at warp speed. It was going to blow her all the way to the planet Dagobah.

"Look out!" she exclaimed, covering her head with her arms. She rolled sideways to get out of the way . . . and landed with a thump on the tiled floor, tangled in the airline blanket. A pair of legs clad in navy blue uniform pants, pushing a floor waxer trailed by an enormous red extension cord, crossed her line of vision.

"Zoë! Are you okay?" Will was bending over her, hands on his knees.

She blinked at his upside-down face. He looked tired, handsome, and solicitous, not necessarily in that order.

"I'm fine. I was just dreaming again." Humiliated, she took his extended hand and let him help her up. "Nobody could sleep through that racket."

Will followed her gaze toward the monster floor waxer. "He's been here for thirty minutes. This'll sure be one shiny floor. Take off your shoes and let's try it out."

Zoë giggled, despite a terminal case of sleep deprivation and an ache in the shoulder that had hit the floor. She pictured herself and Will skating in stocking feet across those miles of tile. "I admit it's as cold as an ice rink in here, but I think I'll pass." She sat down, tugging the blanket around her shoulders. "It's your turn for a nap."

"I'd rather talk," he said, parking himself beside her. He leaned back against the stucco wall and made himself comfortable with his hands clasped across his flat stomach. He looked at Zoë expectantly.

She pulled the blanket up to her chin. "I'm too cold." She let her teeth chatter.

"Well, here." Will got up to retrieve his blanket and tucked it around Zoë's legs. He crouched in front of her, smiling. "How's that?"

"Much better." Unwillingly charmed by his gallantry, Zoë relented. "Okay, Willy, if you're good you can stay up five more minutes."

He sat down again and put his arm around her, tucking her against his side. "For your generosity I'll keep you warm. What were you dreaming about this time?"

"Guess it was that book I was reading. Something about spaceships and laser beams."

"Ah. And romance, I'll bet."

"Not that I remember." Will was as good as an electric blanket. She relaxed, growing drowsy as she thawed out. She felt her natural reserve melt too. "Why don't you tell me how you're going to set up this agency of yours. Are you still hanging around with musicians?"

"I have a lot of contacts in the industry, yes. My partner's been running a studio out of his garage. He's found a couple of possible clients from the Gulf Coast and the Florida Panhandle areas. We're going to start with some kids who—hey, you might know them. They're Miranda Gonzales's cousins."

"Really?" Zoë wasn't terribly curious but enjoyed the animation in Will's eyes.

"Yeah. Did you ever meet Luke, Benj, and Jesse Galloway?"

Zoë tried to remember. "I think I met them once when I went home with Miranda for a weekend, and we ended up baby-sitting. If they're the ones you're talking about, they were only little boys. The oldest was only about eight at the time."

"Which makes them sixteen, fourteen, and eleven now. Very talented kids."

"What are you planning to do with them?"

"Do with them?" He laughed. "You make it sound like child abuse. They're already playing concerts all over south Mississippi, Mobile County, and the Pensacola area. If they hook up with the right record label, they could potentially hit the top of the Christian charts. They just need a little help with venues and contracts." He smiled, looking pleased with himself. "And a demo recording, of course."

She stared at him, twisting the ring on her thumb. This was worse than she'd feared. How could she object without saying more than was safe? "Do you know how much studio time costs?" It sounded lame even to her own ears.

Will's smile faded in a confused frown. "Of course I do. I told you, my partner—Zoë, what's the matter?"

She shrugged and looked away. "It just—it seems like they should be happy just singing in church."

Will was silent for such a long time that Zoë finally sneaked a glance at his face. He was running a finger across his mustache, his gaze unfocused. Maybe she'd hurt his feelings.

*I shouldn't have interfered,* Zoë thought. *Lord, please forgive me and help me mind my own business. . . .*

◎

It was true that Will spent half his time in airports and law libraries, but he'd been in enough courtrooms to know evasion when he saw it. And fear.

He suddenly yanked his grandfather's antique pocket watch out of his pants pocket and dangled it by its chain in front of Zoë's nose. "You are getting sleep-eee," he intoned. "Very, very sleepy."

"Huh?" Zoë's brown eyes crossed.

"I figure if I hypnotize you," Will said, "I can get you to explain what it is about me that makes you so uncomfortable." He pocketed the watch.

He supposed he ought to be running for his life. But contrary to all the rules of common sense, he only wanted to draw closer to Zoë Hancock.

"It's not you personally," she said. "And I'm not uncomfortable." She flicked a glance at him from under those extravagant eyelashes. "Well, maybe a little." Her cheeks were rosy. "You're just so . . . so . . ."

"Persistent?" Will supplied. "That's what my mother says."

Zoë smiled faintly. "Yeah, persistent."

"I think it's a genetic trait," Will said, unperturbed. "So what makes you uncomfortable?"

She looked at him, chin raised. "Well, okay. You had this hunky-dory perfect childhood, and I don't think you understand the dangers of putting children into the public arena of show business."

With an argument to conduct, Will was in his element. "All right, for the moment we'll put aside the issue of my childhood—which you know nothing about—and my method of dealing with minor performers, and we'll talk about what *you* know about kids in show business."

She ducked, giving him a view of the crown of her head. Her hair smelled like strawberries. "It's such a rootless way to live," she said. "I don't recommend life in a Winnebago."

"Well, sure, traveling is part of the deal. It's not for everybody. But young as they are, these boys have a strong walk with the Lord. They're ready to branch out, both musically and spiritually, and they're close to one another." Will peered at Zoë. "I think part of what colors your opinion is the fact that you were a very lonely, shy little girl."

She shifted her gaze away. "This isn't about me."

"Not precisely, but you can't help thinking about it, I'm sure. There are some kids who thrive on adventure. I'm guessing you didn't."

She gave him a wry smile. "The ultimate chicken."

"The perfect lady," Will said. "And I, on the other hand, was the Terror of Yazoo County." He pounded his chest. "Will Fletcher knows no fear. Laughs at danger. Thumbs his nose at caution—"

"In short, you drove your mother crazy." Zoë was laughing now.

"On the contrary, she was one of the few people in the world who believed I'd ever turn into a productive citizen." Perfectly happy to steer the conversation out of dangerous waters, Will grinned. "Even after I dove off a bluff into about three feet of shallow water."

Zoë gasped. "Will! You could've broken your neck!"

"No joke." Will lifted a hank of dark hair off his forehead. "Souvenir."

Zoë examined the two-inch scar that had meandered down his forehead from his hairline since he was fourteen years old. "It's a mercy you lived to tell about it. What were you thinking?"

"Ah, now there's a question I've heard a time or two." Wincing, Will rubbed the scar. "I read somewhere that adolescent boys' frontal lobes don't connect until the age of eighteen or so. Have you ever been to Yazoo City?"

"I've never had the pleasure."

"Well, aside from its distinction as the fertilizer capital of the world, there's not much going on there. You sort of have to make your own entertainment."

"Oh, boy, I feel a story coming on."

Will, the scion of a long line of master storytellers, didn't deny it. "Are you sure you're interested?"

Zoë's eyes sparkled. "It's not like we have anything else to do."

*Except sleep.* But Will wasn't about to pass up the chance to enjoy the company of the sweetest girl he'd come across in years. "Well," he began, "the summer I was eight the river flooded the levee, and the whole town was underwater for a week. My buddies and I went swimming in a cotton field, caught this five-foot king snake, skinned him, and brought the skin home to my mother."

"Ewww!" Zoë shuddered dramatically. "What did she do?"

"Told me I smelled like an old trout and made me take it back outside. But after it dried out she let me keep the skin tacked to the wall in my bedroom."

"I think I'd like your mother," Zoë said drowsily.

"You would. You're a lot like her, believe it or not."

"Says the person who's known me for less than twenty-four hours."

"Now, that's not true. I've known you for nearly ten years."

"Hmph. You paid absolutely zero attention to me when I was Miranda's roommate. I might have been a shadow on the wall." She faltered. "Well, except for one time."

He pounced. "When was that?"

"See? You don't even remember."

Will cudgeled his brain and came up empty. "No. But I don't think it's entirely my fault. I mean, look at you. You used to cover up all that beautiful hair, and you never said a word that I can recall."

"Don't you remember that Sunday morning I tried to get you to come to church with Miranda and me?"

A very vague and strange memory surfaced. "Oh yeah. I tried to talk her out of it because I wanted her to drive down to Biloxi with me for a concert." He pulled one foot up onto the bench and propped his arm across his knee. He looked at Zoë ruefully. "What a moron I was."

"You teased me about not having a life. Which I guess was pretty much true."

Suddenly Will saw the truth of something his mother had been telling him all his life: actions and words and even the expression on your face could affect the lives of others even when you weren't aware of it. *Help me here, God,* he prayed.

"Let's get one thing straight, Zoë. I was another person back then. BC—before Christ. I owe you an apology."

"Oh, Will, you don't—"

"Yes, I do." He caught her hand, which had come out from under the blanket. "I was insensitive and obnoxious and selfish. Besides being a moron."

She laughed then and he grinned, relieved to be so easily forgiven. He kept her hand because he liked the soft, fragile feel of it in his. He examined her fingers. She had delicately manicured nails with clear polish, and her left pinkie was bent at a funny angle. She wore, to his surprise, a pewter thumb ring.

"What are you thinking?" she asked.

"I have an idea."

"Uh-oh."

"It's a great idea."

At Fletcher, Fletcher, and Fletcher, Attorneys at Law, Will was famous for his Great Ideas. Sometimes they earned him an extra week's vacation, and sometimes they put him on a very short leash. This one had the potential to go either way.

He watched Zoë's face carefully. "I'll have to take the Galloway boys out of school while they're recording."

"See, that's what I mean." She frowned. "There's no good reason to disrupt students who're—why are you looking at me like that?" Zoë sat up straight and yanked her hand out of Will's.

"They're going to need a tutor."

"Well, it won't be me! Are you crazy?"

"You wanted to change jobs. You said so."

"I want a permanent, *steady* job with students who don't have anything to do with the entertainment industry. Regular kids. Regular parents. Teachers who meet for lunch in the faculty lounge and complain about the principal." She looked at Will, her mouth set. "Read my lips. N-O."

Will might be persistent, but he had enough sense to know when to back off. He shrugged. "Okay. It was just an idea. But I think you should at least pray about it."

"Will." Zoë closed her eyes and uttered an exasperated little laugh.

Feeling her relax against him, he sat quietly, listening to Zoë breathe. A moment later he knew she was asleep.

*Lord, would it be selfish to pray that she doesn't get that job in Colorado?*

# CHAPTER FOUR

ZOË woke up with a crick in her neck, but at least her hands and feet were warm. Tucked under Will's arm was a cozy place to be. She gulped. A *dangerous* place to be.

Without waking him, she slipped her shoes on and went to the ladies' room to freshen her makeup, brush her teeth, and do something with her hair. A little water and a wide-tooth comb restored it to controlled waves. Maybe she should change clothes. *No. I'm not trying to impress Will Fletcher.*

She touched her cheek where a button from Will's shirt pocket was imprinted. The first time in forever she'd been so close to a man. *You're not going to get mushy over physical touch. Only* morons*—to borrow Will's word—let themselves be swayed by hugs and hand-holding. And a cute grin. Look what happened to Mother.*

Taking off her cardigan and knotting it around her

waist, she surveyed herself in the mirror. She wished that button imprint would disappear.

She had a feeling Will was leaving marks on her heart as well.

After a deep cleansing breath, she exited the ladies' room. She was surprised to find Will leaning against a wall with his cell phone pressed to his ear. He'd shaved and changed into a long-sleeved knit pullover a shade darker than his eyes.

"Listen, Dad," Will said, "I'm sorry I didn't make it back last night, but I'll FedEx the deposition tape from Dallas. Gotta jet. I'll call you when I get to DFW." He flipped the mouthpiece shut and smiled at Zoë. "He's wound a little tight this morning. Let's go look up breakfast."

They found a table in front of the ubiquitous golden arches, whose metal mesh doors had magically risen while they slept. Resting her head in her hand, Zoë nibbled on a plain muffin and watched Will devour a gargantuan pancake breakfast with sausage and hash browns. "You look fresh as the proverbial daisy," Zoë remarked, gratefully breathing in steam from her coffee. "No fair."

"I don't require much sleep." He drained the last of his milk. "Which is fine now, but it nearly drove my parents crazy when I was a kid." He shoved his trash into a bag. "One night they caught me in the woods behind our house, shooting squirrels with a slingshot and a bagful of marbles."

"Will!" Zoë spluttered with laughter.

"Yeah. They'd taken my BB gun away from me because I was using a Kleenex box on my dresser for target practice. So the slingshot was the only weapon handy. My grandfather had made it for my birthday and taught me how to use it."

*"Senator Fletcher?"* Zoë shook her head. "He looks so dignified on TV."

Will snorted. "He's still basically a fertilizer salesman at heart. He kept his farm in Yazoo City, and we spend Thanksgiving there every year."

"A fertilizer salesman?" Zoë was having trouble keeping up with the zigs and zags of this conversation.

"He worked at Mississippi Chemical all the way through college and law school. Then he practiced in their corporate law department until he ran for the state legislature in the sixties."

"Will, you obviously admire your grandfather. Why are you trying so hard to detach yourself from his profession?"

"Because it's just not me! Granddad was able to turn law practice into something noble and exciting, serving his country. But all my dad thinks about is billing hours and depositions and being at the office on time." Will captured Zoë with intent blue-gray eyes. "Yazoo City was a great place to grow up, Zoë, but I'm not spending the rest of my life there."

She stared back at him, perplexed. She knew more about Will Fletcher than was perhaps good for her, but she couldn't understand what was so bad about a close family and a dependable job.

"I suppose everybody wants what they don't have," she said quietly. She looked at her watch. "Hadn't we better check in?"

"Oh yeah. Suppose so." His cheerful demeanor returned. "I'll race you." He was off at warp speed.

Groaning, Zoë grabbed her suitcase and followed.

Will's phone went off as the first boarding call was announced.

"Hey, dude, where you been?" he heard in the put-on

surfer accent that had marked Will and Jed's Excellent Adventure at the University of Southern Mississippi. "I called your place last night and—"

"Oh, hey, Skeet," Will interrupted before his partner could launch into a diatribe on Will's tendency to disappear without notice. Jedediah "Skeet" Lawrence might be wired a little differently from the rest of the human race, but he was as predictable as dirt. He'd grown up in Hot Coffee, Mississippi, but liked to pretend he was from Encino Valley.

Out of the corner of his eye, Will caught the quizzical crimp in Zoë's brow. He winked at her. "I'm in San Jose," he said into the phone, "fixin' to get on a plane headed home."

Skeet whistled. "Dude. Your old man's gonna come uncorked."

"Mount Fuji has already spewed." Will sighed. "Did you need something?"

"Just wondering where you are with the Ewoks. You know, the Galahads."

"Galloways. Still in limbo until their grandma gives us the go-ahead to do a demo."

"Bogus, man." A couple of metallic clanks came over the line, followed by a loud trombone glissando. Skeet worked days repairing band instruments in a music store.

"Another kid sit on his horn?" Will asked.

"*Stepped* on it." Skeet played a couple of experimental bars of "Hold That Tiger," then stopped and said slyly, "So who is the chick?"

"What chick, Skeet?" Will's patience was getting thin. The middle rows of the plane were boarding now.

"The one you're puttin' the move on right now."

Omniscient as well as predictable. And loud. Will's eyes met Zoë's. There was a little grin at the corner of her mouth. "I don't know what you're talking about." He moved the phone to his other ear, farther away from Zoë.

"Yes, you do," Skeet insisted. "You got that drawl, man. Sucks 'em right in. Come on, what's her name?"

If he hung up, Skeet would just call right back and pester him bald-headed. "Zoë," he said through gritted teeth. "Zoë Hancock."

"Dude." Skeet whistled again. "Any relation to Brady Hancock?"

Will released an exasperated breath and looked at Zoë, whose eyes were sparkling. "Skeet wants to know if you're related to Brady Hancock."

Her smile disappeared and her face went perfectly white. "M-my father."

Will heard their section called for boarding. Zoë rushed away, and distracted, he followed her with the phone still attached to his ear. "Listen, I gotta go, but who's Brady Hancock?"

"What's the matter with you, man? He was one of the biggest country-western songwriters and producers in Nashville during the eighties. Got born again ten years ago and disappeared. Nobody knows where he went."

Will noted Zoë's rigid back as she handed her boarding pass to the gate agent. There was something momentous going on here, he was sure.

"I'll call you when I get to Dallas," he told Skeet.

Zoë opened her novel and folded the cover back, grateful to have something to occupy her mind. She had no intention of talking about Brady Hancock, particularly with a music-crazy individual like Will. Fortunately, they were in a three-seat row with a young woman and her fretful baby. Conversation would be next to impossible.

"The change in altitude hurts Addison's ears," apologized the mother, bouncing the stout, apple-cheeked little fellow, who whimpered and butted his head into her neck.

But Zoë had reckoned without the Pied Piper of Yazoo County. Five minutes after takeoff Will was trading raspberries with the hairless little creature. Zoë, parked between them, couldn't help smiling at the baby's fat chuckles. Before long little Addison was sound asleep, as was his harried mother, who had introduced herself as Grace.

"You did that well," Zoë commented, warily meeting Will's gaze.

"Ten nieces and nephews." He shrugged. "Lots of practice."

"Ten?" Zoë blinked. "How many brothers and sisters do you have?"

"Just two sisters. But they're both very, er, prolific."

"Are you the youngest?"

He nodded. "Never had to do a thing for myself until I absconded from college. Which was why that spell of prodigal insanity lasted less than a year."

"I always wondered what happened to you."

"Did you really?" He looked pleased. "Well, now you know. So you have to return the favor. Is Brady Hancock really your father?"

Zoë realized she'd walked into that question. She should have known Will wouldn't forget. "Yes, he's my father, but it's not something I like to talk about."

"Why not?"

"Listen, Will. Brady Hancock was the biggest cokehead in Nashville when he hooked up with my mother. *Irresponsible* doesn't even begin to describe his behavior." Zoë tried hard for a matter-of-fact tone. She was not a tender seven-year-old anymore.

Will looked stricken. "Skeet said Hancock became a Christian a while back. Does he even know about you?"

"Oh, he knows. You have to understand, he was in and out of my mother's life so many times. . . . He'd go through rehab, stay clean and work for a few months or a year, then fall off the wagon again. He did the religion thing regularly. It was all part of the game."

She wouldn't look at Will, but he took her hand in his and squeezed it firmly. "You don't think he was sincere?" There was a sympathetic note in Will's voice.

*For Brady Hancock? For me?* She hated the idea of being pitied. But she allowed Will to continue to hold her hand.

"I know the difference between surrender and expedience. He was a manipulator, Will. I learned not to trust anything he said. The man donated some of my DNA, for sure, but I don't think of him as any real relation. God is my Father."

Will was quiet for a moment. "Maybe this last time Hancock changed for real."

"What last time?"

"Skeet said he disappeared ten years ago. Has he ever contacted you since then?"

"I've gotten a birthday card or two," she admitted. "About five years ago he left a message on my answering machine."

"You didn't call him back?"

"No. I just want to forget about that part of my life." If she sounded heartless, she couldn't help it. She was dead to being hurt again. *"Forgetting the past and looking forward to what lies ahead."* That was what the Bible said. "How did your friend guess I'm related to him? Hardly anybody knows he has a daughter."

"Probably read an article in some trade magazine. Skeet reads CD liners with a magnifying glass. He knows all kinds of weird trivia." Will jiggled Zoë's hand. "What about your mother? Are you close to her?"

Zoë shook her head. For some reason, that question took her off guard. Maybe it was physical weariness. Maybe she was just plain old lonely. She hadn't run across anyone as aggressively friendly as Will in a very long time. Her eyes watered. "I'm sorry," she whispered. "I seem to be very emotional this morning."

He stared at her, head down a bit, in a way she was beginning to recognize as characteristic. Golden striations in his blue-gray eyes made them seem lit from within.

"Don't look at me like that," she said, closing her eyes against that tender expression.

"I can't help it. You're so beautiful."

*"You're so beautiful, baby. Come on, smile for Mama. Smile for the people. Honey, sing a little louder. Put your heart in it and belt it out."*

She didn't know she was crying until Will pulled her into his arms. He enfolded her rigid body, his hand cupping her ear, his fingers sliding into her hair. Her tears soaked the front of his soft, smoke blue shirt.

"I'm not," she muttered incoherently.

"Yes, you are—"

She clutched Will's shirt, stopping whatever ridiculous thing he'd been about to say. "My mother *made* me sing."

The dam had burst, and Zoë found herself blurting out what she'd never told anyone else. "Reeda June wanted to be a singer herself. Played the guitar, dressed like Dolly Parton, took gigs in low-rent dives and county fairs. She went after my father because she thought he'd get her 'in.' The worst thing that could have happened to her was getting pregnant. For a long time she pretended I was her little sister tagging along with her."

She felt Will take a sharp breath but didn't give him time to respond. "But then she realized I could sing, and everything sort of twisted so that I got to be the object of all her dreams."

Will's hand moved lightly in her hair. "So you're a singer, huh?"

"I can carry a tune, but I have no desire to be a performer. It was so humiliating." Zoë sat up and hunted for a tissue in her purse. "She paraded me in front of talent agents and producers, even songwriters, if she could arrange an audition."

"You and I were born into the wrong families. I'd have been in heaven." His mouth curved in sympathy. "Why didn't you just refuse?"

"You'd have to meet Reeda June. She's the ultimate steamroller. Besides, I was afraid she'd leave me too."

She felt his sudden stillness. "Did she actually threaten to do that?"

"She implied it. Little girls can be very paranoid."

Will gently squeezed the back of her neck. His understanding created a perfectly insane desire to fling herself back into his arms. She compromised by giving him a wobbly smile.

Which he returned with a wry one of his own. "I guess this explains why you got a bit testy over my wanting to take the Galloway kids on the road."

"Listen, I've been in the middle of that shallow, cutthroat, worldly environment. It's no place for children."

"But I'm not talking glitz and glamour, at least not in the beginning. The Galloway boys will start out performing in churches and Christian festivals. They're doing mostly gospel music right now, but who knows what influence they can have—"

Zoë placed a hand on Will's wrist. "The influence on *them* is the critical thing. All that craving for attention, glory, and money. There are so many bad people out to corrupt and take advantage—"

"True. But there's also a growing audience of young people who need an alternative to what's out there in the rock-music arena. The Galloways have a message, and I think I'm called to give them a chance to share it—and to protect them in the process."

"I believe you have good intentions. But if it's God's will for these kids to make a *name*—" which sounded weird, but she didn't know how else to say it—"then he'll make it happen without your help."

Will stared at her a moment, his blue eyes blazing into hers. "Have you forgiven your parents?"

"Wh-what?" she gasped. "Where did that come from?"

"I know you've been a Christian longer than I have, and you obviously have a mature faith in most areas. But you were used, Zoë, and I think it's made you cynical in some areas where you need to extend mercy."

Zoë was so angry and hurt that she felt like the top of her head might blow off. Her hands shook with the effort not to pop Will Fletcher on his handsome nose. She managed to say quietly, "Thank you, Dr. Fletcher, for your unsolicited assessment of my character. Do you bill by the hour or by the job?"

Will winced. "Come on, Zoë. It's no accident that I ran into you in Denver yesterday. That you're Brady Hancock's daughter. That you and I have a history together. I believe God wants us to help each other. But no matter how loud he shouts, he won't make you listen, and he won't make you yield. That's your part."

Zoë scowled. Will Fletcher had one enormous nerve, talking to her about yielding to God's will, when he was the one bulldozing ahead without paying any attention to her experience. "Why do you assume I haven't forgiven my parents? Will, I'm *grateful* to them. My childhood made me depend on the Lord at an early age. It made me realize how unreliable people are compared to God."

And what difference did it make to Will whose daughter she was? Unless he'd been planning to ask her to draw on Brady Hancock's influence in the music industry. If that had been in Will's mind, he was truly barking up the wrong tree. Even if Zoë knew where her father was—which she didn't—it would be a cold day in Tucson before she'd ask him to sponsor three teenagers from rural Mississippi in a gospel music career.

"Okay. So *have* you forgiven them?"

Zoë wondered where she'd ever gotten the idea that Will Fletcher was a spiritual lightweight. If he was this dogged on a legal case he could be a millionaire.

She glanced over to make sure Grace was still asleep. She was, but Zoë still whispered. "You can't forgive someone who hasn't asked for it."

"Sure you can."

That couldn't be right. Could it? During high school and college she'd waited in vain for any sign of remorse from either Reeda June or Brady. Then when her father actually made overtures with those silly birthday cards, it had seemed too little too late. Her relationship with her mother was pure fluff. Zoë had enjoyed her position of moral superiority over her parents for so long that the idea of giving it up was almost physically painful.

And now Will wanted her to say "I forgive" and pretend it never happened?

"It's not that simple," she said around the knot in her throat, then looked away.

Will sighed. "No, I suppose it's not."

# CHAPTER FIVE

WILL felt the first jounce in the plane and wished he could have slept through it. From the looks of the lightning outside the window, they had flown into a major storm.

Unfortunately, he was wide awake, reviewing every word he'd said to Zoë and coming to the conclusion that he wouldn't have said anything different. Introspection had never been Will's long suit, but he knew when God was trying to get his attention.

Will's typical style of operation was to run headlong where he perceived his Savior to be working. Occasionally he ran into a painful roadblock, but he would simply pick himself up and get going again in the right direction.

This thing with Zoë seemed to be a wall that loomed to the height of Jericho's walls. He couldn't understand her reluctance to confront the issues in her past, the people in her past. Even Will could see that she'd have a hard time being content in the present if she couldn't forgive and let go of the past.

He wanted her to be content in the present because he wanted to *be* her present.

Zoë sat beside him, huddled into her red sweater, eyes closed, profile serene. He wanted to hold her and share with her the broad base of family support that had given him ballast his whole life. He wanted to hear her sweet laughter.

*Lord, this attraction to Zoë makes no sense. Why now? What do you want me to do? Charge the gates? Walk around her and sing, like Joshua's priests and musicians did? How about a sign—or better yet a billboard?*

The plane dipped, jarring sideways. The pilot's voice came over the intercom. "Ladies and gentlemen, we're experiencing some unexpected rough weather in the Dallas/Fort Worth area. Please be patient while we circle a few times and wait for clearance to land. Stand by."

Zoë's eyes opened. "Will, I think I'm going to be sick."

Will's heart lurched along with the plane. He was no good in emergencies. "Okay, okay, take a deep breath," he said. "Close your eyes—we'll be okay."

Then baby Addison began to whimper.

*Great,* he thought.

Zoë groaned.

"What's going on?" asked Grace, trying to hold on to the squirming baby as she sat up.

"Bad weather in Dallas," Will explained. "Want me to take him?" He held out his arms.

"No thanks, I can—"

Addison jumped out of his mother's arms, crawled across Zoë's lap, and latched onto Will's shirt. Addison blew a raspberry up Will's nose.

"Hey, thanks, buster," Will said.

But Zoë let out a weak giggle, so Will wiped his face on his sleeve and went into Uncle Willy mode.

While he sang "Little Bunny Foo Foo," Grace put a gentle hand on Zoë's arm. "How are you feeling?"

"A little queasy," Zoë said. "I've never flown during a storm before, even though I travel quite a bit."

"Would you believe this is the first time I've ever flown?" Grace laughed self-consciously. "I grew up right outside of Fort Worth. Never went anywhere my whole life until my husband got a job transfer to California." Her voice wobbled. "My mother died this week, so we're coming in for her funeral."

"Oh, I'm sorry," Zoë said with a sincere tenderness that Will admired. "That must have been awful to be so far away when it happened."

"Yes, it was totally unexpected. A heart attack." Grace quickly swiped a hand under both eyes. "She'd never even seen the baby. It was just so far, and I was afraid of flying."

Zoë was silent, and Will knew she must be thinking about the infamous Reeda June. He wondered how long it had been since Zoë had had contact with her mother.

Grace continued, "Now it's too late, and my father is so upset. If this plane doesn't land on schedule I'll miss the memorial service too."

Zoë turned and caught Will's eye. "Would you like us to pray for you, Grace? That always makes me feel better."

Grace looked startled for a moment, then nodded. "Sure, I guess so." She smiled as Addison bounced up, giving Will a drooly kiss on the jaw. "Absolutely, yes."

As the plane rocked and rolled, the three adults bowed their heads—though Will kept one eye open to make sure his charge didn't take a sudden dive off his lap.

"Precious Lord," began Zoë, "we thank you that your

Word says your children are always in the palm of your hand. Thank you for Will's ability to calm the baby, and thank you for your ability to calm us when we're anxious."

Will, watching Zoë as well as Addison, saw her shoulders relax. *Ah yes, thank you, Lord.*

"I pray for Grace," Zoë went on, "that you'll remove her guilt about not being with her mother when she died, and I pray you'll allow her to redeem the time with the rest of her family. Please let the baby be a sweet reminder that times and seasons are in your hands." Her voice faltered a bit as she whispered, "And please give me the courage to redeem time with my own family. In Jesus' name, amen."

"Dah!" shouted Addison, lunging across Zoë to reach his mother. Grace hugged him as all three adults laughed.

"Amen," murmured Will, squeezing Zoë's hand approvingly.

౷

"Bend down just a little more." With a wet paper towel, Zoë scrubbed at an aromatic, Cheerios-textured smear on Will's shoulder. They stood outside the rest rooms in the concourse of the Dallas/Fort Worth airport. "Good thing I didn't see that while we were still on the plane." She crossed her eyes expressively.

"Somehow I would've pictured you as having a cast-iron stomach," Will said, crouching to accommodate the twelve-inch difference in their heights. "Guess I'm going to have to rethink that Hawaiian cruise I'd planned for our tenth anniversary."

Zoë stopped scrubbing and found herself nose to nose with Will. This time she noticed the dark blue outline of his light eyes. "Tenth anniversary of what?"

"Don't play dumb," he said.

"Will, you need an intervention." She laughed, knowing better than to take his teasing seriously. At least their awkward conversation on the plane apparently hadn't left him angry. She wondered what it would take to make Will angry. "Wasn't it great to see Grace's father hug her and the baby?"

"Yup. Sweet lady. I'd like to have a kid like that one day."

Zoë knew he didn't mean with *her,* but an unexpected spear of longing zipped through her anyway. She stepped back and slapped the paper towel into Will's hand. "Okay, you're done. I'm going to get in line for security."

"But I was hoping you'd come with me to the business lounge to take care of this deposition." Will's expression was so forlorn that she nearly gave in.

*He'll pick up some other unsuspecting stranger in less than five minutes,* Zoë assured herself.

"Be brave, little soldier," she teased him, backing up another step. "I'll meet you at the gate." Liszt began to tweedle inside the pocket of Will's slacks. "You know, you are way too available."

Smiling into her eyes, Will held up a finger. She should have taken the opportunity to get out of Dodge right then. But somehow she didn't have the heart to abandon him. Yet.

"Dad!" he said. "My secretary is on her way to mail that deposition tape right now." He paused and grinned at Zoë. "Well, I have one now. Remember Zoë?" Another pause. "What can I say? It's my animal magnetism." Zoë whacked him on the arm. "Gotta go, Dad, before she blacks my eye." He closed the phone and slid it into his pocket again. "Dad says he wants to meet you."

Giving up, Zoë followed Will through a doorway

marked Admiral's Club, annoyed at the flattered zinging of her pulse.

Will had just left his package for FedEx to wing off toward the Mississippi Delta when his phone went off again.

Zoë snatched it out of Will's hand. "Will's Wheel Works. You throw 'em; we cap 'em."

"You're getting really good at this," said Will.

"Hey, dudette," she heard in a deep, lazy drawl edged with a southern California twang. "Where's Wild Man?"

"This is his answering service," she said. "He's out to lunch."

"Truer words were never spoken." Skeet chuckled. "Forget him—I'm the cute one."

Zoë didn't want to give anybody the wrong idea. "I'm sure you are, but my relationship with Will is less than platonic."

"Yeah, yeah. Listen, I did some research on your old man this mornin'. He's livin' in Memphis."

"Oh, really."

"Yeah. Just thought I'd mention it. Listen, tell Will there's a new kink in the works. Roxanne's threatening to kill the deal."

Zoë squelched a surge of interest and curiosity. "Do you want to talk to Will?"

"Nah. Just tell him he might want to lay a little charm on Roxanne."

"I'll tell him." Zoë clicked off the phone and flung it at Will, who caught it one-handed. "Who's Roxanne?"

"Roxanne?" Will blinked; he was going to have to let Zoë answer his phone more often. These one-sided conversations could be very revealing. "She used to be my favorite redhead." He pocketed his phone, looking at Zoë sideways. "I have this thing for older women."

"I'm younger than you!"

He grinned. "Roxanne is Miranda's grandmother and the Galloway brothers' guardian."

"Oh. *That* Roxanne." Zoë blushed. "I met her once when I went home with Miranda for a weekend. We just called her Granny. She is the coolest lady."

"Absolutely. So what did Skeet say to get you riled?"

Zoë straightened her skirt. "He said you need to charm Roxanne. Apparently she's causing a wrinkle in your deal."

"Oh, man." Will scrubbed his hand through his hair. "What else is going to go wrong?" He sighed. "Well, it looks like I'm on my way to the great metropolis of Vancleave, instead of home to Yazoo City."

"But, Will, what about your job? What about your dad? Won't he expect you to come to work?"

"It's easier to get forgiveness than permission."

Zoë looked troubled. "That's not very responsible."

"Responsibility is a matter of perspective."

She laughed. "Now there's a unique motto."

Because Zoë's opinion mattered to him, Will squirmed. "I've got to talk to Skeet. Hold on a minute. I'll be right back."

As he walked outside the door of the Admiral's Club, he took out his phone and pulled up the speed-dial menu. "Hey, Skeet," he said, leaning back against the curtained plate-glass window.

"Didn't your answering service tell you I just called?"

"Yeah." Will rubbed his forehead and sighed. "Jed, I need to ask you something."

"Whoa, man, this must be heavy."

The two of them had been Skeet and Wild Man since

pledging Alpha Chi Alpha fraternity together. Only in times of deep seriousness did it occur to Will to use Jed's given name. "I need to know if I'm a lightweight," Will blurted.

After a blank silence Skeet said, "A lightweight what?"

"You know. Irresponsible."

"Oh, irresponsible." Will could picture Skeet sagely nodding his bleached-blond head. "I'd say joining your dad's law firm wasn't one of your brightest moves, but I think you're coming out of it. We get these Galloway kids squared away, and we'll be in business."

Frustrated, Will propped one foot behind him on the glass. "That's just it. I don't know if I'm mature enough to shepherd those boys through the hazards of a first recording contract."

"Will, listen to me." Skeet abruptly dropped the surfer-dude drawl. "If you can't do it, nobody can. You have unique experience, unique education, and unique contacts, not the least of which is your relationship to Christ. Just do what comes natural and you'll be fine." He paused. "But stay away from that chick who answered the phone. She's scary."

Will laughed. "What do you mean?"

"Remember Jed's dating etiquette rule number one? Never pursue a woman who's smarter than both of us put together."

"I think I'm up to the challenge." Recovering from his unexpected attack of self-examination, Will grinned. "So what's going on with Roxanne?"

"Oh, dude. It's worse than I thought. It sounds like she won't let the kids record."

Will's stomach sank. "You're right. This is not good."

"What time's your plane leave?"

"In a few hours. I'll drive to Vancleave to talk to

Roxanne." Will turned around and pressed his aching forehead against the cold glass window. "She's always had a soft spot for me."

"Well, I'm praying for you, brother."

"Thanks, Jed." Will closed the phone. No matter how bad things got, he could count on Skeet to pray for him. Despite a seemingly vapid exterior, his friend had remained strong in his faith while Will strayed off. He'd been there, too, when Will came crawling back needing forgiveness and restoration.

*Thanks, Lord, for such a good friend. Help me know how to handle this situation. Please.*

# CHAPTER SIX

ZOË looked up from her book to find Will staring at her but not *at* her. He sat with both elbows propped on his knees, brow knit in concentration. He didn't look happy.

Fearing he'd finally gotten tired of her company, she allowed him some breathing space. But she repeatedly caught herself sneaking glances at Will's profile. The generous sweep of his mouth was infinitely more attractive than the swashbuckling hero of *Hearts in Space.*

Alarmed at the direction of her thoughts, she finally cleared her throat. "Will, what's the matter?"

Will's gaze came into focus. He rested his chin in his hand and regarded her with troubled eyes. "Nothing I can talk about right now."

Ooh, that stung. Will could talk about anything. "Okay." She went back to her book.

After a few moments of quiet, she heard Will sigh. "Are you really going to move to Colorado?"

Had she been the object of his thoughts? "I think so. Everything about the job looks good so far."

He pinched the bridge of his nose. "Would you call me when you get home and let me know you're okay?"

"Sure." She stuck her bookmark in her book. "Come on, what's bothering you?"

"I'm a little worried about Benj, Luke, and Jesse. Time is important, so I've decided to drive to Vancleave."

"I see." She took a deep breath. "Did you talk to Mrs. Roxanne?"

Will evaded her eyes. "She's having second thoughts about letting the boys begin a music career, but—" He stopped, as though tangled up in what he could and couldn't say. "Just pray for me, Zoë."

"You know I will." A painful weight seemed to have settled on her chest. Time *was* important. After they landed in Jackson, it was unlikely she and Will would cross paths again. He'd given her his e-mail address, but she knew how difficult it could be to maintain a long-distance relationship.

He looked at her soberly, his eyes mirroring her own thoughts. "Do you want to go check in with me?"

Absurdly relieved at the invitation, Zoë smiled. "Do we have time to stop for yogurt on the way? My treat."

"It's a deal." Looking much more cheerful, Will stood and extended a hand to pull Zoë to her feet. "And on the way you can teach me that trick." He took her book and tucked it under his arm.

"What trick?"

Zoë went breathless as Will leaned close, his breath tickling her ear. "The reading-upside-down trick."

Seated at a little table outside the yogurt stand, Zoë found herself even more aware of the short amount of time she had left with Will. She knew *he* knew she'd been watching him, and there was an amused little twitch at the corner of his mouth.

Finally, she blurted out desperately, "I've been considering calling my mother."

Will picked a gummy worm off the top of his yogurt and popped it into his mouth, delight sparkling in his eyes. "Good for you! Does she still live in Nashville?"

"No. She married an oil baron and lives near Houston."

"What are you waiting for? What's her number?" Will extracted his phone from his pocket.

"You're going to have the mother of all cell-phone bills," Zoë protested halfheartedly.

"Unlimited minutes, unlimited range, compliments of Fletcher, Fletcher, and Fletcher."

The old sensation of feeling her tongue cleave to the roof of her mouth made Zoë's hands shake as she dug her Palm Pilot out of her purse. "It's been almost five years since I talked to her. What should I say?"

"You didn't seem to have any problem sassing my dad." He glanced at the screen of her Palm Pilot and punched the numbers into his phone. "But I'll be happy to get you started."

When Zoë reached for the phone, he dodged her hand with a grin, putting the receiver to his ear. Zoë faintly heard a woman answer.

"Hello," Will said, "I'm placing a call for Miss Zoë Hancock. Reeda June Ellenberg, please." A pause. "Yes, this is her personal assistant. I'll put her on the line in a moment. I'm the warm-up act."

Zoë put her hands to her face, not sure whether she should laugh or kill him. "Will, give me the phone!"

He shoved his chair backward and stood up, out of her reach. "Yes, actually, Zoë and I are old acquaintances, well, close friends I guess you'd say. Ran into each other yesterday in Denver. We were just sitting here discussing our stock portfolios, and she mentioned that she wondered how you and . . . ? Yes, you and Deke were doing these days. I told her no time like the present to find out, so let's just give Reeda June a little ringy-dingy."

*Mother's going to think I've landed in the funny farm.*

But then again, Reeda June had been known to cultivate a few fruitcakes of her own. Since there was nothing she could do about it, Zoë relaxed and let Will go. He wandered off, listening for a few minutes.

Suddenly he faced Zoë, and she watched his eyebrows shoot up. "Yes, ma'am," he drawled like Billy Bob Thornton, "I *do* happen to be from Mississippi. How on earth did you guess?" He gave Zoë a sly look. She folded her arms and crossed her legs. "Oh, she's doing quite well. She wants to talk to you, of course, but I told her, I said, 'Listen, I'm just dying to meet this amazing woman,' so she let me place the call and—yes, of course we'll stop in to see you when we're in town. All right, here she is."

Zoë took the phone, her earlier awkwardness forgotten in Will's merry gaze. "Hi, Mama."

Will watched Zoë's expressive face as she held the phone to her ear. Though he couldn't imagine going five years without a conversation with his own mother, he understood why Zoë had developed trust issues. Two minutes into his conversation with her, he'd pegged Reeda June Ellenberg as a narcissistic charmer with a lethal underpinning of steel in her throaty smoker's voice.

It was a miracle of God that Zoë had survived childhood with any self-esteem at all. She had obviously been dragging around some carefully hidden baggage since then. Will would give anything to help her ditch it.

*Yes, anything, Lord. Please let me be the one.*

"Thank you for breaking the ice," Zoë told Will as they waited in line with a cast of thousands for the interterminal tram.

He looked down in surprise. She'd been quiet, pensive, since saying good-bye to her mother. "You're welcome." He hesitated. "Maybe I was a bit over-the-top."

"She loved it. She said you sound cute." Zoë's smile was edgy. "Same old Mama trying to run my life, though. I almost couldn't convince her you're not my boyfriend."

"My sisters tell me regularly that I'm a clown." Though enjoying the fact that the crowd forced Zoë to stand close to him, Will grimaced. "My father has this theory that women don't respect men who aren't serious."

"You know, Will, you quote your family a lot."

The tram arrived, whereupon a hundred people did their best to squish into a space that would hold twenty. Will grabbed on to a pole, enfolding Zoë in his arms. "You okay?"

"Flat as a granola bar but basically sound."

He chuckled. "Just think, you'll be home by tonight."

"If they ever let us out of this airport. I'm beginning to think I should just marry the floor-wax guy and move in."

Will put his hand on top of her head and tipped it toward his chest. He stared into tea brown eyes shining with mischief. "You're something else, Zoë Hancock," he said slowly and watched her cheeks turn pink. "I know it wasn't easy to talk to your mother."

"Well, I thought a lot about what you said about forgiveness, especially after we prayed with Grace about her mother. I know what the Bible says, too, and forgiving is the right thing to do." She squeezed her eyes shut. "But, Will, it's so hard! It's obvious my mother doesn't really get what she did to me."

"And maybe she never will," he said. "The only heart you can control is yours."

Zoë sighed. "I don't want to stay the same forever, you know?"

The tram swayed, jostling Zoë into Will. The impulse to kiss her satiny forehead nearly buckled his knees. "Me either," he said huskily.

"Will, can I ask you something?"

He nodded.

She continued to look up at him, her golden brows pulled together a bit. "When are you going to stop trying to fulfill what everybody else thinks about you? Just be the *you* God made you to be."

Self-examination being a mostly foreign and embarrassing concept to Will, he chose to joke. "Well, I've always wanted to be groovy. But maybe I should just settle for cute."

"See, that's what I mean." Zoë frowned. "I think all this clown stuff is a ruse to hide the fact that you're a very modest, tenderhearted guy." To his surprise, Zoë wrapped her hands around his. "Since my grandmother died, nobody's challenged me on my relationship with my parents. I've prayed for my mother, but I didn't want to imagine she could really change. Now I find out that, in spite of my lack of faith, she's in a good marriage and seems to have developed a grain of genuine concern for me."

"I'm glad, but I don't think I had—"

"Listen to me, okay?" Zoë's eyes were damp. "You were right about yielding to God and extending mercy. I knew he allowed the experiences of my childhood for some reason, but I didn't want to revisit them." She shrugged. "And I'm still afraid he may be calling me to something I don't want to do. Aren't you ever afraid of that?"

"You mean like going to Africa as a missionary?"

"I'd make a terrible missionary." Zoë gave him a wry smile. "But I think I'd be relieved if that was all it was."

Will shook his head. "I know one thing. Every time I've pushed past my discomfort to do what God wants me to do, the place I wind up is always the place of greatest contentment." The Great Idea suddenly blinked like a hundred-watt bulb in Will's brain again. *Lord, I pray this is from you . . .* "Would you at least consider coming down to Vancleave with me to meet the Galloway boys? I'd really like your insight on how to deal with them, and besides, I bet Roxanne would love to see you again."

Zoë's eyes widened. "Oh no, we're not going there again."

Will sucked in a frustrated breath. "I don't know why you're being so pigheaded," he said rashly. "You've already flown halfway across the United States and back with me. What's one extra little jaunt in the grand scheme of things?"

She glanced away. "This has been a strange couple of days. I don't know what God's saying to me anymore."

"Okay, we've *got* to get by ourselves and pray." He looked at the people all around them. How had he and Zoë had such an intensely personal conversation in such a short amount of time?

Suddenly the tram braked, slamming them into one another again. Centrifugal force was a wonderful thing.

"I'll pray," Zoë said, rubbing her head, which had made violent contact with Will's shoulder, "but I'm not going to Vancleave no matter what you say. I have to start preparations for a new tutoring assignment tomorrow. Pigheaded," she muttered.

"Who would've thought the Dallas airport would have a chapel?" Zoë hovered just inside the door, regretting her impulsive agreement to come here with Will. She had the sensation of rolling downhill in an out-of-control wheelbarrow. The ride might be fun, but a crash at the bottom was inevitable.

She surveyed the room as Will plopped down on a back-row seat. The only concession to religion seemed to be a padded prayer bench at the front of the room and a wooden crucifix hanging on one wall.

"Maybe we should kneel." Oblivious to her hesitation, Will bounced to his feet, grabbed her hand, and led her to the prayer bench.

She found herself kneeling beside him shoulder to shoulder. His left hand—large, warm, and rough—clasped hers. She shyly experimented with the texture of his fingers. There were calluses in odd places, and she wondered if he played baseball or golf. It occurred to her that she knew very little about Will's life beyond airports.

She wished she had time to get to know him better. She could have time—if she went with him to Vancleave.

She shot a cautious look at his face and found him looking up at the crucifix, his expression unexpectedly solemn. A startling image of a bride and groom at the altar popped into her head.

"Why do you suppose so many people's whole concept of Jesus is the cross?"

Zoë tore her gaze away from Will's face. She'd been thinking about him, and he'd been thinking about Jesus. How embarrassing. "The cross is an important symbol of our faith. That he gave himself for us."

"Yeah, but aren't you glad there's more? What would we do if Jesus hadn't risen again to live in us, to give us daily victory?"

The stark truth of that statement suddenly overwhelmed Zoë. Here she was at a crossroad in her life—whether she liked it or not. What if her encounter with Will had been no accident? What if God was trying to teach her something through him, and she coldly turned him off? What if she took a wrong turn and missed God's will? Would he continue to bless her lack of faith?

She put her head down on the rail next to her and Will's joined hands. "I wish God would just put up a billboard somewhere so I'd know what to do," she mumbled.

"What did you say?"

Will's hoarse whisper jerked her head around. He looked like he'd been hit in the face with a mackerel.

"I was just wishing it were easier to discern God's will. How can you know for sure what he's trying to tell you? I mean, not just choosing between right and wrong, but between two good things."

"The billboard thing. You said *billboard.* I heard you."

Zoë grinned, amused in spite of her emotion. "I guess I did. So?"

"That is the exact word I used yesterday. I'm thinking we need to pray for a billboard, Zoë. I want you to come with me, but I'm more interested in knowing if we hear God in the same way. I don't want to pull you away from what the Lord wants for you."

"I'm sorry. I just can't come with you. If I get the job in Colorado, I can't afford to pass it up."

She saw the urge to argue building in Will's expression. Then, just as visibly, he reined it in.

"All right," he said quietly. "Let's pray."

Zoë listened to Will pray, feeling somehow let down. She'd expected him to put up more of a fight.

# CHAPTER SEVEN

ZOË and Will landed in Mobile, Alabama, shortly after eight o'clock.

Zoë hurried to keep up with Will's long strides through the jetway. "Will, just a minute!"

He turned to face her, walking backward. "What's the matter now, worrywart?"

His tone was teasing, but the words stung. *Worrywart* had been her mother's favorite epithet for her. "I'm worried about losing this job. What if I miss the call and they give it to someone else? I need to be home. I can't believe we couldn't land in Jackson."

For once, Will's tone was completely serious. "Everything will work out. Besides—" he gave her his patented cajoling look—"we have our billboard. We're stranded here in Mobile. When I called Roxanne, she said she'd skin me alive if we didn't stay with her." He pantomimed pushing a floor waxer. "Unless you'd rather sleep in an airport terminal again."

"I suppose you're right," Zoë said reluctantly.

Will looked up. "Thank you!"

He charged toward the escalator, leaving Zoë to follow, exclaiming, "Wait!"

Grinning over his shoulder, he hopped down the escalator without slowing. She considered following his bad example, then compromised by carefully stepping down one step at a time as the escalator rolled her to the bottom.

"You're going to get yourself killed doing that!" She scuttled after Will toward baggage claim, where Luke Galloway was to meet them.

He laughed. "Death by escalator!"

A sudden commotion at the lobby door brought Zoë up short against Will's back. Mothers were snatching up children and businessmen were diving for the walls, as assorted airport personnel chased after what Zoë would swear was a lion. Hair standing on end as if electrically charged, the huge yellow animal plunged through the door with galumphing lunges, its nails scrabbling against the tile floor.

Will stiffened. "That looks like Gizmo!"

"What's a gizmo?" Zoë peered around Will in time to see a preadolescent boy with long, flyaway, dirty blond hair round the corner of the L-shaped lobby. He tackled the dog and skidded with a nauseating thump into the base of the baggage conveyor belt.

Will leaped into action. "Jesse, are you okay?" He helped the boy sit up.

Holding his bleeding mouth with one hand, Jesse nodded and grabbed the dog around its wild ruff with his other arm. The animal began to howl.

A second boy, older and dark-haired, pushed through the gathering crowd of passengers and airport personnel. "Jess, I told you to leave that dog at home!"

Will looked up. "Benj! Stay right there 'til I get this straightened out. Zoë!" he shouted over the dog's racket.

Zoë approached the scene of destruction. "What can I do to help?"

"Have you got a towel or something?" Will examined the boy's bloody lip.

Galvanized, Zoë tore into her case, pulled out the first thing she came to, and tossed it to Will.

"Ma'am, is this your dog?" A security guard stood above Zoë, one hand on his gun belt. He did not look amused. "Pets are not allowed in the terminal."

Jesse came out from under Will's arm in gory glory. "He was supposed to stay in the truck, but he got loose."

The guard blanched. "Should I call an ambulance?"

"He's just loosened a tooth," Will said. "We'll get the dog out of here immediately. Come on, buddy, see if you can stand up." He ruffled Jesse's hair and looked at Zoë. "You take charge of him, and I'll get the dog."

Zoë obeyed, dabbing at Jesse's mouth with the clean end of the lacy and very bloody—oh, heavens, it was her nightie—item Jesse still held! She quickly stuffed it back into her bag, relieved that no one else had noticed.

"Let's blow this joint," Will said, maintaining a firm grip on Gizmo's leash.

People parted like the Red Sea as they exited the terminal, Gizmo trotting ahead with a huge doggie smile plastered on his ugly face.

Benj, a fourteen-year-old with Marlon Brando eyes and a James Dean swagger, gave Zoë a speculative look. "Hey, Fletcher, is there something you haven't been telling us?"

"Boys, this is Zoë Hancock. She's a friend of your

cousin Miranda, and she's going to stay with your granny until the weather clears up." Will smiled reassuringly at Zoë, an action that did remarkably little to reassure her.

Zoë looked at Jesse's fat lip in concern. "Will, we need to put ice on Jesse's mouth."

"Okay, we'll stop on the way home and get some." Will seemed unconcerned about their unorthodox reception. "Who drove out here? Your grandma or Luke?"

"Luke," Benj said. "He's driving the truck around in circles because they wouldn't let him park at the entrance."

Zoë's step faltered. "You're in a *truck*? There are five of us!"

"Yeah. It's a good thing you're kinda skinny," Benj told her, deadpan. "Gizmo gets carsick if he has to ride in the back."

"Well, if it isn't the Boy Wonder," said Roxanne Gonzales when she flipped on the porch light and found Will standing there spattered with dried blood. Her thin, artificially arched brows rose to meet her hennaed curls. "What happened to you?"

Will sniffed appreciatively at the smell of cookies wafting from the house. "Jesse's the wounded hero. He's okay, except he'll probably need to see a dentist tomorrow."

Roxanne, wearing plaid pajamas peeking out from beneath a black silk kimono embroidered with exotic birds and flowers, stood on tiptoe to see Jesse and Benj carrying the bags up the gravel driveway. Gizmo followed, making enough noise to wake grouchy old Alvin Goff across the road.

Zoë stood back shyly.

"Come in, come in!" Roxanne hugged Will warmly. "Introduce me to your lovely assistant."

"See if you recognize her," Will said, drawing Zoë into the porch light.

Roxanne might be going on seventy-five years old, but she was still one of the sharper knives in the drawer. She took one look and squealed, "Zoë! Will called and said he was bringing me a surprise. This is wonderful!" She pulled Zoë close with a strength astonishing in one so small and frail-looking, then laid both hands along Zoë's face. "But what are you doing here with *him?*"

Zoë laughed. "It's a very long and convoluted story."

"Ooh, ooh, I love a good romance!"

Before Will could either confirm or refute Roxanne's assumption, the boys reached the porch with the luggage and blond, sixteen-year-old Luke returned from the car shed. Shutting the door to keep the dog outside, they all trooped into Roxanne's tiny living room.

"Granny, did you make oatmeal cookies?" eleven-year-old Jesse demanded.

"Yes, but let me see that lip first." Roxanne *tsk*ed. "Did you put ice on it?"

"Yes, ma'am. Please, can I go have some of your cookies?"

Roxanne chuckled and pinched his cheek. "Knock yourself out."

Will enjoyed watching Zoë slide surreptitious glances at an ornately framed portrait of Elvis in oil on velvet hanging behind the sofa.

"Carrie Ann's husband gave that to me for my birthday last year," Roxanne said proudly.

"Miranda's older sister," Will explained, sotto voce.

"That's their wedding picture right there over the TV,"

said Roxanne. "Right there beside Tony and Miranda and the baby."

"Miranda's got a baby?" Zoë got up to give the pictures a closer look. "Isn't he cute?"

Roxanne smirked at Will. "I'm the one who got Miranda and Tony together. Carrie and Tommy too."

That was Roxanne. Devious as a bankruptcy lawyer. It would be just like her to have arranged for him and Zoë to meet in the Denver airport. He gave Roxanne a suspicious look, which she returned innocently. *No way. Total chance encounter.*

"So, Zoë," said Roxanne, "tell me how you and Will got together, and fill me in on whatever harebrained escapade he's roped you into."

"Oh, we're not together," Zoë protested. "I mean, we've been together, but not—" She gulped and glanced at Will for help.

Will had been looking at the upper half of a plastic doll whose skirt was crocheted onto a pillow. He put it back in its seat in a child's wooden rocker. "Zoë and I have been in about four time zones in the last two days, and it would be really nice to get a shower and go to bed."

Roxanne hopped to her feet, cinching the sash of her kimono tighter around her tubby middle. "I bet they didn't feed you anything but peanuts on the plane. Let's scrounge you two up a tuna sandwich—"

"Oh, thanks, we had supper," Zoë said. "All I need is a place to crash."

Roxanne's elfin face softened in sympathy. "Bless your heart. Let me show you to your room." But as Will started to follow, she gave him a reproving look. "Stay right there, young man. You and I need to talk." Pausing to shoo the boys out of the kitchen and send them off to brush their teeth, she led Zoë into the back part of the house.

In Will's estimation, the only thing worse than a lecture from his mother was a lecture from Roxanne. Reminding himself that he was now a grown man capable of making his own decisions, he prowled the room picking things up and putting them back down again.

"It *was* a billboard, wasn't it?" he muttered to the pillow doll.

She gave him a smug smile.

Eventually Roxanne returned and plopped into a circa 1957 cowboy-print recliner. "I won't keep you up long." Her expression was as bland as Knox gelatin.

Will jingled the change in his pockets, casting about for an innocuous topic. "Those Texas windstorms are something else."

"Oh yeah. But I'm glad you're here. Did Jedediah tell you I visited his studio?"

*Uh-oh.* "He said he'd talked to you."

"On a scale of one to ten in scruffy dumps, that one rates about a twelve. An ambulance chases by there every fifteen minutes."

"It's not nearly that bad in the middle of the night."

Roxanne's frown told Will he hadn't chosen the most prudent remark. "Will, your grandfather is one of my oldest friends, and I love you like you were my own, but I've got to know exactly what you have in mind for the boys. It's been six months since their mother died, and I'm just now getting them settled in school here. It hasn't been easy for any of us."

Will stared at Roxanne, for the first time seeing signs of her years. He supposed worry could do that to a person. And love. "Is it their education that bothers you most?"

"One of many things."

"Well, I've got that covered. I'm working on getting Zoë to tutor them." He sat down on the sofa near

Roxanne's chair, determined to convince her. "Did you know she's an experienced tutor? And she happens to be between jobs right now?"

Roxanne's brows lifted. "I got the impression she's not exactly thrilled to be here."

"The Lord is moving in her life—she just doesn't know it yet."

"Is that right?"

"Yes, ma'am. And I've spent a lot of time praying about this. I'm specifically asking God to give Zoë a heart for Luke, Benj, and Jesse."

Roxanne rubbed her eyes. "I admit there are a lot of things that worry me about the school they're in. Having them under the influence of a godly teacher would be wonderful. . . . But, Will, how am I going to pay her?"

Will felt like break dancing as this major obstacle seemed to crack, but he said cautiously, "Finances are the least of our problems if we get backing from a Nashville label. Would you give me permission to set up a demo recording if Zoë agrees to tutor?"

"I would certainly be a lot more comfortable about it."

Will beamed at Roxanne. Now all he had to do was convince Zoë.

The next morning, wearing a borrowed T-shirt proclaiming "Vancleave: It's Worth an Extra Minute," Zoë followed her nose into the kitchen. She found Roxanne, dressed in a red Nebraska Cornhuskers sweatshirt, jeans, and running shoes, tending a Civil War–vintage, cast-iron skillet.

Zoë sampled a slice of bacon draining on a paper towel.

"Howdy, sunshine," said Will, who was reading the

paper at the dinette table. "Roxanne's famous cheese grits coming right up." At Zoë's expression, he looked struck to the heart. "Don't tell me you don't eat grits."

"Bet she hasn't had them cooked right," Roxanne said. "People up north make 'em too stiff."

"Jackson isn't exactly 'the North.' " Zoë exchanged amused looks with Will. "It's only three hours away."

"Roxanne's such a cultural snob," Will teased, getting up to pull out a chair for Zoë.

"I am *not* a snob. I just know what I like." Roxanne deftly drained the grease out of the skillet and poured in a bowlful of scrambled eggs. "I like to eat my grits with a spoon, not a fork."

"Have you called the airport yet?" Zoë asked Will. "Am I going to be able to get out of here today?"

"Apparently you haven't talked to her yet." Roxanne aimed her egg turner at Will.

He avoided Zoë's questioning gaze. "I haven't had a chance."

"Good. Then I can get an honest response out of her." Roxanne faced Zoë. "As an educator, what do you think about taking my great-grandsons out of public school?"

Zoë ignored Will's pleading look. "I'm not sure I know enough about the situation to make an informed judgment."

"Fair enough," said Roxanne. "But my common sense tells me that uprooting kids from a normal school can't be good."

Zoë felt as if she were walking on a particularly tricky fence—Will on one side and Roxanne on the other. Either way she was going to fall off. "Roxanne, I know the idea of nontraditional school makes a lot of people nervous. Honestly, though, some children actually do better in an environment where they can pursue an artistic bent and be tutored according to their needs. *But—"* she frowned at the triumphant grin building on Will's face—"I have to admit my background makes me uncomfortable about the show-business angle."

"Your background?" Roxanne turned off the stove and began to set dishes on the table.

Zoë had carefully hidden her bizarre childhood from her college friends. She'd wanted so desperately to be normal. "My mother was a country-western singer on the fringes of stardom back in the seventies. My father was a well-known studio musician and producer." Zoë dropped her gaze and twisted her thumb ring. "Mama was the classic stage mother. It's a miracle I finished high school with any kind of scholarship potential. Once I was in college, out from under her thumb, I told myself I wouldn't ever go back to performing."

"Some people don't need *or want* the limelight," Roxanne commented, frowning at Will.

"But there are plenty of people who God made expressly for the stage," he said. "Luke, Jesse, and Benjamin, for example—"

"Will, I've come to a decision." Roxanne's wizened face tightened.

"I'm listening," Will said.

Zoë half rose. "Should I leave?"

"No, you need to hear this." Roxanne sat down between Zoë and Will. "But grace first." She held out both hands to her guests and bowed her head. "Father, thank you for my two young friends. I know they want to serve you and want the best for the boys, as I do. Help us all to know your will and to obey. Thank you for your bounteous gifts. In the name of Jesus, amen."

*To know his will and obey.* Zoë hoped it would be that

simple. She opened her eyes to find her hostess smiling and Will looking wary.

Roxanne tipped her head in her birdlike fashion. "The only way I'll even consider signing the contract is if Zoë agrees to be the boys' tutor."

# CHAPTER EIGHT

WILL felt like he'd been punched in the gut. He knew Zoë wasn't ready to give up on the Colorado job. And if Roxanne wouldn't sign the contract, it might be years before the Galloway brothers got another chance. Their voices were fresh and young, and they had unique stage appeal. It was now or never.

"Okay, let's figure this out." Will tried to think. "How are they doing in school?"

"Not real good," Roxanne admitted. "Three brighter kids with a heart for God you never saw, but the principal is always calling me. Jesse manages to skate by mainly on charm, but Luke got behind and can't seem to catch up. And Benj just walks to the beat of his own drum." Roxanne shook her head. "Nobody knows what to do with him."

"Except you," Zoë guessed.

Roxanne grinned. "Except me. I'm older than dirt, and I've straightened out a few rascals in my day."

Will squeezed Roxanne's knobby, blue-veined hand. "But you shouldn't have to. Zoë and I want to help—"

"Will—," Zoë began, obviously alarmed.

"Just hear me out. You don't have to commit to anything, Zoë, but let's pull Luke, Benj, and Jesse out of school, at least temporarily. Clear it with the principal so everything's legal. Since you're stuck here anyway, you can work with them, start getting them caught up. Meanwhile we'll rehearse for the gig at the fair and get lined up for the demo."

Roxanne still looked reluctant, and he was afraid Zoë was going to come out of her seat. He hurried on, "If it doesn't work out for everyone, I'll go home to Yazoo City and drop the whole idea."

"I don't think—," Zoë tried again.

Roxanne laughed. "Boy, you ought to be a politician," she said. "All right."

"Yeee-hah!" said Will.

"I think he should be a snake-oil salesman," Zoë said glumly.

In uncharacteristic silence, Will piloted Roxanne's bus-sized white Buick along the Pascagoula River, which crawled among swampy lowlands clogged with gnarled oaks, pine, and reedy shrubs. Zoë didn't know exactly where they were, but it still seemed oddly like home. Wondering what Will was thinking, she stole glances at his clean, ascetic profile.

Their heart-to-heart with the principal of East Central High School this morning had convinced Zoë that Roxanne's concerns about Benj were well founded. He could be charming but wasn't particularly concerned about keeping his politically incorrect Christian opinions to himself. There was a good deal of tension between him and his biology teacher, and he'd refused to read one of the novels required for his freshman English class. Zoë was becoming slightly intrigued by the idea of teaching him.

"What are you doing?" Zoë asked when, about a mile inside the Vancleave city limits, Will took a narrow side road that dead-ended at a pier. A stand of scrub oaks lined the river to their left; on the right a small clearing hosted a weathered picnic table, a barbecue pit, and a rusty metal trash can.

"Can we stop for a few minutes and talk?" Will said with his hand on the gear shift. The engine was still running.

"Sure." Zoë leaned against the door, watching him.

He killed the motor and folded his arms, staring through the windshield. His green corduroy shirt woke up odd colors in his eyes. Changeable eyes. He finally looked at her without smiling. "Thank you for what you just did. That woman would've chewed me up, spit me out, and swallowed the bone."

Zoë laughed. "You're welcome."

"No, I mean it. You've got this aura of credibility."

"It's probably the orthopedic shoes."

Will blew out a breath. "You'd think a person with a degree in communications would be better at compliments, wouldn't you?" He flung one long arm across the back of the seat, looking at Zoë ruefully. "Can I ask you something?"

Her blood began to zing. "Maybe. If you'll let me ask something in return."

"Deal." He paused. "When we were in college, why did you color that beautiful hair brown?"

"Isn't it obvious I was trying not to draw attention to myself?" She shrugged. "I thought if I could control my weight and hair color, Mama would leave me alone about singing professionally. I know you don't get this, Will, but I enjoy being in the background, and I really hate crowds."

"Then what made you decide to undo it?"

"I guess it gradually dawned on me that God made me the way I am, and it was arrogant to keep complaining about it."

A smile crept into his eyes. "You seem comfortable with yourself now."

"It's called maturity, Will."

"Guess it is. Got some to spare?"

"You sell yourself short, you know."

"Do I?"

Her midsection gave a crazy bounce when his wistful gaze dropped to her mouth. She could tell he was thinking about kissing her. Powerfully attracted to him, she was thinking about letting him. But if she did, she was going to have a hard time detaching herself from her decision to tutor the Galloway boys.

"You didn't let me ask my question," she said.

Will reached over and picked up her hand, fingering her thumb ring. "Where'd you get this?" He pulled the ring off and squinted at her through it, blue-gray inside pewter.

"No fair. That's two questions for you." Did she sound breathless? "It was my father's. He left it for me with my mother."

Will released a silent whistle and absently stuck the ring on his pinkie.

That made at least three things she'd told Will that nobody else knew. This friendship was going to be very hard to undo when it came time for her to leave.

"Okay," he sighed when she didn't elaborate, "your turn. I'm an open book."

She could ask him about something superficial, like

his hobbies, but she wanted more. She felt like a doctor probing for causes rather than symptoms. "Did Miranda dumping you have anything to do with your leaving college and going off the deep end?"

His eyes narrowed a bit. "Whoa. Go for the jugular."

"I'm sorry. That's way too personal—"

"No, no, it's a fair question." He stroked his finger across his mustache, watching her as if gauging her reaction. "It hurt, sure. But maybe I was too selfish at the time to let it bother me much. You know, plenty of fish in the sea and all that."

"So you don't still—" Zoë's sentence jerked to a halt. "Never mind."

"Hey, don't tell me 'never mind' when the conversation's just getting interesting." Will tipped his head. "You're wondering if I'm still carrying the torch for Miranda, aren't you?"

"I suppose. Are you?"

"Miranda and I are friends." He hesitated. "I'm very careful now about the impression I leave."

Zoë stared at him. The implication was enormous. Will had gone out of his way more than once to remain in her company. What was the impression he meant to leave with her?

And what impression, exactly, did she intend to leave on him?

To Zoë's relief, Will gave her one more wary look and started the car. She could sense pheromones bouncing all over Roxanne's Buick, all out of control.

Zoë and Will walked through a drizzling rain to Roxanne's old toolshed, where the boys had gone to rehearse after supper. Roxanne had spent the morning setting up a temporary schoolroom in the "washhouse"—a tin-roofed, cinder-block building next to the shed, containing Roxanne's washer and dryer and a couple of folding card tables. Now it also had a desk for Zoë, four chairs, and a green chalkboard that Roxanne had bought at a yard sale.

Zoë had spent the afternoon with the boys, getting to know them and discovering where they were in their studies. Against her better judgment, she found herself enjoying her time with them.

As they approached the shed, the music got louder. Aware of Will's strong shoulder just behind hers, she stopped outside the open doorway to listen. "What's this song? I don't recognize it."

He shrugged. "Me neither. Let's go in and listen."

The smell of smoke and cedar, oil and rope permeated the old building. Tools still lined the walls, though the cracks between the planks were covered in acoustical tiling, and amplifiers and speakers occupied every flat surface. The worktable held a collection of percussion instruments. Cords snaked in all directions, and Zoë decided that one good electrical storm would zap the boys into the next county.

She and Will found seats on homemade stools. The three young musicians paid no attention to their audience as they continued the lilting ballad. Benj had a guitar strapped around his neck, his scratched-silver voice covering the lead. Jesse harmonized with his eyes closed, a pair of egg-shaped shakers cradled in one palm, while Luke perched cross-legged on an old anvil, a harmonica cupped to his mouth.

As she listened, Zoë's eyes widened in delight. The innate ability she heard in this tumbledown shed went light-years beyond the boys' ages.

*Teach me, O Lord, to follow your way,*
*Give me understanding and I will obey.*
*I'll do your will, with all of my heart.*
*Make me walk along the path of your commands,*
*For that is where my happiness is found.*
*That is where my happiness is found!*

"Do you suppose one of them wrote that?" Zoë whispered to Will.

"Probably. They've reworked some old stuff from the eighties too, but they've been working on original material for a couple of years now."

"My goodness."

The music stopped. Benj stood with an arm propped across the bow of the guitar, regarding Zoë with intense black eyes. "If you have something to say, Miss Hancock, say it loud enough for the whole class to hear."

Then a slight grin curled his mouth, and Zoë knew he was teasing. "Sorry for interrupting," she said, returning his smile. "I really like the song."

Luke tapped the harmonica against his thigh to remove the moisture. "It's from Psalm 119, but Benj wrote the music." He looked at Will, his hazel eyes hopeful. "You think some record company will like it?"

"It's got a lot of potential," Will admitted.

"Woo-hoo!" Luke hopped off the anvil and did a skipping, sliding dance step across the concrete floor. "We are on our way!"

Roxanne, a wooden spoon in one hand, appeared in the open door to the shed. "If y'all are about through rehearsing, I need one of you to jump on the four-wheeler and ride over to Carrie's for a bottle of vanilla flavoring."

"Me! Me!" Jesse whooped, running out of the shed.

Roxanne brandished the spoon. "The rest of you guys

put away your equipment and go clean up the kitchen. Zoë, I need to talk to you."

"I get to be the supervisor," said Will, who had borrowed Benj's guitar to play a few bars of "Hound Dog."

"In your dreams, Elvis," said Benj. "The guitar case is right behind you."

Zoë and Roxanne walked outside and headed for the backyard glider, skirting a flock of pink plastic flamingos glowing in the moonlight. The night was quiet except for cicadas singing in the woods behind Roxanne's house and the muted commotion in the shed.

"Will was right," Zoë said. "Those are three great kids. And the talent is there—if they've got the dedication to pursue it."

"Thinking about sticking around for a while?" Roxanne pushed the glider into gentle motion.

Zoë didn't answer for a moment. Her plans had gotten so mixed up in her emotions that she could hardly separate them anymore. "I can only spare a couple of days. I have to get home."

Apparently some of her ambivalence must have bled through. "What's going on with you and Will?" asked Roxanne gently.

Zoë found herself both starving to confide and desperately shy about it. "He's not what I expected."

"Which was . . . ?"

"Giddy. Self-centered." Zoë hesitated. "But there's no doubt he's impulsive."

Roxanne laughed. "Never a dull moment with Will. But under that goofball exterior is a very bright, tender-hearted young man who loves God with his whole heart."

Zoë had begun to see the same thing. "I have to admit I've had a lot of fun with him the last couple of days."

"Ha! I knew it!" Roxanne crowed. "Do you love him?"

Zoë wasn't ready to answer that, even to herself. "I don't know. Roxanne, will you pray for us?"

"You know I will."

After Roxanne went back inside, Zoë sat in the glider for another thirty minutes, staring up at a starry, black-velvet sky. When one's life had been turned upside down, a clear view of the vastness of God's creation brought perspective. Pieces of Psalm 8 came to her mind: *"When I look at the night sky and see the work of your fingers . . . what are mortals that you should think of us . . . ?"*

To be thought of by God Almighty. Awesome.

# CHAPTER NINE

WILL woke up the next morning to the rhythmic bouncing of a basketball outside his window. When he looked out and saw Benj Galloway dressed in a pair of baggy nylon shorts, a ripped gray T-shirt, and Nikes without socks, Will quickly pulled on similar clothes and slipped out the kitchen door.

Roxanne's gravel driveway ended in red clay under a freestanding car shed with the basketball goal attached to the roofline. The ground under the goal was dry and hard-packed, rough with shells and rocks, but lack of concrete didn't seem to faze Benj. He shot from six feet out, the ball sweetly whisking through the net. Not waiting for an invitation, Will charged the next rebound. Benj looked around in surprise but beat him to it.

A spirited one-on-one ensued, Will's height and reach compensating for the boy's dead aim and lightning footwork. Twenty minutes later Will was bent double, hands on his knees, heaving with exertion.

Benj danced around him, dribbling the ball. "Hoo, Fletcher, rise and shine!"

Will watched sweat drop off the end of his nose into the dirt, making dark orange pockmarks between his sneakers. "Lay off, kid." He snatched the ball as it went by and sailed it into the hoop. "I'm just out of practice."

"There's a news flash." Benj caught the ball and stood with it tucked under his arm. "You need to spend a little more time in the gym and less on the telephone."

Will grinned and walked over to the garden hose coiled next to the house. After a long, satisfying drink, he turned the water on Benj, who yelped in surprise and tried to wrestle the hose away from Will. They both wound up sitting in the grass, sopping wet and howling with laughter.

"Turn it off before Granny has a stroke," said Benj. "She's got this thing about wasting water."

Will squirted him in the face one more time before turning off the spigot. He watched the boy fling himself back in the wet grass as if he'd been shot, the smile on his face relaxed and open.

Will sat with an arm across one knee, waiting for Benj to break the silence. Just when he thought the boy must be asleep, Benj said, "Granny's not gonna let us loose to record and travel, is she?"

"She might. She mainly wants to make sure you get a good education. I agree. You shouldn't put all your eggs in the music basket."

"So I should go to law school, like you did? No thanks. God's called me to do music." Benj raked back his long, wet hair. "If working with you doesn't pan out, I'll just take off and do it myself."

Benj's deep-set dark eyes were implacable. *That's*

*where I was ten years ago. Father in heaven, please give me wisdom.*

Will thought of something Granddad had told him a long time ago, something that didn't make sense until he was living in a dump with four other knotheads who hadn't wanted to wait for timing and opportunity. "You know C. S. Lewis, the guy who wrote the Narnia books?"

Benj nodded, looking wary.

"He said once, in a book called *Mere Christianity*, that the 'terrible thing, the almost impossible thing, is to hand over your whole self—all your wishes and precautions—to Christ.' But in the long run that's easier than suffering the consequences of going your own way."

There was more, about being "plowed up and resown," a concept that Will doubted a fourteen-year-old was ready to absorb. At least Benj seemed to be listening.

"Benj, I know it's hard to be patient while we wait for God to open doors. Zoë being here is one. Your granny knows and trusts her. And there's the gig at the fair tonight. Don't say anything to the other boys, but Skeet thinks a rep from Pinnacle Records will be there."

Benj's jaw dropped and his eyes lit. He hopped up and extended a hand to Will. "Then what are we sittin' here for? We gotta rehearse!"

"School first," Will reminded him, allowing himself to be pulled to his feet. He squished his way into the house to put on some dry clothes. He hoped that there was still time for Zoë to change her mind about tutoring.

Zoë brushed her hand against the lace curtain, as if she could touch Will's face, then let it slide against the cold iron bedstead. She flopped face-first into her pillow. Awakening to hear Will quoting C. S. Lewis under her window, she hadn't been able to resist eavesdropping.

*Okay, Lord, that did it. I think I should stay here and see how it goes with the boys. Help me do that terrible and impossible thing. Help me to hand over my wishes and precautions to you.*

*Even my wishes about Will himself.*

๑

Freshly showered and dressed in recycled khakis and his only remaining clean polo, Will tried unsuccessfully to open the ancient, warped bathroom door. Its brass doorknob rattled like a loose muffler from being yanked on over the years. Finally, one more grand tug unstuck it, and he surged into the hall.

He nearly stepped on Zoë.

"Oops, sorry," he said, steadying her, pleased that she didn't avoid his touch. She looked wide awake, her eyes bright. "There should be some hot water left."

Zoë smiled, tucking her flaming hair behind her ear. "Thanks. But I need to talk to you first."

"Okay." Curious, Will followed her into the living room. Overnight the weather had turned sunny and windless. What if she'd called the airport and made plans to go home today?

She sat down on the edge of the recliner, lacing her fingers together on her knees. She had on a pair of cutoffs and another one of Roxanne's T-shirts. This one said, "I'm in my own little world, but that's okay—they know me here."

"What's up?" he asked, unable to stand the suspense. He plopped onto the sofa.

She bit her lip. "I've decided to stay."

Will leaned sideways and bumped his hand against his ear. "I must've gotten water in my ear. I thought you said—"

"I did." She took a deep breath and said in a rush, "I prayed about it, and I just don't feel right about going home now. I trust Roxanne's judgment."

"Even though you don't trust mine?"

"That's not what I meant."

Zoë's vulnerable expression made Will sorry he'd showed his hurt. "Never mind," he said. "Of course I'm glad. I'm elated. I'm ecstatic. I'm over the moon. I'm—"

"I get the picture," Zoë said. She jumped to her feet. "Well, that's all I wanted to say. I just wanted you to know what I decided." She shot him a look too brief to be interpreted and bolted from the room.

Will scratched his head. "I don't care how many sisters you gave me, Lord, I'll be a ninety-year-old grandpa before I ever understand women."

Seated at the battered teacher's desk in the washhouse, Zoë surveyed her students. Roxanne was spending the day volunteering at the Singing River Hospital in Pascagoula, and had left her great-grandsons with strict instructions to "mind Zoë and Will or you don't do the fair."

Zoë had to admit—but only to herself—to a few nerves. In the past she had mainly worked with girls. All this rampant testosterone made her jumpy.

The three boys, all dressed in baggy jeans in varying shades of grungy, had been allowed to move the tables to favored spots in the room. In a murky corner where the washing machine and dryer formed an *L* with an upright freezer, Benj sat with his hands folded on top of his textbooks stacked with military precision. His black T-shirt and sunglasses, dark hair, and olive skin made him all but invisible. Jesse, on the other hand, sat under the open window. In a splash of sunshine that lit up his blue shirt, blue eyes, and golden hair, he was happily rapping a cadence with a couple of pencils. Luke had tipped his chair lazily against the opposite wall, chin resting on his chest. Zoë was very much afraid he was asleep.

She looked at Vice Principal Fletcher, perched just behind her on a stool. He smiled encouragingly.

Zoë took a deep breath. "All right, guys, let's begin with prayer."

Benj lowered his sunglasses. "Prayer?"

Though wearing shades indoors struck Zoë as somehow antisocial, she'd decided to choose her battlegrounds. "You have some objection to prayer?"

"No. Actually that's very cool." Benj slid his glasses back into place. "We never got to do that at real school. Carry on."

"This *is* real school," Zoë reminded them. "Just because we're at home doesn't mean we goof off." She caught Jesse's dismayed glance out the window at the bright October sunshine. "But it *does* mean we'll get through earlier in the day than you're used to—if you work hard. And we'll be free to take field trips whenever we want."

Jesse brightened, but Luke's chair hit the floor on all four legs. "Field trips are for babies. When do we get to rehearse?"

"After lunch," said Will, leaning in. "You guys hang with Zoë in the mornings from eight to noon or so; then I'll supervise your rehearsals. When you're ready, we'll go to the studio to start laying down some tracks."

"Just how long are we going to have the pleasure of your company, Fletcher?" asked Benj. Zoë wondered how much of that inscrutable Terminator face was a defense against hurt.

Will seemed to understand the nature of the question. "I'll be available as long as you need me. After the gig at the fair, Skeet can finish up the demo." He paused and fielded Zoë's questioning gaze. "I'll have to get back to my office in Yazoo City to wrap things up there."

Zoë gripped her hands together. *And I'll miss you like crazy.*

*Oh, Lord, do I have to give him up so soon?*

After finishing schoolwork on Thursday, Zoë and Will drove the boys to the Gulf State Fairgrounds in Mobile. After a short rehearsal and sound check, they sent the teenagers off to the midway while the two of them ate supper at a picnic table just inside the main gate. The jumbled whistle of the carousel and the electronic scream of the Himalaya ride, along with the smells of grease and farm animals provided a bizarre dinner ambiance.

"Don't tell me you're gonna eat that with nothing on it." Will watched Zoë take a dainty bite of naked wiener and bun.

"I'm a purist," she said indistinctly.

In many ways she was, he thought, flicking coleslaw off the front of his shirt. She still had on the simple khaki jumper she'd worn all day, with a red polo shirt, thick brown socks, and hiking boots. But a glittering cascade of silver stars dangling from her earlobes gave her an unexpectedly sassy look. Will liked surprises.

Zoë's eyes widened. "Uh-oh."

Will's affinity for the unexpected dropped to zero as soon as he turned around.

Jesse shot toward them like a dart out of a Nerf gun, vaulting over an intervening table while skillfully juggling a funnel cake and a jumbo-sized Styrofoam cup. His light hair hung in his eyes and brushed his shoulders in sweaty hanks. Confectioners' sugar dusted his orange shirt, and his grin revealed blue teeth.

"Hey, Will! It was so cool!" Jesse shouted. "I rode the Venus Venture three times! Didn't even get sick!"

"Great." Will glanced at Zoë, who leaned her chin in her hands, eyebrows raised. "I see you found something to eat too."

"You said no snow cones, so I got a rocket pop instead."

"Well, I hope you brought a toothbrush."

"How 'bout a stick of gum?" Zoë reached into the little shoulder bag resting in her lap.

"Sorry about him," said Benj, stomping up to the table with his fists jammed into the pockets of his baggy black jeans. His hair was drawn into a neat ponytail, the clean, handsome lines of his face marred by irritation with his younger brother. "I tried to keep him from running around too much, but—" he shrugged—"he smells like a goat."

Will had to agree.

"Are you sure this is what you want to do with the rest of your life?" Zoë murmured.

"You're gonna have to go after Luke too," Benj added. "I saw him followin' some girl into the fun house."

"I don't like spearmint," said Jesse, lowering his gamin face to Zoë's level. "Got any green apple?"

◎

After the Galloways' brief opening concert, Zoë made her way through the shadows backstage, where the road crew shuffled equipment and adjusted mikes with practiced efficiency. She found Will standing in a milky pool of light beside an electrical pole and talking to a man who made her think of Friar Tuck in a suit.

Will smiled at Zoë, immediately returning his attention to the round gentleman. "Mr. Jeffries, you just made the smartest decision in your life! I'll catch a flight to Memphis in the morning to meet your representatives."

"Good, good. We'll want to get right on this first album. Never signed kids this young before, but as long as we stay on the right side of Child Protective Services, we should be fine."

Will beamed. "I told you they were incredible! Zoë, I want you to meet Howard Jeffries of Pinnacle Records. Mr. Jeffries, this is the boys' tutor, Zoë Hancock."

The man enthusiastically shook Zoë's hand. "The opener was a barn burner, but it's the voices and those faces I'm most interested in."

The men shook hands; then Jeffries lumbered off toward a knot of roadies.

"Zoë, we've got to talk." Will, bearing a strong resemblance to the smug beagle on his tie, grabbed her elbow. "I would never in a million years have dreamed Pinnacle would show up here!"

"What exactly was he talking about?"

Will picked up her hand and twirled her around. "We're in and you're definitely coming with us."

"Coming where—?"

"Let's go tell the boys!"

The Big Time Diner was crowded with late-night revelers. A friend of Will's had recently become the assistant manager of the popular Mobile diner. Prompted by a call ahead from Will's cell phone, Brad Spencer made sure a corner booth was cleared and ready when Will ushered in his three charges and Zoë.

"We're celebrating tonight, Brad. The boys are signing with a major record label tomorrow!"

"In that case, milk shakes on the house." Brad high-fived all three boys, then called over a teenage waitress. "Suzanne, fix these folks up."

Will felt like a proud papa. He smiled when Jesse scooted closer to Zoë and tucked himself under her arm, saying, "I'm cold."

Zoë squeezed the boy's shoulders and rubbed his arm. Jesse gave a contented sigh, his eyelids drooping. The old-fashioned clock over the counter said it was close to midnight. Will pushed away a twinge of guilt. This was their big night. They deserved a little fun.

"That was some spectacular handspring you did onstage, Luke," said Zoë. "Where'd you learn to do that?"

Luke was smiling at the waitress, who had caught his eye from across the room. Absently he said, "Granny bought us a trampoline at a yard sale a few years ago. We used to mess around on it when we weren't practicing."

The waitress returned, a tray loaded with milk shakes hoisted in one hand. Jesse's eyes popped wide open. "Allll-right!"

Will's phone rang. "Probably Skeet calling me back."

Before he could open the phone, Zoë took it, grinning at him. "Hello, Skeet," she mumbled deeply, apparently trying to impersonate Will.

"Fletcher? Jeffries here." Without waiting for a response, he continued, "Any word yet about getting Brady Hancock out of retirement?"

When Will had called Skeet earlier, he'd turned up the

volume to compete with the fairground's noise. From across the table he could now hear Jeffries loud and clear. He could also see Zoë's stricken face. Because it seemed important to her, he'd given up on using her influence with her father. How did Jeffries know anything about it? She was going to think—

"This is Zoë," she said tightly. "Here's Will." She handed the cell phone to Will.

Distracted by watching Zoë mask her distress, he managed to get rid of Jeffries by promising to call later. He knew he had to talk to Zoë about what had just happened but didn't want to do it in front of these curious teenagers. Will paid the bill, left a tip that would keep the waitress in nail polish for months, and hustled the whole crew to the Buick.

Though in general Will loved being "way too available," as Zoë had put it, at the moment he felt like pitching his phone into the Pascagoula River. Still, he somehow managed to drive home without committing cellular homicide.

Zoë sat on Roxanne's porch steps, listening through the window to the uproar going on inside the living room. Roxanne was bursting with pride over the accomplishment of her boys, and it was clear they wouldn't be ready for sleep anytime this week. Even Gizmo, tied under the porch, was barking his head off.

Only Zoë seemed to be in a silent wilderness of pain.

The screen door slammed behind her, and she heard Will's step. He sat down beside her. "You can't stay out here by yourself all night," he said.

She looked away, though there was nothing to see in the dark yard. She could hear the dog scratching and cicadas tuning up in the hydrangea bush. Pushing her hands into her hair, she leaned her elbows on her knees. Finally she took a deep breath. "I'll get over it, Will. I just need some time."

"Get over what?" He sounded genuinely bewildered. "Jeffries doesn't know what he's talking about. I'll straighten him out—"

"You have been using me all this time, just like I was afraid of."

"You really believe that?"

How dare he sound hurt? Zoë wheeled to look up at Will, but he was backlit by the porch light, leaving his face in shadow. "How can I not think that? You did everything in your power to cajole me into following you down here, made me fall in love with those boys, made me feel needed, and made me—" She stopped. She was *not* going to say she'd fallen in love with *him*.

Will sat silent, his hands dangling between his knees. Finally, he said slowly, "I thought I knew you, Zoë."

"You thought a lot of things that have no basis in reality." Pain gave her short laugh a slight edge. "The ironic thing is, I don't know how to convince you I have absolutely no influence with Brady Hancock. But even supposing I did—if I called him up today, what makes you think he'd want to produce an album for a bunch of young kids he's never met?"

Will reached for Zoë's face. "You're twisting everything, but if you'll just listen—"

She jerked away from him. "Every time I listen to you I wind up way out of my comfort zone, but this time it's just too much. Like I said, I'll get past this just like I've gotten past everything else that's ever happened to me. But don't ask me to live inside your bubble of fiction anymore, Will Fletcher. Good luck with the talent agency. I'm going to bed."

◎

Will woke up early the next morning without the aid of basketballs or alarm clocks or any other wake-up call. He lay knotted up in a sheet, feeling as tired as when he'd laid his head on the pillow.

Zoë's accusations had left him bruised. For someone who prepared defenses for a living, he'd been mighty ineffective last night.

Determined to catch Zoë early this morning and take one more shot at an explanation, he levered himself out of bed and pulled on jeans and a thin sweater. A silver tongue should be good for something besides getting him in trouble.

Hearing wheels crunching on the driveway outside, he frowned and stuck his head out the window to investigate. A yellow cab had pulled in, and the cabbie was stowing a bag in the trunk. Will's heart crashed in his chest when he saw a bright strawberry blonde head disappear into the backseat.

"Zoë!" he shouted into the misty October morning, loud with birdsong. He slammed his hand against the window frame as the cab backed out of the driveway.

She was gone.

# CHAPTER TEN

THE law offices of Fletcher, Fletcher, and Fletcher became a lonely place on a Saturday afternoon, especially the weekend before Thanksgiving. It seemed everybody in Yazoo City except Will Fletcher was either getting ready for company or preparing to leave town for the holiday.

Will listened to a mockingbird warbling in the magnolia tree outside his second-story office window and wondered if he'd ever feel normal again. He was just coming back to the firm after a self-imposed, month-long exile in the DA's office. Because the Jeglenski deposition had arrived safe and sound with time to spare, the Sultan had decided to go easy on him after all. But figuring he had dues to pay, Will had worked hard for the DA and had even been offered a permanent spot with a promotion.

Now he had decisions to make. He very much feared he was being "plowed up and resown."

*Wishes and precautions, Lord. Zoë had problems with the precautions part, but—let's admit it—Wishes "R" Us.*

Feeling like Charlie Brown mooning over his little red-haired girl, he pulled Zoë's ring off his pinkie and squinted through it at the name plate on his open door. William Barton Fletcher III. *Three times and you're out, boy. Well, the first two managed to make a name for themselves. Maybe it's not too late for me. But what do you do when God says, "Read my lips—N-O"?*

Every day for the past month he'd walked by the post office with the intention of putting the ring in a box and sending it off to Jackson. He knew it was important to Zoë as a symbol of hope. The fact that she hadn't called him up demanding that he give it back meant something. Probably she'd given up hope in her father along with faith in Will.

On the other hand, maybe she had let him keep it knowing that good manners would force him to contact her in order to give it back.

Will stuffed the ring into his pocket. Though she was close to being the perfect woman for him, Zoë had blown off their growing relationship and left. He wasn't chasing after her this time. Persistence only went so far. He'd stop by the post office this afternoon to mail it.

Right now, though, he needed wisdom. Will picked up the phone and hit speed dial. "Hi, Granddad," he said. "Had lunch with the president lately?"

Zoë sat in her apartment in Jackson, packing about a million books into boxes.

As she went about the business of preparing for her new position at the Colorado boarding school—completion of medical check-ups, transferal of transcripts, FBI fingerprinting, and the like—she found it just that. A business she could accomplish in her sleep.

Emotionally, however, she found herself beset by what C. S. Lewis called "the dangers and perturbations of love." The heart, once cracked open, required a conscious effort to heal: the medicine of Scripture, bandaging with prayer, and a constant self-reminder not to pick at the scabs of remembrance.

She found that she'd become inordinately fond of C. S. Lewis, discovering a powerhouse of encouragement and strength in *Mere Christianity.*

*Lord, I wish I had a chance to assign this to Benj for a book report.*

But Benj would have some other teacher, likely one who would let Will Fletcher talk her into doing everything his way. Jesse would go around with blue teeth because Will wouldn't think to carry gum. And Luke would grin that lazy, heartbreaker smile and get away with murder.

*Oh, Father, I wanted so much to be their teacher. I wanted to be Will's girl.* Her throat clogged with tears. *Okay, I wanted to be his wife. I know we were only together for a short time, but it felt like the biggest part of my life.*

How in the world could that be?

*Will changed me. No, you changed me through him. Opened my eyes and made me vulnerable. Helped me to call my mama and move closer to forgiveness.*

Zoë picked up her Bible off the coffee table and laid her forehead against its smooth leather cover. *Why was it so petrifying when Will disappointed me? Why is it so hard to forgive him?*

She knew she should, but her feelings wouldn't cooperate. She'd heard it said that love is a decision.

*Decide, beloved.* The words seemed to pour like heat from the book against her face. *Decide to forgive. "You can pray for anything, and if you believe, you will have it. But when you are praying, first forgive anyone you are holding a grudge against, so that your Father in heaven will forgive your sins, too."*

"I want to, Abba," she said aloud. "You know I do." She looked at her two hands grasping the Bible. Both thumbs were naked, even the left one that should have worn her father's ring. She'd never been able to explain to herself why she wore that ring, but now it made a weird kind of sense. She'd always yearned for a connection with her father, even when he least deserved it.

Will had absentmindedly taken the ring, but somehow she knew his keeping it had been very much on purpose. And she'd let him. Would he still be wearing it? Would he be thinking of her?

Suddenly she knew what she had to do. She had to contact her father.

Will watched his father line up for a drive off the ninth tee at the Yazoo City Country Club. The old man was in great shape for a grandfather of ten. Worked out every morning at the Y, drank a Slim-Fast for lunch daily, and of course, being a Baptist deacon, never touched a drop of liquor. He also had the added satisfaction of always being right.

Will wondered how it would feel to live without the burden of a load of I-told-you-so's.

To Will's enormous satisfaction, William Fletcher's drive sliced forty yards to the right of the fairway, winding up in the trees.

"Good shot, Dad," Will said, earning a dirty look from the Sultan.

"Let's see you do better," growled William, backing up.

Will set up, took a practice swing or two, and nailed

the drive straight down the middle of the fairway. He met his father's rueful smile with a modest shrug. "I'll help you find your ball."

They picked up their bags and fell into step together across the neatly clipped green grass of the fairway. Will cleared his throat. "Dad, I have to tell you something."

William shook his head and unconsciously picked up the pace. "What is it this time?" he asked. "You're not taking off for some godforsaken—"

"No, nothing like that." Will remembered telling Zoë that responsibility was a matter of perspective. *Lord, what an oatmeal-brained thing to say.* He'd learned a lot from falling in love and getting socked in the emotional solar plexus. "I'm taking the job with the DA's office."

William screeched to a halt, dropping his bag with a thud, and stared slack-jawed at Will. "You can't do that. This is a family business."

"Granddad thinks it's a good idea. The firm obviously won't fold without me. Besides, I need to gain independent experience and responsibility before I try to step into your shoes. I'll come back when I'm ready, if you still want me."

William's eyes narrowed. "The DA's office will soak up every particle of your time. What about your obsession with starting an entertainment agency? What about the Galloway boys?"

"I've decided to yield to Roxanne's wishes. At least wait until the end of the school year—if it happens, it happens. I'm not running ahead of God again."

William picked up his bag. "I never would have sent you over there if I'd thought you'd stay," he grumbled. "I really have to meet this young woman."

"What do you mean?"

"You've been a different man since that last trip."

"I know." Will slung his arm around his father's shoulders as they walked on. "Thank you for putting up with me, Dad. I love you."

Everything Zoë owned was packed and ready to be moved to Colorado. She had resigned from the tutoring agency, and only the formality of signing with the boarding school remained. The school had called to say her contracts were in the mail. She was to start teaching second semester, but she planned to move before Christmas to give herself time to acclimate to the surroundings.

Now, two days before Thanksgiving, restless and bored, she wandered into her bedroom, considering giving her mother a call. She had located her father's address and phone number after a lot of on-line research, starting with Memphis, where Skeet had said he'd been at one time. Initiating contact with him had been difficult, but she was glad she did it. She'd found that Will's claim that Brady Hancock had become a believer was true. He was sober, married with three small children, and served his church as a guitarist in a praise band. Zoë and her parents still had a lot to work through, but she wanted to reconcile with them, no matter how long it took.

New cell phone in hand, she plopped on the bed, which was still covered in sheets and a light blanket. But as she looked for her mother's number on the phone's speed-dial list, the name *R. Gonzales* popped into the menu window.

Roxanne. Seized with a sudden urge to hear her wise, laughing voice, she pressed the Talk button. *I'll just check on the boys, see how the recording's coming along. . . .*

Roxanne answered the phone immediately, and Zoë

found herself so choked she could hardly speak. "Roxanne, this is Zoë. How are you?"

"A lot more relaxed, now that people aren't breathing down my neck about signing recording contracts."

"Oh my. Did something fall through? Aren't the boys disappointed?"

"Sure they are." Roxanne sighed. "But they need to learn early on how to wait for God's timing. If they're supposed to record, the good Lord will provide a way. In his time."

Zoë winced. This was a good lesson for her as well. "Would you tell the boys I'll pray for them? I know God has blessed them with a special gift. Their music certainly ministered to me."

"I'll tell 'em." Roxanne paused. "Did you know that Will is the one who backed off on the contract?"

Zoë caught her breath. "I wonder why he did that. He was so set on it."

"I think you shook him up." There was amusement in Roxanne's voice. "The boys and I are headed for his grandpa's farm for Thanksgiving. Want me to give him a message?"

"No, I-I think I'll give it to him myself."

"That's my girl," said Roxanne.

Zoë made the short drive from Jackson to Yazoo City in a state of high nerves. She had called Skeet for directions to Senator Fletcher's farm, because she wanted to surprise Will. As a result, she'd discovered that Jeffries's knowledge about her father had come from Skeet. Will had never discussed the subject with the record executive.

Apparently, many things were not as they had

appeared. She couldn't wait to talk to Will and apologize for leaving.

Unfortunately, Skeet's directions were less than concrete. It had been late afternoon when she left the apartment, carrying a change of clothes in a gym bag. By the time she'd turned off the highway onto a two-lane county road lined with kudzu vines, it was nearly dark and raining buckets. She called Skeet on the cell phone again.

"Skeet, this is looking very weird. I think the road's coming to an end. Where's the church I'm supposed to turn at?"

"I don't know, man." She'd noticed he called everybody "man," regardless of gender. "Do you see a white rail fence?"

"No. It's raining and the road's turned to mud and gravel all of a sudden. It's going to destroy my—" a pothole jarred the phone away from her ear—"oil pan."

"Okay, just slow down. Man, I wish you'd let me come with you."

He'd offered to meet her at the Yazoo City exit off I-55 and guide her to the farm, but Zoë wanted to do this on her own. "Should I keep going?"

Suddenly Skeet's voice was gone. The gravel disappeared at the top of a steep hill, and it was so dark she was afraid to keep going. What if the road totally dropped off? She pulled over.

She didn't know how long she sat there praying before she saw rain-blurred headlights appear across the top of the hill. *Oh, thank you, Lord. The cavalry has arrived.*

But there was no way she was going to unlock her door and let some stranger into her car, even to tell her how to get where she was going. Everybody knew not to do that.

Therefore, when her rescuer, dressed in a yellow slicker and a fishing hat held on by elastic under the chin, knocked on her window, she shook her head and stared straight ahead. From the corner of her eye she could tell he was getting wetter by the minute. And madder, too, if the way he was jumping up and down was any indication.

He knocked on the window again, and she realized he was screaming, "Zoë!" Surely an ax murderer wouldn't know her name.

She rolled the window down an inch, far enough to see a pair of light blue-gray eyes, rimmed in pewter and streaked with gold. *Will!* But he hadn't known she was coming.

"What are you doing here?" she said.

"I might ask you the same question, except I'm about to drown. Would you please let me in?"

"Oh!" She hit the door locks while Will ran around and fell into the passenger side, smelling of wet rubber and Yazoo clay.

"How did you know I was here?" she asked, and at the same time he said, "Why are you sitting here, when the farm's just over the hill?"

"You first," they said simultaneously.

They eyed each other warily. "I'm keepin' my fat mouth shut for a change," Will said.

Zoë grinned. "Why start now?"

"Ha-ha. Skeet called and told me not to tell you he called, but that you were almost here and apparently lost. He didn't know this patch of road's out."

"You mean if I'd kept driving I would've been there?"

"In about two seconds."

"How humiliating." Zoë laid her head on the steering wheel.

"I think it's cute." Will yanked off his hat and tossed it into the backseat. The top of his head was dry, but water dripped from his beard. He looked like Poseidon in yellow rubber. "You came all this way to tell me you're sorry."

Zoë gave him an exasperated look. "I came all this way to hear *you* say *you're* sorry."

"Oh yeah, right. *I* was the one who took off running without waiting for any kind of explanation."

Zoë looked at Will uncertainly. "I did come to say I'm sorry."

"Huh?"

"Okay, I did run away without letting you fully explain. I thought I had myself together, but you know how—" she gulped and risked it—"the more you care about someone the more they can hurt you."

He smiled a little. "I know. I would've come after you eventually, but I needed a little time to locate my nerve again." He shifted uncomfortably. "You rattled my cage, lady."

"I did?" Zoë felt her lips turn up. "Guess it was mutual." She looked away. "Anyway, Skeet said *he's* the one who spilled the beans to Jeffries about my father."

"Aha. And when did you get so chummy with Skeet?"

"You're jealous!" Zoë clapped her hands in delight.

"Of course I'm jealous. I've never even kissed you, and already you're trading cell phone numbers with my best friend."

"You know we can fix that," she said. "The kissing part." Will's eyes lit, but Zoë stopped him with a hand on his wet chest. "Hold on. Where is it, buster?"

"Where's what?"

"My thumb ring. You kept it. You knew my dad gave it to me and it meant a lot to me, which reminds me." Will shook his head, obviously bewildered, as Zoë excitedly put both hands on his face. "I called Brady to thank him for the birthday cards. He wanted to know what I've been doing, and we talked for nearly an hour. Oh, Will, I really wanted to give up that resentment."

"Zoë! Help me out of this crazy raincoat so I can hug you!"

Zoë was almost sorry she did so when Will nearly squeezed the breath out of her. But the long, slow kiss that followed more than made up for it. Ignoring the fact that they were rapidly sinking into a mudhole the size of the Okefenokee Swamp, she lay against his damp shoulder, stroking her hand along the fine skin of his cheek where it met silky beard and mustache. *Lord, I'd like to have this the rest of my life. Please?*

"I nearly mailed that ring back a million times, but I kept hoping you'd come and get it." He dug it out of his pocket and slid it onto her thumb. Then kissed her hand. "Zoë, I'm going to tell you something, but it has nothing to do with recording contracts or cell phones or rings or anything else except just us. Do you know what I'm saying?"

She nodded, spellbound by the ardor in his eyes. "Tell me, Will."

"It wasn't any accident that we were standing in line together in the Denver airport. I think God put us together for a reason. I think I'm the other half of you, and you're the other half of me. I love you, Zoë, so much."

She shyly kissed the corner of his mouth and said it back to him. "I love you, Will."

A tinny electronic "Hungarian Rhapsody" went off inside Will's shirt pocket. He ignored it because he was busy kissing Zoë.

Zoë plucked the phone out of Will's pocket and mumbled, "Hello."

"Well, it's about time," said a woman, presumably Will's mother. "Will said if he wasn't back in fifteen minutes to call him. Are you coming home for dinner?"

## A NOTE FROM THE AUTHOR

*Dear Reader,*

*Has anyone ever told you, "You can't get there from here"?*

*In the summer of 2000, my family flew to Colorado to visit relatives and enjoy a much anticipated vacation. I went prepared with notebooks and camera; I just knew I was going to get a great story out of this trip. And I did, but it had nothing to do with old mining towns and trains . . . the magnificent Rocky Mountains . . . the U.S. Mint and Capitol Building in Denver . . . the Celestial Seasonings Tea Factory . . . a butterfly museum and art galleries galore.*

*No, indeed. I wound up with a story about airports.*

*If I've learned anything from writing, it's that most interesting and memorable things in life are often the most frustrating—and funny! As Zoë and Will learn in this story, God often uses the derailing of our plans to teach us to trust him more. I pray that when difficulties, whether small or large, come into your life, you'll learn to look for what God is teaching you. He has a bigger purpose in mind for you than anything you could imagine! He loves you with an everlasting and unshakable love.*

*Yours in Christ,*
*Beth*

## ABOUT THE AUTHOR

Born in Mobile, Alabama, and reared in north Mississippi, Beth White spent most of her life pursuing a career in music education. A voracious reader and daydreamer, she always found time to make up stories from the perspective of her lifelong love for Jesus. She finds herself amazed and delighted to now have the privilege of sharing those stories with others.

Besides writing, Beth enjoys playing flute in the church orchestra, painting portraits in chalk pastel, and teaching second-grade Sunday school. She resides on the beautiful Gulf Coast of Alabama with her minister husband, Scott, teenagers Ryan and Hannah, and an ADHD Boston terrier named Angel.

Other novellas by Beth are included in the Heart-Quest anthologies *Prairie Christmas* and *Sweet Delights*. Currently she is working on her first full-length novel.

Beth welcomes letters written to her in care of Tyndale House Author Relations, P.O. Box 80, Wheaton, IL 60189-0080, or you can e-mail her at bethsquill@aol.com.

Kathleen Fuller

*To my husband, James,*
*who believed in me,*
*even when I didn't believe in myself.*

# CHAPTER ONE

Annika Goran sat in her light blue Escort, pain shooting through her fingers from their death grip around the steering wheel. Before her loomed the Moreland Institute of Music, its gleaming windows reflecting the fading afternoon sun. The bright rays bounced off the building and shot directly in her eyes, adding blinding pain to the sickening lump forming in her stomach.

Sitting in the car merely delayed the inevitable. She had to go inside, despite the dread that kept her frozen in her seat. She inhaled deeply, closing her eyes. *Lord, get me through this. Give me the strength I need when I see Simon.*

Simon Tunney—she had hoped never to be in the same room with the man again. How her attitude had changed from when she had first started at the institute as a student four years ago, when the mere mention of his name had sent her heart fluttering. At the time, Simon had been a senior and concertmaster of the concert orchestra. He was an excellent violinist and a charismatic performer, and Annika had been deliriously happy when he asked her out. That he possessed an ego that surpassed his talent was inconsequential. But in a short time she made an important discovery: no one thought more of Simon Tunney than Simon Tunney.

Their three-month relationship ended on bad terms. She readily accepted responsibility for it; however, she believed Simon got exactly what he deserved. When he graduated from the institute and moved to New York to pursue a career as an orchestra conductor, Annika believed she'd never see him again.

Until last night.

Her best friend, Stephanie, had called, telling her how Simon had agreed to replace Peter Van Sant, the orchestra's current conductor who'd been seriously injured in a car accident a week earlier.

Annika had nearly dropped the phone. "Why would he come back to Moreland?" she asked, clutching the receiver tightly. Simon had always looked down upon the small institute, despite its impeccable reputation for turning out world-class musicians. He felt he had done the school a favor by attending it.

"Who knows?" Stephanie answered. Annika could hear the popping sound of Stephanie's chewing gum as she cracked it between her back teeth, a constant substitute for the cigarettes she'd given up a year ago. "I just heard about it today when I stopped by the school office. I guess it was supposed to be a surprise, an alum returning to conduct at his alma mater. I thought I'd warn you though, since you two were . . . um . . . involved." She paused. "He'll be at rehearsal tomorrow."

Annika had appreciated the warning but not the consequences of it—a sleepless night and an empty bottle of antacids. Now, with the minutes ticking down and her stomach twisting in a configuration rivaling a roller coaster, she couldn't procrastinate any longer. She grabbed her violin off the passenger seat and hurried to the building.

Jogging up the steps leading into the institute, she tried to see the upside of the situation. After years of sweating blood and shedding tears during endless hours of practice, she had finally reached her goal—concertmaster of the Moreland Chamber Orchestra. And what a year to hold that position! In two weeks the orchestra would embark on a six-week European tour—a first for the school. Annika had never been overseas before, and in the months leading up to June she could hardly contain her excitement. But spending six weeks in Europe paled in comparison to what she considered her pinnacle achievement—being the featured soloist on the tour.

She wouldn't let Simon Tunney ruin what she'd worked so hard for. With renewed determination, Annika opened the door to the concert hall and made her way backstage. Musicians had stopped milling around and were finding their seats. A peek at her watch told her that she'd made it with a few moments to spare.

Annika went to her seat, weaving through chairs, music stands, and musicians. She waved at Stephanie, who flashed her a grin and continued popping her gum while she tuned her cello. Simon was nowhere to be seen. Relieved, she started to sit down when she heard a shout behind her.

*"Vorsicht!"*

Annika spun around to see a tall, slim man snatch a well-worn violin out of her chair, muttering several more words she didn't understand. German words, maybe, but she wasn't sure.

"You almost sat on it!" he snapped in slightly accented English.

Speechless, Annika's mouth opened to apologize but clamped shut when she realized whose violin she'd nearly put out of commission. Standing a few inches from her, clutching his instrument protectively as if it were a priceless treasure, was Josef Gemmel. *The* Josef Gemmel.

She couldn't believe it. Josef Gemmel—considered the best of the best violinists in the world, standing on the same stage she was. Only twenty-five years old, the Austrian virtuoso had won every award and accolade possible, plus the admiration of a multitude of adoring fans. What was he doing at her small school? And why had his violin been in *her* seat?

Her thoughts were interrupted when Simon entered and stood in front of the orchestra, scrutinizing the music that lay on the stand in front of him. *He hasn't changed much since I saw him last,* Annika thought. Same sandy brown hair, perfectly combed in the latest style, same muscular build, perfectly dressed in the latest designer labels, same haughty expression, perfectly suited to his overblown personality.

Simon hadn't so much as flicked a glance in Annika's direction. Obviously she'd gotten worked up over nothing. She was a different person now than she had been four years ago; perhaps Simon was too.

The steady tattoo of a baton tapping on the fiberglass stand, slow at first, then growing louder and more insistent, cut through the sounds of scattered conversation and the tuning of instruments. Still stunned by Josef's presence, Annika watched as he slipped into her chair, leaving her with no alternative than to sit in the seat next to him. The *second* seat.

Simon waited until everyone quieted down before

speaking. "People, let's get started. I didn't spend hours rearranging my complex schedule just so I could baby-sit some social club. I expect all musicians in your seats with your instruments tuned by five minutes to four. If you can't do that, stay home. I don't have time to waste on amateurs."

After hearing his opening statement to the orchestra, Annika knew Simon hadn't changed at all. "Oh, brother," Annika muttered. It was going to be a long two months.

For the first time Simon looked in her direction, causing her heart to jump to her throat. To her surprise, he didn't acknowledge her at all. Instead he gestured to the man sitting next to her.

Simon's lips formed a smile. Annika recalled how it used to dazzle her. Now she could see how fake it was, like the pink plastic flamingo that decorated her grandmother's front yard.

"I've also managed to arrange for Josef Gemmel to join us on this tour," Simon continued with exaggerated pride. "I'm sure all of you are aware of who he is. Let's welcome our new concertmaster."

Josef tipped his head lightly as the orchestra members applauded. Annika couldn't move. *New concertmaster?* She furrowed her brows in confusion and looked at Simon. Fury replaced the numbness as she met his eyes, the look of cruel triumph in them explaining everything. Not informing her of Josef's arrival or her replacement as concertmaster hadn't been an oversight.

Simon turned and addressed the rest of the orchestra. "I'd like to start with the concerto. From what I understand, a few of you are having difficulty with the middle section. You won't leave here until it's perfect." He gave Annika another pointed look.

Annika scrambled to pull the concerto out of her music folder. Frustrated by Simon's heartless actions, she had trouble finding the piece. She finally located it in time to see Simon raise his arms for the downbeat as the musicians held their instruments at the ready.

To her horror, she realized her violin was still in its case.

Her cheeks flaming, she fumbled with the clasps on the case as Simon lowered his arms and the musicians relaxed their stances. With shaky hands she hastily lifted her violin and bow from the soft blue velvet, nearly losing her grip on the instrument. Anger and humiliation rushed through her as she set the case on the floor and shoved it under her chair with the heel of her shoe.

"We're all waiting on you, Ms. Goran," Simon said, barely hiding the scorn in his voice.

*This cannot be happening,* she thought, placing her violin under her chin. She readied her bow and waited for Simon's downbeat.

As the orchestra began playing, she forced her brain to concentrate, despite feeling as if she'd been plunged into her worst nightmare. She consistently had problems with the concerto, but she refused to give Simon any more ammunition to embarrass her further. To her satisfaction, she played the piece flawlessly, albeit a bit out of tune. He either didn't notice or didn't care.

While Simon paged through the music on his stand, a low, smooth voice reached her ear. "The concerto is certainly not a problem for you."

Annika turned and frowned. Josef's remark had been said in a friendly manner, but she wasn't in the mood to chitchat with the usurper of her coveted position. Besides, Josef's reputation preceded him—and not just his musical one. Typical of prodigious performers, she had heard rumors about his vanity, self-absorption, and philandering nature. She'd had enough of conceited violinists to last a lifetime.

The piece on the program after the concerto was her feature. At least she still had that. Annika flipped through her folder and pulled out the music, visualizing the notes in her head before she looked at the paper.

"I've made a slight change in the next piece," Simon said as he rubbed the baton between his hands, appearing to relish what he had to tell the orchestra. "Josef will take the solo."

Annika froze. She shot a glare at Simon, then at Josef, who at least had the grace to feign surprise at this latest announcement. She fought for control, to maintain her dignity, when what she really wanted to do was hurl her bow like a spear at Simon's head. She closed her eyes briefly. *I asked for help before, Jesus. I really need it now.*

Within moments she managed to pull her emotions under control, yet the anger still simmered beneath the surface. Her position as concertmaster, her featured solo, everything she'd sacrificed to achieve, gone in the span of thirty minutes, taken away from her by a megalomaniac still nursing a grudge. She'd remain silent for now, pretending that her ego hadn't been destroyed and her confidence shattered in front of her friends, fellow musicians, and Josef Gemmel. No, she'd hold her peace, until the end of the rehearsal. She'd speak to Simon in Peter's office, privately.

Then she'd let him have it.

Josef felt like a heel.

None of it was his fault, but he didn't find much consolation in that fact. He wished, not for the first time, that he'd turned down this job the minute he'd been offered it. He had come to Moreland as a favor to Peter Van Sant, a lifelong friend of his father's. That Josef admired Peter as a conductor and a person had helped sway his decision. Now he was in a difficult position, something he didn't appreciate at all. But he would honor the commitment; he'd never broken a contract before and wasn't about to start now.

He glanced at the woman sitting next to him. Apparently there was some kind of feud going on between her and Simon Tunney. Josef didn't care much for Tunney, whom he considered a mediocre conductor at best. The man should have continued with the violin, Josef thought, but then Tunney would remain a follower instead of a leader. Simon Tunney, exceptional violinist and average conductor, was above all a control freak.

The recipient of Tunney's high-handed tactics was valiantly trying to hold herself together. Josef admired how she held her head up during the rehearsal—even as an outsider he could tell she was humiliated by it all. He'd seen conductors reduce young musicians to tears over less. Obviously the solo he'd been given to play had been hers; after the announcement Josef had observed the death grip she had on the neck of her instrument. He deduced the woman would have been pleased to replace the violin with Tunney's neck.

It didn't matter to Josef whether he had a solo or not. Lately, nothing seemed to matter much at all. For months something had been missing from his playing. A few weeks ago, after a little self-analysis and a lot of prayer, he'd managed to pinpoint the problem. He'd lost the *joy*. That ebullient feeling he got every time he picked up his instrument, the high he experienced after each performance, the oneness he achieved when he played in private, for himself and for the Lord. His reason for performing—no, his reason for *living*—had mysteriously disappeared. The violin had become a dead piece of wood in his hands, and while his performances were technically correct, they were emotionally hollow. He feared people would begin to notice.

Another fear—stronger and more penetrating—haunted him. What would he *do* without his music? From the time his father had placed a tiny violin in his hand at age three, Josef had known what he was destined to be. He had trained under elite teachers, each one agreeing that his talent came straight from God. Performing on the stage, touring the world with the finest musicians—this was what he was created to do. The thought of it vanishing terrified him. He had never considered doing anything else. Without his music, without the joy, he would be lost.

The last country on the Moreland tour was Austria. They had performances scheduled for Innsbruck, Salzburg, and Josef's hometown of Vienna. He planned to stay on in Vienna after the six-week job. He needed to see Franz Schneider, his former teacher and current mentor. Talking to him on the phone hadn't been enough, hadn't helped him come to any conclusions about what to do. Hopefully a visit in person would be the answer.

God certainly wasn't giving him any answers. He'd asked the Lord why, after so many years of loving his work, did he feel so empty inside. What was he supposed to do next? Over and over he'd hit his knees in prayer and meditation, beseeching the Lord for answers. He received silence instead.

There was nothing left for him to do but keep going, keep praying, and announce his retirement. This would be his last concert tour. Until he could conquer the problem, Josef wouldn't expose himself to a slashing by the critics. Josef Gemmel would finish on top, even if it meant he'd never darken another concert hall again.

Tunney tapped on his stand again, a habit Josef found

a little annoying. That he treated these students, many of whom were superb musicians, like beginning orchestra pupils annoyed him a *lot*. Especially Ms. Goran—was that her name? Her technique wasn't perfect, but the emotion she put into it was. She definitely had the joy.

They played the final selection of the program, a composition by Vivaldi that was one of his favorites. He played it from memory, having performed it several times before. There weren't too many pieces that he didn't know by heart because of his photographic memory for music. He discovered that he knew the orchestra's entire program. The lack of a challenge didn't help his situation any, and he knew he'd have to make a supreme effort to inject energy into the upcoming performances.

Rehearsal finally ended, three hours after it began. Josef thought of speaking to Ms. Goran again but changed his mind, remembering the frosty reception his earlier comment had received. He watched her as she wiped down the strings with a soft cloth, then placed the violin and bow in their case with almost reverential care. He used to treat his instrument the same way, as if it were an extension of his own body. Considered priceless, his Stradivarius was insured for millions. But despite its monetary value, the most emotion Josef had felt over it in the past few months was a stab of panic at the sight of Ms. Goran nearly splintering it with her backside.

She snapped the clasps of the case shut and stood to leave, but he blocked her way. Actually his long legs blocked her way.

"Excuse me," she said, her voice strained and tight.

Josef shot to his feet, allowing her to pass. "Hey," he said, touching her on the arm, "I am sorry about this. I did not know about the solo."

She yanked her arm from him, her eyes flashing with

ire. "Save it." She walked away, but not before he heard her mutter under her breath, "You egomaniacs are all alike."

Josef didn't know whether to laugh or be insulted. It wasn't the first time he'd heard that term used in reference to himself, usually second- or thirdhand. Never to his face, however. What bothered him more than the direct slam on his reputation was that Ms. Goran considered him in the same league as Tunney.

He put his violin away, slung the case over his shoulder, and followed her. A few minutes later he spied her slipping into Van Sant's office. Josef approached, intending to go to Tunney and refuse to take the solo, figuring that should settle the issue. He felt uncomfortable taking it from a student anyway. When he neared the door, he stopped at the sound of them arguing.

"You can't do this to me, Simon," she said, her voice rising an octave higher. "I've *earned* the right to be concertmaster."

"It's out of the question, Annika," Tunney said, sounding as if he were addressing a recalcitrant child. "Why do you think I convinced Josef to join this tour? Big names attract big crowds; big crowds make big money. Do you believe people will flock to hear the Moreland Chamber Orchestra featuring Annika Goran? Hardly."

Josef couldn't believe Tunney had the gall to take credit for something he had nothing to do with. He fought to stay calm.

"I-I'll go to the dean about this," Annika said.

"Go ahead. See the president of the institute if you like. But you won't get very far. They will abide by whatever decisions I choose to make. The administration has given me complete control of this orchestra."

"No doubt one of the requirements of your contract," Annika remarked sourly.

"Of course."

A long pause. "O-okay." Josef could tell it cost her to admit that Tunney held the upper hand. "But to take my solo away—"

"Same reason. It's business."

Josef peeked around the doorjamb, ignoring the guilt he felt over eavesdropping on a private conversation. He could see them both clearly. Tunney leaned back in his chair, his hands clasped across his lap and a smug look plastered on his face. Annika paced in front of his desk, chewing on her bottom lip. The wall of indifference she'd maintained during the rehearsal seemed to crumble around her.

She stopped pacing and turned to Tunney. Josef couldn't see her expression, but he could hear the desperation in her voice.

"Simon, please. If this is about what happened four years ago . . . I told you I'm sorry for that. You know I'll never have this opportunity again. Please . . . don't take it away from me."

Her words had an odd effect on Josef. He felt sympathy for her. Sympathy and something else he couldn't define. Something that made his heart beat a little faster.

"Please, Simon," she repeated, choking on his name. She was begging, pleading for Tunney to reconsider.

Josef clenched his fists. She shouldn't have to beg.

Tunney unclasped his hands, rose from his chair, and leaned forward until their faces were inches apart. "This is an important tour. The institute's reputation is at stake."

"Since when did you care about the institute?" she sneered.

"Since I put my name and reputation on the line to conduct this orchestra! You don't have what it takes, Annika. You never have. When I met you, you were struggling to keep up with the least talented musicians in the orchestra. Pitiful, really, how you had to spend hours and hours practicing the easiest compositions. We both know you were lucky to be accepted into the institute to begin with, not to mention this orchestra." Simon smirked. "I can only imagine how you used your . . . talents . . . to get Peter to hand you that solo."

Annika stuttered, apparently trying to defend herself.

As for Josef, he'd heard enough. Tunney's implication was explicitly clear. He stepped through the office doorway and cleared his throat loudly. "Simon, a word?"

Annika's head jerked at the interruption; her face flushed. For an instant their eyes met, and he was startled by the underlying sadness he saw in hers. And the beauty. Her eyes were the most striking color, not a true blue or green, more like aquamarine. The unfamiliar emotions he'd experienced moments earlier returned full force.

She turned away from him quickly, as if trying to hide what he'd already seen. She picked up her violin from the floor and hurried past him, brushing his arm as she went by.

Tunney shut the door behind her, smiling as if he had been discussing the weather with her, instead of shredding her character and leaving the remains at her feet. "Josef. What can I do for you?"

He counted to ten. He needed the time to collect his thoughts, to keep from saying something he would regret to this cocky fool who showed no remorse for shattering a young woman's dreams. During those ten seconds he made a decision.

"There will be a change in the program," Josef announced, telling Tunney his plan. When the conductor began to sputter in protest, Josef raised his hand, cutting him off.

"Do not worry, Simon; it is nothing personal. Just *business.*"

# CHAPTER TWO

THE next afternoon, Annika sat in her Escort in the same parking space as the day before. No sunlight bounced off the windows this time. Flat gray clouds cloaked the sky, mirroring her foul mood. A bizarre sense of déjà vu hit her, along with the thought that at least yesterday she'd had a flicker of hope that things would be civil between her and Simon. Today she had nothing.

She'd cried last night, too many tears to count. She railed against Simon, then turned her anger on God. *Why?* She kept asking the question over and over, certain her cries were landing on deaf ears. Why would God allow this to happen? He knew the desires of her heart. She'd felt his presence in her life nearly every moment since becoming a Christian three years ago. Didn't he want her to achieve her goal? Annika had thought she'd been given a divine blessing the day Peter had offered her the chance of a lifetime. Now she didn't know what to think.

What chafed the most was that her dream had dissolved at the hands of Simon. Her hatred of him had increased exponentially throughout the course of the night. It had taken all the strength she could muster to let go of it before she fell asleep, her Bible lying on her bed, open to the book of Ephesians. "Don't let the sun go down while you are still angry." Annika had taken the apostle Paul's words to heart, asking Jesus to help her let it go. While the scorching hate no longer consumed her, nothing could stem the deep disappointment that penetrated her soul.

With a deflated spirit she entered the institute. From the corner of the practice hall she could see Josef, his height making him visible over most of the other musicians. He was tall and thin. *Too thin,* Annika judged, slightly satisfied that Josef Gemmel had at least one imperfection.

He couldn't be faulted for anything else. Even in her agitated state, Annika had to admit he was extremely handsome. Pale blue eyes, angular jaw, hair the color of spun gold. His playing was pure genius. If she hadn't been so distracted yesterday, she would have enjoyed being so close to musical heaven. God had blessed Josef's face and fingers, no doubt about it. It made her resent the man even more.

She hadn't realized she'd been staring at him until he lifted his hand and waved in her direction. Dismissing his gesture, she started to turn her back on him when Stephanie appeared.

"Annika, are you okay?" Stephanie asked, stepping in front of her. "I was worried about you. I tried calling a dozen times last night, but your line was busy."

"I took the phone off the hook."

Stephanie nodded. "I don't blame you. What a jerk! I don't understand what you ever saw in Simon Tunney."

"Me either," Annika agreed.

"Well, if you ask me, I think what he did yesterday was bogus. I hope you straightened him out."

"I tried. He wouldn't listen to me."

"Let Gus and me have a shot at him," Stephanie offered, referring to her boyfriend, who happened to be the orchestra's timpani player. He was also an amateur bodybuilder on the side. "Give us a few moments alone with him, and I'll guarantee you'll have two solos on the program."

Annika gave her a halfhearted smile, then glanced at Gus, his massive biceps bulging as he picked up and arranged his timpani on the percussion platform. "I appreciate the offer of brute force, but it's not necessary. I've accepted that Josef will do the solo. For me, I guess it wasn't meant to be."

At the sound of shrill feminine laughter Stephanie turned around, and both women saw Josef smiling, surrounded by several females flirting outrageously with him. "At least you have one thing going for you," Stephanie said, sighing.

"What?"

Stephanie pointed her thumb in Josef's direction. "You get to sit next to *him*. Imagine, Josef Gemmel, playing with our little orchestra. It's too good to be true."

Annika rolled her eyes. "C'mon, Stephanie, don't tell me you've been sucked in by his so-called charms too."

"What charms? Just looking at him is enough for me." She leaned forward and whispered conspiratorially. "Don't tell Gus I was drooling, okay? He has a bit of a jealous streak." She spoke the last statement with pride. "You know, Annika, half the women in this orchestra would give their right arm to trade places with you."

Annika frowned. "I don't want anyone's arm. I want things back the way they were."

Annika stood across from Josef, still trying to figure out how she ended up in the practice room alone with him. It had all happened so fast—she had just finished tuning her violin when Simon started passing out new music, saying there had been *another* change in the program.

All these changes didn't sit well with her, especially being made less than two weeks before the tour started. She liked to have plenty of time to practice. She *needed* the extra practice sessions. Unlike Josef, and even Stephanie, Annika's talent wasn't natural, which was why she'd been so surprised when Peter had chosen her as soloist. She had to work at it constantly to make it appear that way. The hard calluses and permanent dent marks on the fingertips of her left hand were testimony to her perseverance. Occasionally she still had to apply bandages to her hands after a particularly long session. But what she lacked in talent she made up for in determination and a complete love for her instrument and her music.

While the idea of performing a solo in front of an audience made her knees shake and her stomach do flip-flops, she couldn't help but feel pride that someone had appreciated her efforts. This was her last year with the orchestra. After she finished school in December she wouldn't move to New York or Boston or London to join the big orchestras. The competition was too fierce, the other musicians too talented. Instead, she planned to find a job teaching music to elementary students. This trip would have been her one chance to experience what up to a few months ago she had considered only a fantasy.

Thanks to Simon, it would remain a fantasy.

As soon as the musicians had a copy of the new piece in their hands, Simon had dismissed her and Josef without an explanation, telling them to go to practice room 219. Josef hadn't seemed confused at all as Annika led him down the hall and into the room. When they entered, he reached for two music stands and set them next to each other, spreading the sheet music across both.

He looked up at her expectantly. "You can read music from over there?" he asked, a teasing smile playing on his lips.

She wouldn't budge until she got some answers. "I want to know what's going on."

"A change in the program," he replied, gesturing to the stands in front of him. "A duet."

She shook her head, not comprehending. "With who?"

"With me."

Annika rubbed her lips together, still unsure of how to react to this latest news. Josef wanted her to play a duet? With him? Then reality hit—and caused her nervous system to surge into overdrive. Josef had performed for monarchs, presidents, and sultans. She surmised he probably had played in every major concert hall in every major city in the free world. She'd never been beyond the Illinois state line. How could she possibly measure up?

"I-I can't do this," she said quietly.

Josef arched an eyebrow quizzically. "Why not?"

"Because you're you, and I'm . . . me."

He smiled again. "Now that we know who we are, you can come over here. I promise, I do not bite." His smile dissolved somewhat when she didn't react to his attempt at a joke. "Okay. Let us start. This is a rather difficult piece, and we do not have much time to go over it."

His words made her blood run cold. If he thought it was difficult, she would think it impossible. Suddenly she saw the situation clearly. This had to be Simon's idea—

a way to hack down her ego another notch. "You can tell Simon to forget it. I'm not doing this." Annika folded her arms across her chest, her violin and bow dangling on each side of her torso.

Josef stepped from behind the stands and walked toward her. She had to raise her head to look him in the face. He had at least six inches on her. With him this close, she could see exactly what Stephanie and a legion of other female admirers were talking about. The fluttering sensation that unexpectedly appeared in her stomach had nothing to do with nervousness or her renewed irritation with Simon.

*Stop it!* She had to be going crazy. The stress of the past twenty-four hours was getting to her. That had to be why she was experiencing such an intense attraction to him. No way she was getting involved with another musician. Never, ever, ever. Even if he did have gorgeous blue eyes and a lightly accented voice that could melt butter.

"You think this was Simon's idea?" he asked, seemingly taken aback that she would suggest such a thing.

"Who else?" She took a step away from him. "He knows I can't keep up with you."

"But you are wrong about that. I think you can keep up with me just fine." Annika swallowed as he extended his hand toward her. "Come, Annika. Try it. You may surprise yourself."

She stared at his hand. It looked strong. Inviting. Tempting. Then she realized her hands were full.

Uncrossing her arms, she sailed past him, trying to appear nonchalant, like handsome virtuosos offered their hands to her all the time. "I'll take a look at it, but I'm not making any promises."

"Agreed. No promises." If he was bothered by her rebuff, he didn't let on. He also didn't seem like the conceited artist she'd heard about. Then again, they'd only been together for a few minutes. Annika would have bet her left hand his true colors would show anytime now.

Simon had fooled her once. She wouldn't be fooled again.

෴

Two hours later, Josef and Annika were still working. He was pleased that his intuition about her had been correct— the woman would not quit. He had been straight with her in describing the difficulty of the piece. There were several tricky passages; he'd had trouble with a few of them the first time he played it. But as with other compositions, he had this one memorized. For her sake, he pretended not to.

"I can't do this!" Annika cried out in frustration. She stomped away from the music stands and plopped onto a hard-backed wooden chair, her head dropping into her free hand. "It's too difficult," she whispered, defeated.

Josef laid his violin in its case, dragged a chair from across the room, and sat next to her. "We will take a break. We can get some coffee—"

"I don't want any coffee!" She lifted her head up and looked at him, strain and weariness etched on her face. Thin strands of her dark brown hair had fallen from her sleek French braid, adding to her fatigued appearance. She tried to smooth a couple of them back, but they fell forward again.

"All right, then, we can resume this tomorrow," Josef assured her.

"Why don't we just forget the whole thing," she retorted.

"So you are having a little bit of trouble. Do not worry about it. We will practice some more."

She scowled at him, pointing her finger at his chest. "You don't understand. It comes so easy for you. I can tell you're holding back—" Annika dropped her hand and looked down at the floor—"because of me."

Josef hadn't counted on her being so perceptive. It made him like her even more. "Annika, I have played this before. Not in public, but I have rehearsed it and learned it. I have an advantage over you."

"Don't patronize me!" she shouted, then slumped her shoulders. "Where did you find this *Die Verfolgung,* anyway? I've never heard of Franz Schneider."

That didn't surprise him. Over thirty years ago, Franz had been in the same position Josef was in now. After an illustrious career touring the world, Franz abruptly retired and now shunned the limelight, content to teach his few students, advise their careers, and compose music that came from his heart. Josef spoke of him fondly. "He is a friend of mine, a very good friend. He wrote this piece for me last year, then told me to find a partner to perform it with. I chose you."

Annika sighed. "You obviously chose wrong."

"No, I do not think so. Maybe if I explain the story behind it, you will better understand the movement of the piece." He told her how Franz had been inspired to compose the duet when he'd read an old story about two young lovers, one who pursued the other relentlessly, courting her until she gave in.

"So you're chasing me, is that it?"

"Exactly." Josef hid a smile at the blush that rose to her face. "The measures you are struggling with are the scenes where you are running away from me. You have to stay a few beats ahead. It is a complicated rhythm."

She remained silent for a few seconds, in deep thought. "Maybe if I heard the rest of the arrangement . . . "

"I will get the tape of it from Simon tomorrow before rehearsal. I asked him to record it today when the orchestra goes over it."

"I'm surprised you convinced him to do this." She paused, her eyes narrowing at him suspiciously. "You heard us arguing yesterday, didn't you?"

This time Josef turned pink. "Just a small part of the conversation—"

"Oooh, I don't believe this!" Annika shot from her seat and retrieved her case. She practically threw her violin in it and slammed the lid shut. "I suppose I should kiss the ground in gratitude over the privilege of playing with the great Josef Gemmel." Shaking her head, she walked toward the door.

"Now wait a minute," Josef said, growing irritated with her sarcastic tone. "I am only trying to help you."

Annika stopped and spun around, her eyes filled with anger. "And what will you demand in return for your offer of 'help'?" She marched to where he was seated and glared down at him. "I don't know what Simon told you about me, but let me set the record straight *right now.* I'm not some starry-eyed schoolgirl you can seduce with a favor and a few compliments. I know what you're after, and you won't be getting it from *me.*"

Slowly Josef rose from his seat and looked at her, trying to contain his temper. He couldn't believe he'd just been lambasted, not to mention insulted, when his motives had been pure. This time he towered over her, feeling more than a little satisfied that he was now looking down at *her*.

"I do not have to listen to this," he stated in a clipped tone. "I have needed a partner for this piece of music. You had something unfairly taken away from you. I thought this might be the answer for both of us." He brushed by her, grabbed his instrument and case, then walked to the door. "You have acted very much like a schoolgirl today. When you are ready to act like a professional musician, let me know."

"Josef—"

He turned and opened the door, then spoke over his shoulder. "And do not ever assume you know what I want, Ms. Goran. You do not know me at all."

# CHAPTER THREE

"YOU'RE a twit, Annika."

Annika froze at Stephanie's barb, a pastrami sandwich halfway to her mouth. They were eating lunch at Bruno's, their usual hangout. The small deli was filled with customers, their noisy conversation filling the air.

"What did you call me?" Annika asked, thinking she might have misunderstood her friend. She set down her sandwich on the red-and-yellow-striped plate in front of her.

"Look, I've always been honest with you, right? We've been friends for three years now. We accepted Christ at the same time. We've been there for each other through the good and the bad. So when I tell you you're a twit, I mean it."

Annika pouted. "That's harsh, Steph."

"I'm sorry, but I call it like I see it. I don't understand what the problem is with you and Josef. If he wanted to do a duet with me, I'd faint from the thrill."

"There're extenuating circumstances." Annika didn't want to acknowledge the mortification she'd felt at discovering Josef had overheard her conversation in Simon's office. Every insult Simon had hurled her way replayed in her mind. That there had been a grain of truth in Simon's assessment of her musical talent cut her deeply. That Josef had heard it poured salt into the wound.

Stephanie cracked her gum. "You're scared."

"No, I'm not."

"Yes, you are and I know why. You're afraid he's like Simon."

"I'm sure he's exactly like Simon," Annika asserted.

"I don't get that impression."

"You don't know him."

"And you do?" Stephanie stared her down. "Annika, you've only known him two days, and the first day doesn't count because you didn't talk to him."

"I know his type," Annika said defensively, yet realizing what she said rang false. *"You do not know me at all."* Josef's words in his ridiculously formal English bounced around in her head. Her sandwich lay on the plate, untouched, her appetite gone. She spread out her hands, palms up. "Look, I've heard the stories, the rumors about him. They say he has a girl in every city, so to speak, and he's left a trail of broken hearts that would span the Atlantic. What else am I supposed to think?"

Stephanie scolded her. "I can't believe you actually pay attention to those stupid rumors. You of all people should know how damaging gossip is."

Annika folded her fingers into tight fists, remembering what happened four years ago. "Simon spread those lies out of revenge. There wasn't a grain of truth to any of them."

"Of course not. Still, some people did believe what he said about you sleeping around."

She flinched. "I know. It took months for me to restore my reputation. Why are you laughing? I don't see anything funny about this."

Wiping her eyes, Stephanie fought for control. "I'm sorry. I can't help it. That happens every time I think about that right hook you gave Simon."

Annika's face slowly broke into a grin. "He deserved it—I'd had it with him pressuring me into giving him what he wanted. Sex was—*is*—all that man ever thinks about."

"Well, I think breaking his nose taught him a lesson. He had black bruises under his eyes for weeks!"

"How was I supposed to know he had sensitive skin?"

With that, both women burst into laughter. *Thank God I can laugh at it now,* Annika thought. At the time it had been anything but funny.

Stephanie became serious again. "Annika, this thing with Josef—you need to give him the benefit of the doubt. It's no more than you would have wanted for yourself. Besides, there are some other rumors that contradict the ones circulating around."

Annika was skeptical. "Like what?"

"That he's a Christian, for one. That he's a nice guy for another. Take him at face value, and see for yourself if the stories you've heard are true or a bunch of fairy tales." Stephanie slurped her strawberry soda, the shade of the beverage matching the latest color of her cropped hair. "Look at it this way: Simon snatched your golden moment right out from under you. Josef's giving you the opportunity to shine again."

Annika started to tear tiny sections of crust off her bread, waiting a few long moments before admitting the real basis of her fear aloud. "What if I can't match him, Steph? Josef's in a class by himself musically. What if I drag him down?"

"I'm sure he'll adjust," Stephanie replied dryly. "The point is, he chose you, so he must have some confidence in your abilities. I know I do. Now you need to look inward and heavenward and find that confidence for yourself."

Sensing another presence in the practice room, Josef opened his eyes and stopped his bow. Annika entered and placed her violin case on an empty chair, then flipped up the clasps.

He threw her a cold look. "Are you back to play, Annika? Or are you here to pick another fight?"

Turning toward him, she took a deep breath. "Josef, I owe you an apology. I've been a little . . . stressed lately. That's a lousy excuse, I know." Her fingers twisted the hem of her lavender shirt. "I'm here to play if you still want me as a partner."

Reading the genuine remorse in her eyes, Josef's attitude softened. "No harm done," he said, meaning it. Annika smiled, causing Josef to notice again how lovely she was. He liked how she wore her dark brown hair braided and pulled back from her face, showcasing her irresistible aqua eyes and creamy complexion. He hadn't realized he'd been staring at her until she cocked her head to the side and looked at him oddly.

"Everything okay, Josef?"

"Uh, yes," he said, quickly recovering by lifting up his violin. "We should, um, tune, *ja?*"

*"Ja,"* she mimicked good-naturedly.

After they tuned their instruments, Josef went to the tape player and popped in a cheap white cassette. "The orchestra," he indicated, pressing Play.

For the next three hours they practiced. By the second

hour Josef thought they sounded good, but Annika wasn't satisfied. By the end of the third hour she was less sure than before.

"Josef, this is a disaster. I sound horrible."

He disagreed with her assessment but had noticed that the last thirty minutes hadn't gone well. She seemed to be caving in from the pressure she was placing on herself. This was a different Annika from the woman he'd heard play his first day at the institute. Before her confrontation with Tunney.

"You have to let go. Trust yourself. It does not have to be perfect every time."

"Yes, it does! I have to be perfect because you're perfect!" She groaned, as if she hadn't meant to voice her thoughts aloud.

Josef wanted to put his arm around her, to give her the reassurance she desperately needed, but he sensed she wouldn't appreciate the gesture. *What do I tell her, Lord? How do I help her believe in herself?*

"No more practicing," he blurted, not knowing where the words came from.

Annika shot him an incredulous look. "What?"

He now knew what he had to do. "You can practice on your own if you want. When we get to London we will do a quick run-through before the first concert, but I am through working on this." He gathered up the sheet music and handed it to her, wincing inwardly as he saw the color drain from her face.

"Josef, don't leave. Please! I need you to help me."

The note of sheer terror in her voice tugged at him, but he stood firm. "I believe you are ready, Annika. Now it is time for you to figure that out for yourself." He picked up his violin and left as she started to object again.

Shutting the door behind him, he was grimly aware that for the second time in two days he was walking out on her.

꩜

Two weeks later, the Moreland Chamber Orchestra departed for Europe. Several hours into the flight, Annika felt someone grasp her earphones, pulling them away from her head.

"What are you listening to?" Stephanie asked, letting the ear pads drop onto Annika's neck.

"The duet," she replied, more than a touch annoyed at the interruption. "I recorded my part right before we left, and I've been reviewing it."

"For five hours?" Stephanie tossed her a disapproving look as she sat down in the empty seat next to her.

Annika checked her watch. Had she really been listening to the same song for five hours straight? That couldn't be possible, yet time didn't lie.

"You're obsessing," Stephanie commented, popping her gum.

"And you're irritating." Annika pressed the rewind button on her portable tape player. "What are you doing up here, anyway?" she asked. Stephanie's and Gus's seats were several rows behind hers. "Don't you need to go bug your boyfriend or something?"

"Gus is sleeping like a baby. You know men—they can conk out anywhere."

Annika nodded her agreement. For the thousandth time since the flight from Chicago began, she looked across at Josef, who was leaning back in his seat, his lanky legs stretched out into the aisle. Watching the steady rise and fall of his chest as he slept, she remembered his refusal of the first-class ticket the institute had offered him. Instead of enjoying the spacious leg room and special treatment that Simon had insisted on, Josef had his ticket downgraded to coach. That gesture was the exact opposite of what she'd expected of him. She didn't know what to make of it.

"You're staring at him again."

"No, I'm not," Annika shot back, not in the mood for Stephanie's ribbing. She lifted the headphones from her neck. "I don't want to be rude, but I need to work on this. We'll be in London soon—"

"Where you'll pull out your violin and practice for another five hours while the rest of us are out sightseeing. The concert isn't until tomorrow, Annika. Give it a rest."

"I can't." Annika put her headphones back on and closed her eyes, hoping Stephanie would get the hint, and was relieved when she did. After her friend left, she pressed the play button on her cassette player and turned up the volume. Musical notes danced in her head while her left hand played an imaginary fingerboard, complete with vibrato. Her fingers were moving through a run of sixteenth notes when she suddenly felt a warm hand cover hers.

Startled, she lashed out. "Stephanie, I told you to leave me alone!" Too late she realized the hand holding hers was far too big to be Stephanie's.

She opened her eyes to see Josef sitting in the seat next to her. He threaded his fingers through hers.

Annika ripped off her headphones. "What do you think you're doing?"

He smiled playfully. "If I have to, I will hold your hand all the way to London."

Was it her imagination, or did the temperature in the airplane suddenly rise ten degrees? The sensation of their entwined fingers, along with his charming grin, caused her to experience a confusing mixture of excitement and wariness at the same time. A small part of her enjoyed the contact, but she had to work hard at getting the image of Josef as a Casanova out of her head.

"You have a lot of nerve," she said, sounding more annoyed than she actually felt. "Besides," she added, attempting to yank her hand from his, "it really isn't necessary."

Josef shook his head. "I disagree. You have been fingering the same notes for hours, Annika."

"No, I haven't," she lied. "I've been listening to different pieces."

"I recognized the finger positions."

She felt her face heat. That's what she got for lying. Embarrassed at being caught fibbing, she tried to pry her fingers loose, only to have them squeezed gently for her efforts. When she looked at Josef, she saw the twinkle in his eye.

"You're not that good," she said, realizing he'd been pulling her leg.

"No, I am not," he agreed, chuckling as he settled more comfortably in his seat.

Closer to her, she noticed, secretly pleased. Their shoulders were nearly touching, and she knew she should put more separation between them. But for some reason all the mental stop signals that usually lit up in her head were out of order. Suddenly tired, Annika leaned her head against the back of her seat and turned to him, noticing for the first time that his eyes weren't a pure shade of blue, but flecked with tiny spots of hazel. *He has the most amazing eyes.* Instead of looking away like she should have, she continued to gaze at him, an activity she thought she could indulge in all day.

"Tell me what it's like to be a famous virtuoso," she said, suddenly wanting to know more about him.

Josef shrugged, still holding her hand. "Not much to tell. A concert here, a concert there."

Annika closed her eyes, feeling relaxed for the first time since the plane had left the ground. Her mind felt thick and fuzzy, her hand turned into a deadweight in Josef's palm. "Surely you have some fascinating stories to relate." She yawned. "Leading the glamorous life you do."

"I would not call it glamorous," he said, his voice sounding strange and far away. He made some other comment, but she didn't catch all of it. The last thing she remembered was her head landing on something warm and extremely comfortable.

Annika's eyes flew open as the jet's landing gear hit the ground with a loud thudding screech. She glanced at her hand, still comfortably cradled in Josef's. Her eyes grew wide when she realized her ear was pressed against his shoulder while his cheek rested against the top of her head.

"Josef, wake up!" she ordered, nudging him with her elbow. How long had she been sleeping on him? She extracted her hand from his and scooted as far away from him as she could, attempting to smooth back her hair, which had come out of its braid again. Annika frantically hoped Stephanie had stayed in the back of the plane with Gus. If her friend had spotted them using each other as pillows, Annika would never live it down. Turning her head to stare out at the gray blanket of mist smothering the runway, she couldn't help but glance briefly at Josef while he calmly stretched his arms over his head and unfurled his long legs in the aisle.

"Ah, we have landed," he said, casually leaning near her to look out the window, so close she could feel the warmth of his breath against her ear, causing an involuntary shiver to run down her spine. "Good old Heathrow—covered in fog as usual."

Annika remained silent and continued to stare out the tiny oval window as if the London fog was the most interesting thing England had to offer. She could feel his eyes on her, as if he was waiting for a response. When he sat back in his chair, she exhaled, unaware until that moment that she'd been holding her breath.

Within minutes they were at the terminal. After they deplaned and collected the baggage and instruments, the orchestra members flagged down several taxis that took them to a quaint little village outside of London. Amid the hectic confusion, Annika and Josef were separated.

They had arrived in London shortly after noon, and with the concert eight hours away, some of the musicians, including Stephanie and Gus, discussed their plans for the rest of the day. Annika declined their offer to join them, instead choosing to practice in the room she and Stephanie shared. Saying "I told you so," Stephanie dragged Gus by the hand and left, in a hurry to catch the bus to London.

Now alone, Annika's relaxed mood had completely dissipated, leaving near panic in its place. She wished she could somehow halt her unnatural fear of performing tonight. Though she was used to a touch of stage fright, she'd never experienced uncontrollable trembling in her hands and a sick sensation in her stomach this early before a performance. *If I feel like this now, how am I going to make it through the concert tonight?*

Annika went to the tiny bathroom in her room and turned on the tap. She splashed her face a few times with the chilly water, the liquid cooling her hot cheeks.

Although the windows were cranked open, the room still felt warm. Annika quickly changed out of her navy pantsuit and into a pale green T-shirt and white shorts, then freed her hair from its braid, ran a brush through it, and clipped it back into a ponytail at her neck. Feeling refreshed and a little less anxious, she took her violin out of her case and began to tune it, plucking the first string when she heard a knock on the door.

"Just a minute." Annika laid the violin on the bed, thinking Stephanie must have left her key behind. When she opened the door, she was stunned to see Josef standing there, his violin tucked under his arm.

"I thought you'd be sightseeing with everyone else," Annika remarked.

Josef shook his head. "I have seen London already. Several times," he added with a touch of weariness. "I told you we would practice before the concert, remember?"

She had forgotten. Taking note of his appearance, which she inexplicably seemed to be doing a lot of lately, she saw that he'd changed into a black T-shirt and a pair of khaki shorts. She also noticed how incredibly good he looked.

For a few awkward seconds she stood gaping at him in the doorway while he remained in the hall.

# CHAPTER FOUR

"GET your violin," Josef said. "I know a place where we can practice."

Annika paused before picking up her violin and bow. With no one else around, Josef had a clear opportunity to make a move on her. She knew Simon certainly would have tried under the same circumstances. But instead, Josef remained in the hallway, keeping a polite distance. Not exactly the behavior of a lecherous lady-killer. She already respected Josef Gemmel musically. Now she was beginning to respect him as a man as well.

She retrieved her instrument, slipped her room key into her pocket, and slid her feet into a pair of sandals. After locking the door, she followed him down the hall of the very unusual hotel. It wasn't really a hotel—more of a cross between an inn and a huge bed-and-breakfast. Annika thought the quaint decor and sincere hospitality of the staff were charming.

"Where are we going?" she asked, having to take two strides to Josef's one.

He glanced down at her, the glint back in his eyes. "Always full of questions," he replied cryptically.

"Why do you have to be so evasive all the time?" she parried back.

Josef laughed. "Another question—I am right, *ja?*"

*"Ja,"* she said through gritted teeth. "Would you mind slowing down?" she requested irritably, her legs starting to ache as she tried to keep up with him.

"Sorry." He slowed his steps, but only slightly, a smile still on his face. "I forgot that you are so little."

Despite his jovial tone, she took his words as an insult. "I'm *not* so little," she insisted, gripping the neck of her violin tightly. "In case you hadn't noticed, you are *unnaturally* tall."

Josef suddenly stopped, then turned toward her. She halted but barely missed colliding with his chest as he stepped forward. Her own chest felt like it would explode when he placed two long fingers underneath her chin and tilted it up.

*"Nein,* Annika," he said, his voice low and husky. "I do not think I am too tall for you."

*Please, Lord, no. I cannot fall for this guy! No musicians, remember?*

But it was Josef who broke away first, so swiftly that maybe she'd dreamt he'd touched her. When they resumed walking, she had to take three strides to match his pace.

Annika was breathless by the time they reached the lobby, whether from the brisk walk or her encounter with Josef she couldn't tell. She was grateful when he left her side to speak with the owner of the inn, giving her a chance to settle her emotions.

When he returned, the woman's bright laughter

echoed through the room, and a mischievous grin shone on his face. "Ready to practice?" he asked.

"Where?"

"No more questions," he said. "Follow me."

As they walked out the door, Josef snatched a short, round, brass kettle off a small table near the entrance of the inn. The pot was empty, a part of the inn's eclectic decor.

They walked down the cobblestone path and onto the sidewalk in front of the establishment, next to the street. He set the container in front of him and lifted his violin to his neck.

"Let us start," he said, playing what she recognized as an Irish jig on his strings pizzicato style with his index finger.

She scanned the area, then looked at the pot near his feet. He couldn't be serious. The fog of the morning had melted off; now sunshine filled the sky. An unusual aromatic mix of freshly cut grass and industrial exhaust permeated the air. People in the surrounding houses were tending the flowers in their yards or sitting in plastic and metal lawn chairs, enjoying the warm summer day. Everywhere she looked she saw people—sitting, walking, driving cars on the wrong side of the road. It was a busy neighborhood.

"Here?" she queried, thinking he'd lost his mind.

Josef kept plucking. "Why not here?"

"Because there are tons of *people* around, or has that little detail completely escaped you?"

"Who do you think you will be playing in front of tonight—cows?"

She laughed at the image of several hundred bovines crowded into the elegant London concert hall. "Okay, point taken. But still . . . "

"Annika," he said sternly, "no more stalling. Lift up that violin or I will do it for you."

She didn't think she could handle being that close to him again, so she complied. They were well into their duet before she realized it was the first time she had played it without the reassuring presence of sheet music in front of her. She stumbled a bit, then recovered nicely.

Soon they had an audience. Annika skimmed the crowd, and before long she heard the plinking of coins being tossed in the brass pot. She looked at Josef, who winked and flashed her a wicked grin.

As they continued to play, all trepidation and nervousness left her. More people gathered around, but Annika began to lose herself in the beautiful music she and Josef were making together. When the piece was almost over she had no idea if she'd played it accurately or not. For once she didn't care. From the appreciative looks on the listeners' faces, no one else seemed to care either.

Still running through a tricky triplet passage, she strolled toward Josef, staring at him with wide-eyed innocence as her fingers abandoned the romantic classical tune they were playing and flew into old-fashioned Kentucky bluegrass, proving he wasn't the only one who could spring a surprise.

Annika reveled in the shock she saw in his eyes, which quickly changed to delight as he switched gears without missing a beat. What started out as one lover chasing another turned into dueling fiddles, the crowd applauding its approval. Rivulets of sweat ran down her back as she played faster and faster, trying to outduel the virtuoso in front of her. She noticed a lock of his blond hair had fallen over his forehead, the color of it darkened by perspiration. Her eyes never left his, and she was mesmerized by the unabashed happiness she saw in them, thinking they reflected the mirth in her own.

Each time she sped up, he matched her. When she

slowed down, he stayed with her. Anything she did he reacted to without a misstep, until her arm began to ache and strands of horsehair on her bow began to split apart. Notes flew fast and furious in the air. The crowd—which had grown considerably larger since the couple had changed musical styles—was clapping and cheering along. But she couldn't keep it up much longer. He was too fast, too strong for her. Reluctantly, she gave in, finishing her last stanza with a flourish.

"Bravo! Good show! Encore, encore!" Onlookers voiced their approval as coins and bills fell into the pot, filling it to the brim. Exhilarated and gasping for breath, Annika took a small bow. Josef did the same.

It wasn't until the crowd had finally dispersed that she saw members of her orchestra approach, still clapping.

Stephanie ran up to her and caught her in a big hug. "That was fantastic! Unbelievable! I had no idea you two could do that. Who knew an Austrian could play bluegrass like an Appalachian country boy?" Stephanie, never stingy with her hugs, put her arms around Josef as well.

Annika watched him return Stephanie's hug a bit stiffly at first; then he relaxed and embraced her completely. She felt a tingling sensation up and down her arms as she imagined for a split second that she was the one embracing him, instead of Stephanie.

"You have to do that tonight at the concert," Stephanie ordered after she and Josef had parted.

"We can't play bluegrass at a classical concert," Annika said, unnecessarily stating the obvious.

Stephanie shook her head. "No, not that. What I mean is you two need to play together on the stage, just like you did here."

Confused, Annika questioned her again. "What are you talking about? We already do that."

Stephanie let out a long-suffering sigh. "Not the way you did here. In rehearsal you guys just stood next to each other, playing to the audience. Here you played to *each other.* Do that tonight and you'll knock 'em dead."

Josef smiled slowly. "Good idea, Stephanie. *Sehr gut.*"

Annika wanted to be as confident as he was. She'd had fun, and from what she could tell, he'd enjoyed himself too. Could they duplicate it onstage? Self-doubt plagued her again as she thought about it.

Josef appeared unconcerned. He picked up the pot loaded with money and tucked it under his arm. "I am going to take a rest before the concert." He looked at Annika. "Do not worry," he told her. "You are more than ready." He gave her a reassuring smile, then turned to go inside.

Watching him walk away, Annika wished she could believe him.

"Hey, Josef!" Stephanie shouted after him. "What are you going to do with all that cash?"

His only response was to give Stephanie a backhanded wave as he entered the inn.

Josef arrived at the concert hall early, something he did before every performance. He liked having the stage to himself for a few minutes. It gave him a chance to tune, to practice, and to pray.

Tonight he had more to pray about than his own playing. He wasn't nervous; stage fright was something he'd conquered years ago. If he made a mistake, he never let it affect the rest of his performance. Contrary to what Annika believed, he wasn't perfect. He knew he never would be.

Backstage he absently ran through a few scales, his thoughts not on the music but on Annika. There was no use denying it—he liked her. A lot. Not just her physical beauty, although in his mind she had plenty of that. No, the attraction went deeper, beyond her feelings of insecurity about her playing, past her wariness and distrust of those she felt threatened by.

He remembered holding her hand on the plane, the tender softness of her palm against his. When she'd fallen asleep on his shoulder, he'd taken the opportunity to examine her hand, noting the toughness of her fingertips and the scarred lines embedded in them. To him, the contrasting textures of her hand represented the woman herself—soft and vulnerable on the inside, tough and scarred on the outside. More than anything he wanted to break through her veneer of fear and self-doubt and discover the real Annika.

She had shown her capabilities during their feuding fiddles on the sidewalk. He'd also gotten a glimpse of her true self. With her doubts and insecurities stripped away, she'd been able to let go and play without fear. She had played with an exuberance and a reckless abandon that he hadn't heard from another musician in a long time. It was a stark reminder of the way he used to play.

Josef placed his violin in its case and walked out on the stage. The curtain was still raised, and he looked at the rows of plush red seats that would soon be filled with music enthusiasts. A far different crowd from the one he and Annika had played for earlier.

Performing on the sidewalk had been an impulse; something he'd never done before. His audiences usually consisted of stodgy classical music buffs who could spend a large sum of money on a concert ticket and not blink an eye. The response of the afternoon crowd to their impromptu duet had been invigorating, and for a brief instant he thought the joy might have come back.

The feeling disintegrated the moment he entered the concert hall.

Soon other members of the orchestra started to arrive. He turned to watch the double bass player and two of the percussionists as they set up their instruments on the podium, greeting Josef with a nod. He genuinely liked these students, who weren't much younger than he was. Being a part of this particular orchestra was a different experience from the other tours he'd been on. He felt like a member instead of a guest. He'd already made friends with many of the musicians, and they continually impressed him with their musical ability. Some had promising futures. It wouldn't surprise him if he were to perform with several of them again in a few years, as members of one of the elite orchestras.

*If* he performed again.

Never had he been at such a crossroads before, with both his career and his faith. Yet in spite of the growing separation he felt between himself and the Lord, he was turning to Scripture and prayer more than ever. But lately he was finding more questions than answers.

From the wings of the stage he heard the clicking of heels against polished wood, the sound pulling him from his thoughts. Turning, he saw Stephanie rush toward him, her normally sanguine expression replaced by genuine worry.

"Josef, I need your help. It's Annika."

A shot of alarm ran through him. "Has something happened to her?"

Stephanie responded by tugging at the sleeve of his suit jacket. "Come with me—I think you're the only one who can get through to her."

Springing out of the way as the curtain began to lower behind him, he moved to follow Stephanie backstage to a long corridor until they stopped in front of a brightly painted red door. He read the brass placard bolted to the front of it—Women.

Gus stood in front of the door. With his close-cropped brown hair, legs spread apart, and arms crossing his large chest, he looked like a soldier guarding a bathroom full of Fort Knox gold.

Stephanie shot Gus a questioning look. When he shook his head, she turned to Josef. "You've got to talk to her," she begged.

"All right. When she comes out, I will speak with her."

She shook her head vigorously. "She won't do it. I've tried. Even Gus called through the door trying to coax her out. I think she's having an anxiety attack."

Surprised at Stephanie's assumption, Josef glanced at the door again. "She has had one before?"

"Once. It was when she first applied to the institute. I didn't know her then, but she told me about it. It incapacitated her, and she failed the admissions test. She had to wait another semester to apply again." Stephanie's jaw was moving at lightning speed, her chewing gum cracking and popping along with it. "You've got to go in there. I know she'll listen to you."

Josef's mouth dropped open. "You cannot be serious." But he could see she wasn't joking.

"Don't worry; no one else is in there," Stephanie explained. "Gus has been guarding the door."

Looking to Gus for confirmation, Josef groaned when the big man nodded and stepped aside.

"Josef, please!" Stephanie sounded desperate. "The concert is starting in fifteen minutes!"

His concern for Annika outweighed any remaining

reservations he had about entering the women's rest room. He placed his hand on the door, gave it a shove, and walked inside.

"Annika?" he called out, her name bouncing off the walls in the seemingly empty room. He took a few steps forward and briefly scanned the row of stalls, not daring to actually check inside any of them. He didn't see her anywhere. Trying to ignore the discomfort and odd curiosity he felt at being in a public ladies' room, he jumped at the sound of a hinge squeaking behind him. He spun around and saw the door to the last stall slowly open.

Annika peeked around the beige metal door, her eyes wide with disbelief. "Josef? What are you doing in here?"

"Asking myself that same question," he muttered.

Releasing the door, she stepped around it. Immediately he could see that Stephanie hadn't exaggerated. Annika's skin, naturally fair under normal circumstances, now had a ghostly hue, her black dress intensifying the effect. The crimson lipstick and silvery eye shadow she wore stood out sharply against her pallor, giving her a clownish appearance.

Her bottom lip quivered when she spoke. "I'm so sorry," she said, hanging her head, her voice barely above a whisper. "All those people out there—you, the orchestra . . . I've let everybody down."

Josef went to her and grasped her hand, disconcerted by the icy feel of it. "You have not let anyone down yet," he said gently.

She clung to his hand but refused to look at him. "I'm terrified," she admitted, her voice almost inaudible. "This . . . it's happened to me before . . . I've tried at least ten times to walk out that door, but I can't. It's like . . . I'm paralyzed with fear or something."

He pulled her closer to him but resisted the sudden

urge to embrace her completely. More than anything he wanted to comfort her, to ease her fear. "Do not worry," he said softly. "It is natural to be afraid before a performance. Especially your first one on the tour."

She lifted her gaze to his. "You're not afraid," she pointed out.

"True, but I used to be." His eyes darted in an exaggerated back-and-forth motion, as if he were checking the vacant bathroom for hidden spies. "I would never admit this to anyone else," he said in a loud stage whisper, "but I used to get so worried before a concert I would blow up."

A puzzled look crossed her face. "Blow up?"

"You know . . . get sick . . . "

"Oh, you mean *throw* up." She let out a nervous giggle at his intended slip. "And here I thought you had a perfect command of English."

Josef sobered. "I am far from perfect."

She glanced at the floor for an instant, then looked up at him again. She didn't acknowledge his assertion, instead choosing to stay on the subject. "I can't imagine you ever getting that worked up over performing."

"Believe me, I did." He didn't think it necessary to tell her that he was ten years old the last time it happened. But he was completely candid with his next statement. "What helps me now is prayer."

"You pray?"

"Before every performance."

"Me too," she said, a bit of the wild look in her eyes dissipating. "That's what I've been trying to do in here for the last half hour. Normally praying helps calm me down, but right now I'm so unfocused. . . . "

"Would you like me to pray for you?" he offered.

She answered with a tremulous smile. "Yes."

Taking her other hand, he prayed for both of them.

And despite the strange setting, amid the stalls and sinks and flowery wallpaper, praying with her felt completely natural. "Dear Lord, be with Annika and me tonight. Please fill our hearts and minds with peace as we step onto the stage, and may the music we play glorify you." He gently squeezed her hands. "We ask these things in Jesus' name. Amen."

When he finished, he opened his eyes and took a step back, glad to see some of the tension gone from her face. "Better?" he asked.

She nodded. "Some. But I'm still shaky." She held up her trembling hand.

"Then I will offer another suggestion. Be someone else. That is another trick I learned long ago."

"Acting?"

"Yes, acting. Remember the story behind the music. Forget you are Annika Goran and become Isabel, the woman I am desperately after. And I am Marco, the man you are desperately fleeing from." He wiggled his eyebrows devilishly, which earned him another giggle.

"You are incorrigible, Josef—I mean, Marco."

A sharp knock sounded on the door, startling them both. "Is everything all right in there?"

Annika went to the door and pulled it open partway. "We're fine, Stephanie."

Stephanie slipped inside and looked to Josef, who had moved next to Annika. He mouthed the word *yes,* and Stephanie sighed with relief. "That's good," she said, "because Gus and I are running out of excuses to tell those women why they can't come in here."

"What women?" Annika asked.

"These," Stephanie said, moving past her and flinging open the door, causing Josef and Annika to take a few steps backward. Stephanie waved to a line of ten women, many with irritated expressions on their faces. The irritation soon changed to curiosity, accompanied by giggles, as Josef realized he was standing center stage in the middle of the ladies' room—flanked on one side by Annika, on the other by Stephanie.

Never ill at ease in front of an audience, Josef reached for Stephanie's hand, kissed the top of it, then let it drop slowly.

He did the same to Annika, letting his lips linger on her smooth skin longer than necessary. "I will see you in a few minutes, Isabel," he said, giving her a wink.

"Yes, you will," she replied with a smile. He was warmed by the rosy blush that had suddenly blossomed on her cheeks.

# CHAPTER FIVE

STANDING in the wings, Josef waited for the rest of the orchestra to take their seats. Before walking onstage, Annika appeared by his side, her chin lifted proudly. Josef suppressed a chuckle as, without a word, she thrust her violin and bow in his free hand, then made a show of smoothing the folds of her shiny black dress. More of her color had returned, and with her long brown hair swept high on her head, the square set of her shoulders, and the arrogant look in her eyes, Josef knew "Isabel" had arrived to perform. But when she reached for her instrument, he noticed her hands were still unsteady. While the transformation may not have been complete, at least she was here, ready to play. He watched as she and the rest of the orchestra took their places.

When the musicians were seated, the curtain, which had been down while the audience members filled their seats, began to rise. As concertmaster, Josef was the last musician to go onstage. Applause and whistles saturated the air as he headed for his seat. The adulation used to excite him, making his adrenaline pump and his heart race. But tonight he felt nothing. No, he did feel something—a combination of grief and loss for how satisfying his career had once been.

For Annika's sake, he hid it and forced a smile. She gave him a weak one in return. He sat down next to her, then waited for the oboist to play the tuning note.

Tunney, in full white tie and tails, entered the stage. Josef rolled his eyes. He had left his own tuxedo at home in Vienna, knowing most, if not all, of the students wouldn't have their own formal wear. Of course, a simple black suit wasn't Tunney's style.

They opened with an excerpt from a Wagner opera. Judging from the audience's response, the orchestra had gotten off to a good start. A few songs later, at the midpoint of the program, it was time for the duet.

Josef leaned close and whispered in Annika's ear, "Ready, Isabel?"

Closing her eyes, her lips moved in what Josef assumed was a silent prayer. When she opened them, they were filled with determination. "Just try and stop me."

He held his hand out to her and led her to the front of the stage. They faced each other, locking eyes. Bows in position, Josef signaled to Simon, and the orchestra began to play.

When it was time for her to come in, Annika faltered. Fear leaped to her eyes, and Josef thought she might lose it completely. Within a few measures, however, she managed to dig deep inside herself and pull it together, infusing new energy into her playing. She seemed to let go of whatever held her back, not totally, but just enough to cause Josef to spur her on. Soon he began to play as if he really were Marco pursuing his darling Isabel, enticed by her many wavering refusals of his advances.

Annika appeared to *become* Isabel, her lovely eyes flashing dark and luminous, even teasing at times. They never left Josef's, and he lost himself in their blue-green depths, the pulsing beat of his heart slamming hard against his chest. It exhilarated him far beyond what any prior performance had. They played their parts in a rising crescendo, the notes crashing together in sweet harmony as they acted the part of lovers finally dropping all pretenses, declaring their feelings for each other.

The audience was on its feet before they finished the last note. Josef beamed at Annika, who appeared stunned by her own performance. With her eyes sparkling like rare jewels and her cheeks the color of a pale pink sunset—Josef thought her enchanting. Finally she broke through her trance, and the glow of her smile lit the stage more brightly than any spotlight could.

He motioned for her to bow, which she did tentatively. Not willing to take the credit for such an inspired performance, he took a shallow bow himself, knowing he and Annika had not made the magical music alone.

As for the rest of the concert, he couldn't recall any of it, playing as if he were a machine, with little emotion or thought for the music. Instead, he wondered how it happened, how in front of hundreds of people, during what should have been a normal, uneventful concert performance, he'd fallen completely in love with Annika Goran.

The concert ended to more thunderous applause. Tunney basked in it, taking several deep bows, yet gesturing to the orchestra only once. When the curtain lowered, Tunney blurted out a few congratulatory words, announced the time of the next rehearsal, and rushed off the stage to meet and greet the patrons.

Josef stepped back as Annika's fellow students crowded around her, congratulating her on a job well done. They extended their appreciation to him as well, but it didn't bother him that their focus was on her. His focus was on her too, but for different reasons. However, there was one thing everyone seemed to be in complete agreement on. Tonight, she was the true star.

A short while later Josef, Annika, Stephanie, and Gus left the hall, Gus carrying Stephanie's cello. The bright lights of the streetlamps and late-night merchants open for business matched the buoyant mood of the quartet as they walked down the sidewalk.

Annika skipped ahead a few steps, then twirled around, hugging her violin case close to her chest and letting out an exultant cry. "Incredible! A standing ovation! It was so . . . exciting. So wonderful . . . so . . . "

"So over!" Stephanie reached out and hugged her. "You were brilliant, Annika. I knew you could do it!" She turned and winked at Josef. "You were okay too, Gemmel."

Josef pretended to be offended. "I think I was better than *that.*"

"Not compared to this gal." Stephanie checked her watch. "It's late. We're heading back to the inn. Are you coming?"

Annika pouted. "Oh, c'mon! The night is still young—why let it go to waste?"

"It's eleven-thirty. We have rehearsal at eight in the morning."

"I don't care. I want to see London." She swept her arms wide. "Look how beautiful it is tonight."

Josef watched her appreciatively as she spoke. Several strands of hair had fallen free from her upswept hairstyle, framing her delicate face and brushing the top of her shoulders. The loose strands looked like shining threads of chocolate-colored silk, and he imagined how it would feel to rub one of them between his fingertips. No, whatever beauty the city of London had to offer couldn't compare to Annika's.

"Suit yourself," Stephanie said. "Gus and I are heading back. What about you, Josef?"

"I will stay with Annika. I can show her the sights," he quickly added.

Stephanie gave him a knowing smile. "I'm sure you can. You two stay out of trouble, okay?"

"What kind of trouble could we possibly get into?" Annika said dreamily, still floating on air.

Josef reddened. "Never mind," he said, thankful she missed Stephanie's less-than-subtle insinuation.

Accepting Stephanie's offer to take their instruments back to the inn, Josef and Annika turned their violins over to her.

After she and Gus had left, Annika surprised Josef by wrapping her arms around him. "Oh, Josef! I had no idea how thrilling performing like that could be! No wonder you love it so much."

She surprised him, but only for an instant. His arms slid easily around her slim shoulders, and he closed his eyes, enjoying the feel of her body so close to his. Then just as unexpectedly as she'd hugged him she pulled away, leaving him bereft.

Disgruntled, he addressed her remark about performing. "What makes you think I love it?" he muttered.

"But you must," she said, giving him an inquisitive look. "How can you not? I've only had a taste of what you've experienced for years, and I'm still reeling from it. I can't imagine what it's like to feel that kind of passion while you play, to hear that kind of applause night after night." When he didn't answer, she looked at him. "Is there something wrong?"

He wanted to tell her, to explain all that he felt. How radiant and beautiful she'd been onstage tonight. How her enthusiasm and joy for her music had touched him in a place in his soul he hadn't been aware he had, making his problems and worries evaporate. How in two short weeks she'd managed to capture his heart completely, stealing it from him as easily as a rosined bow glides across violin strings. Gazing into her mesmerizing eyes, he was tempted to speak it all.

But he held back, wondering if his hesitation was because he feared scaring her off by revealing his feelings for her. Maybe it was because *he* was scared by the depth of his emotions. This was unfamiliar territory for him. Life on the road wasn't conducive to establishing and maintaining relationships, and his few forays into dating hadn't lasted long. He couldn't just throw his feelings at her feet and expect her to understand them when he didn't understand them fully himself.

Thrusting his hand into his pocket, his fingers touched the envelope of bills he had placed in it earlier. Remembering why he'd brought the money and glad for a diversion, Josef took the pound notes out of his pocket and showed them to her.

Annika looked down at the bills in his hand. "Wow! That's a lot of money. You shouldn't carry that much on you, you know." She glanced up at him. "You could get mugged or something, flashing it out on the street like this."

Giving her a wry grin, he walked toward a crosswalk. "Do not worry. We are safe here. Come with me," he said, pocketing the money. "I have something to show you."

For once she didn't ask where they were going. She simply followed.

Again, Annika had to rush to keep up with Josef as they walked the streets of London. *Why does he have to have such long legs?* Not that she would change a thing about him. As far as she was concerned, he was perfect in every way.

Looking at his profile, she couldn't believe how wrong she'd been about him. How had she ever considered him too thin? When she gave him that hug—something she'd been wanting to do all evening—she realized what a well-muscled body he had. Strong, like his personality and his faith in God. Before tonight, she would have questioned where he was leading them. Now she would follow him anywhere he asked.

Josef pointed to a large building a few blocks away. "That is where we are going."

The dim lighting in this part of London made it difficult to see what it was. As they approached, she could barely read the letters engraved on a rectangular concrete slab above the doorway.

"Cotteridge Home?" she asked when they were in front of the building.

"It is an orphanage."

Annika watched him pull out the plain white envelope filled with money and shove it into the mail slot. Through the door she heard it land with a thud on the other side. "I don't understand. Why would you give so much of your money to an orphanage tonight?"

"It is not my money. It is ours."

*Ours?*

"From this afternoon," he said, answering her silent question. "I exchanged the coins for bills before the concert. We made a tidy little sum today." Josef ran his hand against the rough wooden door of the orphanage. "My grandfather was raised here during the second World War. He was the only one of his family to escape Austria when the Nazis invaded. He returned to Vienna as an adult and met my grandmother." He turned and looked at her solemnly. "The time he spent here was not always pleasant, but he had a place to live. Many children did not."

Annika wondered how many young boys and girls were inside the old building, tucked in their beds, asleep for the night. The thought of any child without a parent made her heart ache.

His gaze was thoughtful. "I am sorry. Perhaps I should have asked you first before I did this. I did not mean to spoil your happiness," he said, a note of regret in his voice.

"You didn't spoil it. I'm pleased you thought of giving the money away."

Josef looked relieved. "The orphanage can use it." Placing a hand to her waist, he gently led her away from Cotteridge Home. The warmth of his touch sent pleasant shivers through her, but then he pulled his hand away, leaving her disappointed. Side by side they walked, retracing their earlier steps, heading toward the main area of the city.

"Now, enough of this somber mood," he said in a bright tone. "You wanted to see London, and I promised to show it to you."

Suddenly, the idea of touring London lost its appeal. "If you don't mind, I think I want to go back to the inn."

"Are you sure?" he asked, appearing confused.

"Yes. I'm kind of tired. I must be coming down from the high of the concert." But she realized that her words weren't totally true. Tired as she was, she now floated on a high that had nothing to do with the concert and everything to do with the man standing in front of her. It still amazed her that he had thought nothing of going in the ladies' room and soothing her shattered nerves when she needed it. Then he'd prayed for her, and now he'd given away a sizable amount of money to a small London orphanage anonymously. What other man would do those things?

When they came to the end of the block, she stopped walking. "Thank you, Josef," she said, turning to look at him.

A puzzled look crossed his features. "For what? Being a terrible tour guide?"

A small smile settled on her lips. "No, not that. For praying with me earlier."

"My pleasure. It was not the most eloquent prayer—"

"It was wonderful," she interrupted, charmed by his sincere modesty. "Deep in my heart I know I need to draw my strength from Jesus. Thank you for the reminder."

"I think we all need a little reminding every once in a while."

She met his gaze and felt her breath catch. A warm summer breeze kicked up and ruffled his hair, leaving it a bit disheveled. Her hand seemed to have a mind of its own as it reached up to brush aside the thick blond lock that covered his forehead. Coming to her senses, she snatched it back quickly, instead smoothing back a strand of her own hair.

Was a future with Josef out of the question? Suddenly her vow to stay away from musicians didn't seem valid anymore. She certainly hadn't been looking for romance, not since Simon had put a bad taste in her mouth concerning relationships. Yet she couldn't help but feel that God had placed Josef in her life for a reason.

But she had to be realistic. They had their belief in Christ and their music in common; however, she couldn't be certain that was enough to bridge the gap between them. They came from different backgrounds, lived in separate worlds. Still, there was an undeniable attraction between them. She had first been aware of it on the plane, and it had grown stronger during their performances this afternoon and tonight. Earlier she thought it might be one-sided on her part, but the way his blue eyes now glowed with intensity in the bright light of the city streetlamp made her whole body feel weak.

She placed a hand on his upper arm to steady herself, then dug her fingertips into his muscle when he took another step forward, slowly lowering his head toward hers.

*He's going to kiss me! Do I want him to? Yes, yes, I do . . .* She closed her eyes and tilted her face to him, waiting with breathless anticipation for his lips to cover hers.

For the second time that day, Josef nearly kissed Annika.

The first time had been in the hallway at the inn, when she had so adamantly—and so adorably—protested his joking comment about her size. He'd come so close to kissing her then that he almost hadn't pulled away.

Now, standing together on the deserted street corner with his mouth hovering over hers, he felt a thin wisp of her soft hair brush enticingly against his cheek. He could smell the irresistible scent of her perfume, could imagine the sweet taste of her soft lips. Yes, it would take an act of

God to pull him away from her now. Closing his eyes, he moved to eliminate the space between them.

*Honk!* The blaring of a car horn jolted him back to reality, and he jerked his head up in time to see a large black taxicab come to a screeching halt at the end of the corner. His nerves raw from being deprived of what was sure to be the sweetest kiss of his life, he stifled a moan of frustration when he saw Tunney exit the car.

"Simon!" Annika hissed. Josef saw that she was shaking. "What are you doing here?"

Tunney put one foot forward on the curb, only to miss it completely, barely managing not to fall flat on his face. He made it on his next attempt, and when he spoke, Josef realized the reason for his clumsiness.

"Past curfew, you two," he said, speaking directly to Josef. The strong odor of English ale hung in the air between them. With a leering grin he turned to Annika. "Time to end the extracurricular activities."

"Seems to me you've been up to some extracurricular business yourself," she retorted, crossing her arms over her chest.

"My business isn't any business of yours," he said with equal venom. "Now get in the cab."

She didn't move. "I don't have to take orders from you."

"Oh yes you do. You're my responsibility on this trip."

"What a comforting thought."

"Well, what you think doesn't matter," Tunney said, trying to stand up a little straighter. He failed and ended up tottering a few steps to the right.

Up until that point, Josef had observed their exchange in silence, mostly because he knew she could handle Tunney without his interference. However, Josef wouldn't stand idly by while Tunney hurled his insults her way. "That is enough, Simon," he said, his tone slightly threatening. "Annika is with me. I will see she gets back safely."

Tunney turned bloodshot eyes on Josef. "No. You do what you want, Gemmel, but it'll be without her. She's coming with me."

Anger surged through Josef. His hand curled into a tight fist, and he was ready to slam it right into Tunney's face when he felt Annika's hand curve over his clenched fingers.

"Okay, Simon, you win," she conceded, giving Josef's fist a squeeze. Somehow she'd known exactly what he'd wanted to do and had inconspicuously stopped him from doing it. Tunney didn't know how close he'd come to getting a broken nose. "I'll go with you," she continued, releasing Josef's hand and going to the car.

Unwilling to let Annika ride in the cab alone with Tunney, Josef followed behind her. She got in the backseat first, but when Josef tried to get in beside her, Tunney moved past him with an awkward shove and slid into the seat next to her. Josef had no choice but to sit next to him, separated from her again.

The passengers were silent on the way back to the inn. Tunney occasionally piped up with an inane comment or two, but neither Annika nor Josef responded. Finally he got the hint and clammed up for the rest of the ride.

Josef stared out into the inky darkness through the car window. He'd never been so enraged at another human being as he'd been with Tunney. Normally he prided himself on his ability to remain cool and collected under pressure. It seemed all of his emotions were at a heightened level now. Fortunately Annika had kept him from hitting the man. Fighting with someone who'd been drinking would have been stupid, not to mention wrong. And unfair too—in Tunney's state, Josef had no doubt he would have knocked him out cold with one punch.

The cab stopped in front of the inn. Josef paid the fare, as Tunney didn't have enough cash on him to cover it. They all exited the car, Annika storming up the cobblestone walk, several strides ahead of Josef.

"Annika?" he called after her, leaving Tunney to make his wobbly way toward the inn.

She whirled around quickly, the skirt of her black dress flaring around at the knees. "Look, Josef, I'm tired. Thanks for everything, but I need to get to bed." She looked at him for one long moment, as if she might change her mind and let him get near her again. Then with a slight shake of her head, she told him good night and went inside the inn.

He stood and watched her go, dumbfounded, not knowing what he'd done to bring about her sudden change in attitude.

"Don't waste your time, Gemmel."

He hadn't heard Tunney come up behind him. Now the man was practically standing toe-to-toe with him. Josef muttered his irritation in German.

"What?" Tunney slurred.

"Forget it," Josef said tersely, stalking up the walk to the entrance of the inn.

Tunney followed at his heels. "She's a cold fish. Frigid as an iceberg. You'll never get anywhere with her."

Josef halted but held himself in check. "I am not interested in getting anywhere with her," he stated.

Tunney smirked. "You misunderstood me. I'm not talking about going someplace with her. I'm talking about getting her to—"

"I know exactly what you are referring to!" Josef had spun around and was now looming over him by four inches.

"Hey, back off! I'm only giving you some friendly advice. No sense in casting out your line when the fish won't bite."

"When I want your opinion, I will ask for it," Josef sneered. "Although it is unlikely I would want your thoughts on anything, be it women or *music*."

His words had a sobering effect on Tunney. The man's steely gray eyes narrowed with ire. "Well, here's a word of warning," he shot back. "Fraternization within the orchestra is not tolerated."

Josef scoffed. "What rule is this? I certainly have not seen it enforced."

"For some, the rule doesn't apply. For others . . . " His voice trailed off, and his mouth formed a cold grin. "I'll give you one more warning, Gemmel. This is one you'd better heed. If I see you and Annika alone together, under any circumstances, she'll be sent back home."

"You cannot do that."

Tunney's smile turned cruel. "Maybe I can; maybe I can't. Do you really want to risk it?"

He was bluffing and Josef knew it. In fact, if anyone had the power to ruin this tour *he* did. One phone call to the institute and Tunney would be the one packing his bags. Right now that idea was very tempting.

But he wouldn't go through with it. As much as he reviled Tunney, Josef wouldn't take his personal frustrations out on the hardworking students of Moreland. And the more he thought about it, he realized that Tunney might actually be doing him a favor. However, Josef had no intention of letting him know that.

"I will do as you say." The words tasted foul as Josef said them. Capitulating to him required all the self-control he possessed.

Tunney gloated. "Then we have an understanding.

You're on my turf now, Gemmel. Don't ever forget who's in control here."

Josef fought the urge to laugh at the ludicrous statement. That this conceited man thought he had complete control over *anything* showed how lost he was. Josef pitied him.

Tunney went inside, leaving Josef to brood alone. Instead of following him, Josef turned in the opposite direction and walked down the sidewalk. His emotions were in chaos—he couldn't sleep if he wanted to.

*What was I thinking?* He'd let his attraction to Annika cloud his judgment. How could he possibly have a relationship with anyone when his own life was in shambles? It would be unfair to drag her down into his abyss of unhappiness and confusion. And he couldn't expect her to put her life on hold while he sorted through the mess of his career. His profession and his life were so intertwined that it was impossible to separate the two. For the first time he regretted not having an existence outside his music.

Josef yanked on the knot of his necktie, which he had loosened earlier after the concert had ended. Shoving the black silk tie into his jacket pocket, he stopped walking and stared up at the twinkling night sky.

*So what do I do about this, Jesus? When I'm near Annika I can't think straight. I only feel. Tunney gave me an easy out—staying away from her is the best thing for both of us. But that doesn't change my heart. Tell me . . . how do I stop loving her?*

How long he stood there, he didn't know. Minutes, hours—time seemed to stop while he waited for an answer from his Lord.

He never got one.

# CHAPTER SIX

"WHAT'S the deal with you and Josef?"

Annika stood motionless, the white T-shirt she'd lifted from her suitcase dangling over her left hand. "I don't know what you're talking about," she told Stephanie, refolding the shirt. "There's nothing between Josef and me."

"Liar."

"It wouldn't hurt you to use a little tact, Steph. Try it sometime."

Stephanie chuckled. "Believe me, I do. I walk the tactful tightrope with Gus quite often. How do you think we've managed to stay together so long?"

"That's always been a mystery to me."

"Very funny." Stephanie slammed her suitcase shut and slid it underneath the bed. Having toured three countries in three weeks, the women were becoming experts at packing and unpacking their belongings. The orchestra had arrived in Venice, Italy, that morning, and the two women were getting organized before spending the afternoon sightseeing. "Anyway, we're not talking about my relationship, which couldn't be better, by the way. We're talking about you and Josef."

"There *is* no me and Josef." Picking up her black dress, Annika went to the tiny closet she and Stephanie shared and hung the outfit carefully on a hanger. "What do you want to do first? Shop for souvenirs or tour St. Mark's Cathedral?"

"Quit changing the subject."

"Quit asking dumb questions," Annika said sharply, then sagged against the closet with a sigh. "I'm sorry. I don't know what's wrong with me."

"I do," Stephanie replied, walking over to her. She grinned. "You're in *love.*"

She started to shake her head, then stopped. No sense in denying it, especially since Stephanie already guessed the truth. "You're right," she said quietly, moving to sit on the side of the bed.

"I knew it!" Snapping her fingers and cracking her gum with enthusiasm, Stephanie sat next to her, giving Annika's shoulders a squeeze. "From the moment I saw him I knew he was the man for you. You two are *so* perfect for each other."

Annika stiffened. "I can't think of two people more unsuited for each other than Josef and me," she said.

"You're wrong," Stephanie insisted, her smile fading into a frown.

"No, I'm not. Think about it, Steph. Josef's not interested in me. Why would he be? He's gorgeous, charming, kind—"

"And since you're so ugly, bland, and cruel, of course he wouldn't like you. Give me a break."

"Our lives are so different," she continued as if what

Stephanie said hadn't registered. "He's European. He's toured the world. He's a musical *genius.*"

"I fail to see the problem here."

"The problem is that I love him, and he couldn't care less about me!" The lump that suddenly appeared in her throat both surprised and annoyed her. She swallowed hard, determined not to dissolve into tears in front of Stephanie. She wouldn't let anyone see her cry over Josef Gemmel. "We've been on this tour for three weeks now. You see how much time we spend together offstage. None. *Zero.* When we do run into each other, he acts like we're strangers. Always polite but never friendly." She ran her damp palms across her jean-clad thighs. "He acts more interested in you than in me."

Stephanie furrowed her brows. "But you're missing something here. He watches you. I've seen him, and those looks he keeps casting your way are definitely more than just *friendly.*"

Annika blinked. *He watches me?* The very idea sent a wave of warmth through her entire body.

"And what about when you two are performing together? You could set a blaze right onstage with all the sparks you guys put off. Don't tell me you haven't noticed that."

She *had* noticed, which confused her all the more. When Josef performed he was a different person altogether, more like the man she'd known in London than the stranger he was now. His interpretation of their duet was intoxicating, and the way his eyes held hers while they played, as if she were a treasure he desperately wanted but couldn't have, merely deepened her love for him. But after they left the stage, he ignored her until the next performance. Then it started all over again. His contradicting behavior threatened to push her right over the edge.

Annika didn't want to share all this with Stephanie, despite her being her best friend. She'd already said more than she should by admitting her love for him. Her feelings were too private, too painful to share with anyone except God. Over the past weeks she had grown closer to him, relying on him to help keep her frayed emotions in check. Drawing nearer to God had been an unexpected benefit in an otherwise depressing situation.

She turned to Stephanie. "You're a great friend, and I appreciate what you're trying to do. But I can't talk about this, not with anyone." Annika rose from the bed, then paused. "And what I said about loving Josef? Pretend I never mentioned it."

"But—"

Annika lifted her hand, swallowing again. "Please," she said, her voice cracking slightly. "Forget it, okay?"

"Okay," Stephanie agreed as she stood up, then gave her a halfhearted smile. "So . . . are we going shopping for outrageously priced souvenirs or not?"

"Let's go." Grabbing her purse off the bed, Annika headed out the door, grateful Stephanie understood.

Two hours later dozens of gray-and-white pigeons surrounded Annika and Stephanie as they strolled through the plaza of St. Mark's Cathedral. The birds rose and soared against the blue sky, and others poked and pecked at the crumbs of food stuck in the cracks of the cobblestones.

"You know," Stephanie commented, looking up at a particularly large flock fluttering a short distance above her head, "I wish I'd worn a hat."

Annika nodded, noting the numerous blotches of white that dotted the ground, evidence that Venetian pigeons were definitely well fed. "You'd think they'd mention this kind of hazard in the brochure."

Stephanie smirked. "I can see it now—'Attention tourists. Beware of pigeons bearing . . . gifts.' " Chuckling, she linked her arm through Annika's. "Forget about the birds. Isn't Venice marvelous? Such a *romantic* city."

"Maybe," Annika replied, wanting to change the subject to anything but romance. Of course her friend could speak easily of the Italian city's romantic allure—she had Gus. Annika had . . . her violin.

"Well, for goodness sake!" Stephanie exclaimed, tugging on Annika's arm. "What are *they* doing here?"

Annika eyed her suspiciously. Ultracool Stephanie would never say anything as old-fashioned as "for goodness sake." When she looked in the direction that her friend was pointing, her heart dropped to her stomach like a rock.

Seated at a small round table on the edge of an outdoor café were Gus and Josef. Annika's gaze zeroed in on Josef as he casually perused a menu. Suddenly her heart leaped from her belly to her throat as Stephanie started dragging her toward the café. They swiftly made their way through the crowd, and before Annika could find her voice to protest, they were standing in front of the two men.

Stephanie leaned over and kissed Gus lightly on the lips, then looked at Josef. "Well, isn't this a coincidence," she said, her voice much louder than normal. "Imagine running into the two of you here."

"Yeah, right," Annika muttered, elbowing Stephanie in the ribs before unlinking their arms. If she'd had any doubt that her *former* friend had orchestrated this little surprise, they were put to rest when she saw Stephanie casually step on Gus's toe as he started to contradict her.

Stephanie slipped into the wrought-iron chair next to

Gus, leaving Annika standing and feeling foolish. The only other empty chair was next to Josef. The rich, delicious aromas of hot coffee and freshly baked bread floated around her as she waited a few seconds to see if he would invite her to sit down. Instead he continued staring at the menu, not even acknowledging her presence.

*Fine,* she thought, grabbing the empty chair and yanking it as far from him as possible without appearing ridiculously obvious. *If he can be rude, so can I.* She angled the chair so that most of her back was to him, then snatched a menu off the table. More than a few moments passed before she noticed she was holding the cream-colored folder upside down.

"So, what brings the two of you here?" Stephanie asked with round-eyed innocence while Annika swiftly righted the menu.

Josef shifted in his seat. "Gus mentioned he liked espresso. Here they serve the best in all of Venice."

"Really?" Stephanie asked. "What's so great about it?"

Before long Josef and Stephanie were discussing the merits of Italian espresso, with Gus throwing in an occasional comment or two. Annika sighed and tossed her menu on the table, feeling like a neglected cup of coffee. A green thread of envy wound around her heart as she listened to the easy way Stephanie and Josef talked. Why couldn't she talk with him that way?

She longed to recapture the magic of that evening in London before Simon had shown up and spoiled everything. That night she'd gone to bed, imagining what kissing Josef Gemmel would have been like. She thought it would have been incredible, a thousand times more thrilling than any standing ovation could be.

Now she would never know.

"Annika? *Annika!*"

Blinking, she turned her attention to Stephanie, who gave her an impatient look. "Where'd you go? I was just telling the guys here that you and I have always wanted to take a gondola ride."

"We have?"

"Yes, *we* have." Stephanie's brown eyes bored into her. "There's just enough time to catch one before we have to get ready for tonight's concert." She quickly rose from her chair, bringing Gus immediately to his feet. "There are some gondoliers over there," she said, pointing to a couple of men dressed in black pants and white-and-black-striped shirts, beige straw hats resting jauntily on their heads. "C'mon, let's go before someone else takes our boat."

"Gondola," Annika corrected, rising reluctantly. She noticed Josef stayed in his seat, shaking his head.

Stephanie rounded the table and grabbed his hand. "Oh no you don't, Josef. You can get that fabulous espresso later. You're coming with us, and I won't take no for an answer. I'm very stubborn when I want to be."

He looked to Gus, who nodded his head vigorously. "All right," Josef said, with all the enthusiasm of a man being forced to walk the plank.

Annika and Josef lagged behind in silence as Stephanie and Gus approached the gondoliers. Stephanie went to the taller man, her hands moving as she spoke. After a few moments she returned to Annika and Josef. "Okay, it's all set. Let's go."

They walked toward the first of two gondolas tied to the side of the canal. The gondolier stepped into the narrow boat and motioned for the foursome to get in.

"We'll get in first!" Stephanie squealed with childish glee, practically shoving Gus onto the wooden board that served as a seat, then hopping in after him. Annika moved to follow them, but the gondolier was too quick. With one blurry motion he untied the gondola and shoved off, leaving her and Josef standing on the bank of the canal.

*"Ciao!"* Stephanie called out, her laughter fading as the gondola glided through the water. Gus shrugged helplessly, a wide grin plastered on his face.

Annika shoved her fists against her hips, the red plastic shopping bag she'd been carrying slapping against her thigh. *Great, just great. Now what? Stand here and wait for them? Take a gondola ride by myself? Oh yeah, that would make me feel* much *better.*

She turned to look at Josef, taking in his handsome profile as he continued to watch the traitors disappear in the distance. His expression was blank; if he was upset with Stephanie and Gus he didn't show it.

"It is your turn, *si?"* The second gondolier looked at Annika expectantly. With a wide sweep of his arm he gestured for her and Josef to get into his boat.

Glancing at the line of people forming behind them, she swallowed. *What do I say now?*

Suddenly the entire situation seemed absurd. Here she was in Venice, probably for the only time in her life. And she was seriously considering turning down her one chance at a gondola ride, all because of a fickle Austrian. Well, she wouldn't let Josef spoil her good time.

Carefully she stepped into the boat, clasping the gondolier's hand when he offered it. *At least* he *acts like a gentleman.* When she'd situated herself on the seat, she glanced at Josef, who was still standing at the edge of the canal. The late-afternoon sun glowed brightly behind him, obscuring her view of his face.

Shading her eyes with her hand, she looked up at him. "So? Are you getting in or not?"

꩜

Although he maintained a cool exterior, Josef knew he'd have difficulty keeping it up much longer. After spending three torturous weeks trying to keep his distance from Annika, the entire pretense was close to shattering, thanks to one spunky redhead and her partner in crime.

He knew he couldn't keep Annika waiting. The steady tapping of the toe of her shoe against the bottom of the gondola, along with the irritated expression forming on her pretty face, conveyed her impatience.

"Never mind." Waving her hand at him, she then nodded to the gondolier. He put his pole in the water and prepared to shove off.

*Good,* he thought. She'd made the decision for him. Now he could walk away, keeping his vow not be alone with her. He could go back to his hotel room and practice before tonight's performance. He could even go back to the café and have that espresso.

Trouble was, he didn't want to do any of those things.

"Wait a minute," he said on impulse, straddling the widening gap between the canal and the gondola with one long leg. The gondolier steadied the boat as Josef scrambled in, landing ungracefully in the seat opposite Annika at the front of the gondola. His eyes met hers as he settled back onto the seat, and he thought he saw a flicker of disappointment in them. A sinking sensation washed over him. Had she really wanted to ride alone?

Heavy silence hung between them as the gondola cut smoothly through the water of the canal. Annika appeared deeply interested in the apartment buildings they were gliding past, so Josef took the opportunity to watch her covertly, his gaze skimming her lovely features. As usual she wore her long brown hair pulled back from her face, this time with a navy blue headband that matched the shade of her T-shirt, the words *Moreland Institute* emblazoned in white on the front. The fading sunlight cast a peachy glow on her smooth skin, enhancing her aquamarine eyes.

*Her eyes.* They always drew him to her, from the moment he'd first noticed them that day at the institute, to each time they performed onstage together. During their duets her emotions were always evident in them. The joy she experienced as they played. An underlying fear that never seemed to go away completely. And lately the hint of something different—an emotion that threatened to touch his heart and soul.

But while he couldn't be absolutely sure of Annika's feelings toward him, his own were crystal clear and becoming more and more difficult to hide.

"So," she said, looking at him with those incredible eyes, "I suppose you've done this before."

"Yes," he answered. *But not with someone as beautiful as you.* He caught sight of her hands, which were tightly twisting the brown leather strap of her purse. She should be enjoying this; instead she was mutilating her handbag.

"What do you think of Venice so far?" he asked, trying to put her at ease despite feeling very uneasy himself.

"It's . . . different," she replied, then gave him a small smile. "But wonderful. Where else can you ride in a funny-looking boat down the main avenue of a major city?"

Leaning forward slightly, Josef clasped his hands between his knees. "Not in Chicago, that is for sure."

She chuckled and let go of the purse strap. "Absolutely not in Chicago." She peered over the side of the gondola and made a face at the murky brown liquid. "For some reason I thought the water would be blue. I've always imagined myself lounging in one of these things, letting my hand trail through the water, strains of a Puccini aria running through my head." Quickly she averted her gaze. "Silly romantic notion," she whispered, so low he barely caught the words.

Josef didn't think it was silly. He definitely thought it was romantic. *Oh, why bring Annika into my life now, Lord? Why send me the woman of my dreams—a beautiful, talented woman after your heart—when I have nothing to offer her?*

Her voice broke into his thoughts. "Oh my," she said, pointing behind him. "How breathtaking."

Shifting around on his seat, he saw what she was referring to. The sun had dipped past the horizon, filling the cloud-streaked sky with translucent shades of purple, pink, and orange.

"God's signature," he said, mesmerized by the gorgeous sunset.

"Yes," she agreed softly. "The divine artist at work." She paused, and he turned around and looked at her. "Josef, there's plenty of room for you to sit here next to me. That way you won't have to twist around to see the sunset." She placed her palm on the spot beside her.

The water lapped quietly against the boat as he stared at the space where her hand rested. More than anything he wanted to go to her, to sit next to her and enjoy the sunset, holding her hand as they traversed the canals of Venice. He wanted to wrap his arm around her shoulders and feel her cheek rest against his chest.

He wanted more than he could ever have.

"I am fine here," he said, his voice sounding hoarse and unnatural. He cleared his throat. Twice. "Besides, I think our ride is nearly over."

The gondolier steered the boat to the edge of the

canal near the same place where they had departed twenty minutes earlier.

After he and Annika disembarked, she looked around. "No sign of Stephanie and Gus," she said with a sigh. "Not that I'm surprised." She checked her watch. "I suppose we should head back to the hotel." Josef saw her take a deep breath. "Would you like to share a cab?" she asked tentatively, as if she were taking a big risk by asking him.

First the gondola ride, now the cab. He realized it would be too easy to accept her offer and just as easy to forget his promise to keep his distance. But that was one promise he couldn't afford to break. "No," he said, stepping away from her, hating himself for doing it. Remembering that this was supposed to be for her own good didn't help at all. "I need to pick up a few postcards before I go." *Postcards!* he thought lamely. *Why couldn't I come up with something better than that?*

"Oh. Well . . . I guess I'll see you later tonight." With that, she turned around and left, but not before he saw the disappointment in her eyes. Again.

This time there was no question in his mind he'd caused it.

# CHAPTER SEVEN

ANNIKA lifted her violin from its bed of blue velvet and picked up her bow. Normally she would have repeatedly glanced at the backstage entrance waiting for Josef to arrive, fully aware that it was a useless endeavor. He hadn't shown up early for a performance since that first night in London.

The gondola ride in Venice had been an eye-opener, however. She'd put herself on the line—twice—and he'd rejected her both times. She didn't have to be a genius to understand he wasn't interested in her. Even Stephanie had accepted reality and stopped her matchmaking schemes.

Annika had spent the last three weeks coming to terms with her feelings for Josef. She hadn't imagined that unrequited love could be so painful, especially when she had to face the object of her affection nearly every night onstage. His last couple of performances had become so intimate, it was as if the rest of the audience hadn't existed and he'd played only for her.

But that's what they were—performances. With each one he twisted the knife a little deeper into her heart. She knew he was pretending. Hadn't he suggested back in London that they act out their parts? He was simply following his own advice, and she felt like a lovesick sap, falling for it every time. But not anymore.

The tour was winding down, and tonight the orchestra was performing at the Large Festival House in Salzburg, Austria. Then they would travel to Vienna for the final concert. After that she would never see Josef again, so why waste the rest of her time in Europe pining for him? *Forget about him. He certainly won't remember me when it's over.*

As usual, backstage before the concert was a busy time. Instrument cases were strewn everywhere and discordant sounds filled the air as the musicians warmed up their instruments. Annika searched for a quiet corner where she could think and pray. When she located a semiprivate area, she headed toward it, only to have Simon step directly into her path.

"Josef's in the hospital," he told her without preamble.

A stab of panic cut through her. "Is he okay? What happened?"

"Food poisoning. He ate a bad cream puff or something."

"How serious is it?"

He shrugged, as if the severity of Josef's illness wasn't important.

She scrutinized Simon's flat expression. Something was wrong, other than Josef's being sick. The fact that Simon wasn't ranting and raving about the duet being ruined made her immediately suspicious. "You don't seem too upset about it," she accused.

"Of course I'm *very* concerned for him," he said with derision. "May he get well soon."

His callous attitude appalled her. "What is your problem?" she said, her voice rising with every word. The formerly noisy backstage area immediately became eerily silent, and she could sense everyone staring at them. She didn't care. "He's in the *hospital*, Simon! Don't you have a compassionate bone in that arrogant body of yours? Or is Josef too much of a threat?"

Obviously caught off guard by her outburst, his eyes shifted back and forth, taking in the group watching them raptly. When his gray eyes reached hers, they hardened like chips of stone. "Watch it, Annika," he said, lowering his voice in warning.

"Or what? I'm not afraid of you. There's nothing you can do or say that will bother me anymore." And it was true. For the first time she realized that Simon Tunney no longer had a hold over her, and the thought of it brought a smile to her lips. *I'm free of you, Simon.* It was a liberating revelation. She lifted her chin slightly. "Go ahead. Give it your best shot."

*Uh-oh.*

She watched as the corners of Simon's mouth lifted in an ugly smile, his predatory grin telling her she'd crossed the line. "I'm always up for a challenge," he boasted, his eyes slowly traveling the length of her body.

Her cheeks flamed at his bold perusal. He was no longer concerned that they still had an audience. "Don't forget what happened to that pretty face of yours," she reminded him through clenched teeth. She thought she saw his nose twitch.

He stepped toward her until he was so close she could tell he'd had onions for lunch. "I don't forget a thing," he said. His eyes softened for an instant, his voice turning low and husky. "You know what the most memorable thing about you is?"

His tone unnerved her. She'd rather deal with an angry Simon than a lusty one. She didn't respond to his question; instead she gripped her violin tightly, preparing to protect herself. She'd strike him upside the head with it if he so much as laid a finger on her.

She needn't have worried.

"You're a coward, Annika," he said harshly, stepping away from her. "We all know it." He swept his arms out wide, gesturing to the rest of the orchestra. "Attention, everyone. We will not play the duet tonight. Instead, Annika will perform her solo." He spoke to the orchestra members, but his eyes never left hers.

Completely blindsided by his announcement, she remained frozen as his exultant expression mocked her. The only sound she heard was the painful pounding of her heart. She couldn't possibly perform her feature, not without adequate time to prepare. She hadn't practiced the solo in over two months and wasn't sure if she even remembered it. How could she perform onstage alone? She needed Josef . . .

*"God has not given us a spirit of fear and timidity."* The passage from Second Timothy came swiftly to mind, immediately slicing through the terror quickly overtaking her. *Help me, Jesus. Not because I need to prove anything to Simon. I need to do this for me.*

"Okay," she said evenly, gaining more confidence by the second. "No problem."

Apparently surprised, Simon paled. "We don't have time to run through it," he stressed, trying to undermine her further. "You'll have to play it cold."

"I know."

"There'll be hundreds of people watching you, listening to your every note."

Annika gave him a slow, cocky smile. "I hope so."

The orchestra members broke out of their silence, whispering and twittering while Simon shoved his hand through his hair, ruining its perfect style. "You'll make a fool of yourself," he muttered, storming away and getting the last word in as usual.

Not that it mattered to her anymore. *Thanks, Lord. That wasn't so hard. Now if you could get me through this concert I'd appreciate it.*

Josef glanced at the white medical tape plastered on his left wrist and grimaced. He'd received the IV yesterday, when he'd been brought into the emergency room after having lunch at one of his favorite cafés in Salzburg. The rich Austrian pastry he'd had for dessert had tasted great, but apparently the whipped cream had been spoiled. He'd spent the rest of the afternoon and most of last night in gastronomical agony. But while he was glad that the fluids and medication the doctor had prescribed had made him feel better, the idea of a hollow tube penetrating his vein gave him the creeps. He'd always hated needles.

Lying on the uncomfortable bed in his room—a private room, one of the perks for being famous, he supposed—the only thing he could do was think. And pray. *Not that anyone's listening.* He was no closer to making a decision about his future than he'd been five weeks ago. Of course, concentrating on his career or seeking the Lord's guidance was nearly impossible when Annika continually haunted his thoughts.

Keeping his word to Simon had been the easy part—with the exception of Venice, he'd had no problem staying away from her offstage during their travels through

Europe. And with each passing moment away from her, Josef believed he had successfully purged Annika Goran from his system.

Then he would see her at the concert hall, with her lustrous hair pinned up high on her head, a few dark tendrils framing her exquisite face, and he knew he'd been deluding himself. He could keep his feelings at bay away from the stage, but when they performed together, he became powerless to control them. Each performance of their duet was bittersweet. While the unbridled passion with which he played brought him intense joy, it became more difficult to rein in when the song was over. More than once after the final note emanated from his violin he'd wanted to go to her, draw her in his arms, and let her know how he felt. But he couldn't, because of Simon's warning, because of the uncertainty of his life, because—

A sharp knock on the door pulled him out of his thoughts. "Come in," he said, expecting and hoping the doctor had arrived to sign him out of the hospital. Josef pushed a button on the side of his bed and the head of it raised up. His eyebrows rose in surprise as Annika tentatively entered the room.

"Hi," she said softly as she approached his bed, then stopped several feet away, as if afraid to move any closer to him. He watched her twist the bottom hem of her yellow T-shirt. "I-I wanted to see . . . um, how . . . are you doing?"

"Better," he answered, amazed that his voice could sound so steady while his turbulent emotions felt anything but calm. "I will be leaving here soon, so they tell me."

"Good." She rocked back on her heels, her head moving around as she surveyed his room. He noticed she seemed to take in every aspect of the drab hospital room but refused to look at him directly.

After a few awkward moments he broke the silence. "What time is it?"

"Six-thirty."

He was stunned. Not only because she'd come to see him at that hour in the morning, but he also knew it was at least a forty-minute cab ride from the hotel. He could tell by her neat French braid and freshly scrubbed appearance that she hadn't simply risen from bed and thrown on her clothes. She must have been up for at least a couple of hours already. The idea touched and puzzled him at the same time.

"Why are you here?" he asked quietly.

She turned her head and met his eyes for the first time since she'd come in the room. "Because I'm worried about you."

The note of caring in her voice made his heart lurch.

She moved toward him until she stood near the edge of his bed, then saw the IV line poking out from under the bandage. "Does that thing bother you?"

"No," he lied, unwilling to show more weakness than he already felt with her standing close enough to touch.

Annika looked at him again, her gaze telling him she saw straight through his facade. *Has she seen through me all this time?*

"I hoped we could talk," she stated. "About us."

That was a topic he *definitely* didn't want to discuss. "How was the concert last night?" he asked, changing the subject.

"Fine. I played my solo."

He couldn't help but grin at the bright smile that instantly appeared on her face. "You played well, *ja?*"

She nodded. "*Ja.* I knocked them dead, to use Stephanie's words."

"Then you are no longer afraid?"

"Not of performing. I think I've finally conquered my

stage fright with God's help. And yours." Her smile faded and uncertainty crept into her aqua eyes. She stared at him intently. His attention strayed to her mouth as she licked her slightly trembling lips. "Josef, I've . . . oh, last night was great, but it wasn't the same without you up there with me." Taking a deep breath, she continued, her words rushed. "I've sensed this connection between us when we play. I thought maybe you . . . ah . . . felt it too."

Josef remained silent, unable to tear himself away from her intense stare. The stark honesty he saw in her darkening eyes, coupled with the revelation that he hadn't hidden his feelings nearly as well as he should have, both excited and scared him. He had to take control of the situation before she ended up controlling him.

"I am tired," he said bluntly, looking away. "I would like to be alone now."

"No!" she cried out. Jerking his head back in her direction, he caught the now familiar look of determination on her face. "You can't run from me this time, Josef. You owe me an explanation, and I'm not leaving here until I get one."

In that instant, he realized she'd given him the opening he needed. Forcing a scowl he spoke harshly. "I *owe* you? How exactly am I in your debt?"

She paled. "I-I—"

"It is always about you, yes?" he interrupted. *"Your* fears, *your* problems, *your* insecurities!" She began to back away, her lips forming a red slash against her pallid skin. His words shot at her like arrows, each one aimed straight and true. "Have you ever thought about anyone but yourself, Annika? Has it ever occurred to you that other people have problems?"

Tears pooled in her eyes. "I'm sorry." She choked on the words.

Her tears moved him, but he didn't soften. He couldn't, even though he didn't believe any of the things he was saying to her. His barbs had the desired effect. She looked ready to flee. But she surprised him by standing her ground.

"What about us, Josef? Can you dismiss what's between us so easily?"

"There is nothing between us!" he shouted, not caring if he disturbed the entire ward. "Why would there be? You are a mere student, whereas I am a virtuoso. Why would I waste my time with someone so . . . *unworthy?"*

Thin streams of moisture slowly ran down her cheeks. "Now you sound like Simon," she whispered.

"Perhaps Simon and I have more in common than you thought."

"I can't believe that."

"Believe it," he sneered. "Now . . . get *out!"*

Without another word, Annika whirled on her heel and fled.

Josef pounded on the bed rail with his fist, forgetting about the IV still stuck in his wrist. Pain shot up his arm, and with a shout of frustration, he ripped off the tape and yanked out the tube. A stream of blood gushed from his vein, and he grabbed the corner of his white bedsheet and tried to stem the flow. Grinding his teeth, he pressed the call button for the nurse, then dropped his head back against his pillow in defeat.

*I have made a mess of this, Lord. But it had to be done, right? Please, God, tell me I have not made a huge mistake.*

# CHAPTER EIGHT

ANNIKA tried to calm down. She was no longer sobbing, but she couldn't stop the steady flow of tears that continued to come. Sitting in the hallway outside Josef's ward, she attempted to collect her emotions before she called a cab to take her back to the hotel.

Unable to sleep and tired of denying her feelings, she'd spent last night in prayer, asking God to give her the courage she needed to tell Josef how she felt. That morning as she'd ridden in the cab to the hospital, she could sense the Lord's presence, knew she was doing the right thing. Never had she imagined Josef would turn on her like he did.

She'd been so sure he was different. Now after their argument, she wasn't sure about anything. How could she love a man who spoke to her so cruelly? She'd taken verbal abuse from Simon and vowed never to be a victim of that again. Was this a pattern for her? Would she always fall for the wrong man?

But she didn't believe that, just as she didn't believe that Josef and Simon were the same type of man. What she didn't understand was why Josef had lashed out at her. She replayed the conversation in her mind, searching for something she'd said that might have set him off. She'd wanted to clear the air between them. Instead, everything was cloudier than before.

He'd insinuated that she was selfish. Perhaps he was right. The more she thought about it, she realized she'd made a huge mistake by coming to see him. *He's in the hospital! Instead of trying to cheer him up, I draw him into a fight. No wonder he thinks I'm self-centered.*

Hearing the sound of footsteps approaching, she sniffed and reached in her purse for a tissue. She blew her nose rather crudely just as the footfalls stopped in front of her.

A man with a bushy salt-and-pepper mustache smiled down at her. "Ms. Goran?" he asked, white teeth gleaming through the thick hair fringing his top lip.

Wiping her nose with the damp tissue, Annika wondered how he knew her name. "Yes?" she answered thickly.

"Ah, I thought so." He spoke English with the same accent as Josef. "I saw you perform at the Large Festival House last night. You play very well."

"Thank you," she replied blandly, his comment failing to make a dent in her miserable mood.

He eyed her silently for a few seconds. "Do you mind if I join you?" he asked, gesturing to the empty chair next to her.

Suddenly wary, she waited before responding. "I'll be fine, thank you."

"You do not look fine. You look as if something—or maybe *someone*—has upset you."

Now she was unnerved. Who was this guy? "I don't think this is any of your business," she snapped, rising from her seat.

Placing his hand gently on her shoulder, he kept her from leaving. "It might be. Stay." He extended his hand. "Franz Schneider. Josef has mentioned you to me. I am glad to finally meet you."

Annika let out a sigh of relief. "Mr . . . er, *Herr* Schneider, it's an honor to meet *you,*" she said, shaking his hand enthusiastically. They both sat down. "You've written a beautiful piece of music. I've enjoyed playing it."

"Good. That makes me very happy. From what I hear, you and Josef play it very well. And please, call me Franz." He cocked his head in the direction of Josef's room. "Have you seen him?"

"Yes."

"I suppose he is the reason for the tears."

She didn't want to admit it, but Franz looked at her with such kindness she felt she'd found a friend. "I just don't understand him," she admitted with a sigh.

"I think he speaks English rather well," he teased.

A small smile came to her lips as she shook her head. "Not that kind of misunderstanding. There's a barrier between us that doesn't have anything to do with language."

Franz tugged at his chin. "I have known Josef a long time, since he was a child. Because of his talent, he grew up under unusual circumstances and has led a sheltered life. At times he has difficulty seeing . . . how do you say . . . beyond the bottom of his nose?"

"I think you mean past the tip of his nose," she offered, smiling again.

"*Ja,* that is it. Anyway, do not judge him too harshly. He is a good man but not a perfect one." Franz checked his watch, then stood up. "I have to be in Vienna by noon. Good luck, Ms. Goran, and please, do not give up on him. You two will work this out."

As she watched him head for Josef's room, a sense of calm came over her. *I won't give up on Josef. I can't. . . . He means too much to me.*

Josef yelped and lashed out in German at the nurse holding his wrist in her viselike grip. "Are you trying to cut off my circulation completely?"

"Next time you want to play doctor on yourself, Herr Gemmel, do it at another hospital. Quit whining so I can get this bleeding stopped."

After what seemed like an eternity, the nurse bandaged his wrist again. "Now don't touch anything else. I'll find the doctor so he can sign you out of here."

*"Danke,"* Josef responded a little sheepishly.

Her reply was caustic as she left the room. "Don't mention it."

Seconds after she disappeared, Franz entered the room. "Have you managed to upset all the women at this hospital, Josef? The nurse I passed in the corridor was mumbling something about you under her breath, and it wasn't complimentary."

"Franz!" Josef exclaimed, pleasantly surprised to see his friend. "Come in, come in. It's good to see you."

Franz crossed the room and sat down in a hard-backed chair opposite Josef's bed. The men talked for a short time. Franz explained that he wouldn't be able to see the Moreland orchestra's performance in Vienna because of a conflict, so he'd traveled to Salzburg last night to see Josef and Annika play their duet.

"Sorry I disappointed you," Josef said glumly. "I seem to be doing a lot of that lately."

"Nonsense. I thoroughly enjoyed the performance, especially Annika's."

"I heard she did well."

"Yes, very well." Franz eyed the bloodstained sheet on the bed, a look of alarm crossing his features. "What happened there? Are you all right?"

Josef followed his gaze and gestured to the bed. "Other than acting like an idiot, I'm fine." He told Franz everything that happened and all that he'd been keeping inside for weeks. The words flowed from him as if a dam had broken. When he was through, he felt as if a heavy weight had been lifted from his shoulders.

Up to this point, Franz had listened silently. When Josef finished, Franz paused for a few moments, then spoke. "I see the problem here. You're afraid."

"Of course I'm afraid!" Josef responded in exasperation. "Didn't I just say that? I'm afraid of the future, afraid of my feelings for Annika, afraid that I've severed my connection with God somehow. Why don't you tell me something I don't already know?"

"You're a Christian. You've accepted Christ and you serve the Lord. I can tell you that you haven't broken your relationship with God."

"Then why do I feel so alone?"

Franz leaned forward in his chair. "It's because you're afraid."

To Josef the conversation seemed to be going in a circle. "But isn't he supposed to calm my fears?" he asked, his tone desperate. "I pray constantly, asking for answers, asking for something, anything that will let me know he's still in my life. All I get is silence, and it terrifies me."

"Then let it go."

Josef frowned. "Let what go?"

"The fear. You're not sensing God's presence because you've closed yourself off to him. You've allowed fear and worry to control your life, Josef. It's created a wall between you and God. Letting go of that fear is the only way to break down that barrier."

"But how do I do that? It's not like I enjoy being miserable."

Franz nodded. "Of course not. Acknowledge that God is sovereign in your life and give up trying to control the future. Remember God's plan for you is perfect." He leaned back in the chair and crossed his ankle over his knee. "In your mind you already know these things. Put them into practice and believe them with your heart."

Falling back in his bed, Josef regarded the man he'd considered a father since the death of his own father five years ago. Franz had led him to Christ, and Josef had consistently trusted his counsel. This time was no exception. *He's right, Lord. I do know these things. Now is the time to start trusting you with Annika and with my future.*

Both men turned at the sound of the door opening. The nurse walked in with a doctor trailing close behind. She handed Josef a sheet of paper, a satisfied smile on her face. "Your discharge notice, Herr Gemmel," she said smugly. "And stay away from the cream puffs for a while."

Feeling more lighthearted than he had in months, Josef threw back his head and laughed. "Impossible, they're my favorite dessert. I'll take my chances." He looked at Franz, who returned his grin. "I'm ready to get out of here. Want some company on your trip back to Vienna?"

๑

Blotting her raspberry-shaded lips with a tissue, Annika surveyed her appearance in the mirror. Her makeup wasn't flawless, but it would have to do. Snapping the clasp shut on her purse, she left the ladies' room and made her way backstage to warm up with the rest of the musicians.

The mood backstage was somber, the reality of the end slowly setting in. This was their last concert. Tomorrow they would all leave Vienna and return to Illinois, have a four-week break, and start the fall semester. Their summer in Europe would soon be a memory.

Annika lifted her violin to her chin and slowly slid the bow across the strings. The sound the instrument made barely reached her consciousness. Her mind wasn't on her music but on her upcoming performance. It would be the performance of her life.

Tonight she would reveal her feelings to Josef. That he'd left Salzburg without a word to anyone but Simon didn't deter her. She wouldn't give up on him, not until there was absolutely no hope left. After this concert she would know for sure.

Stephanie appeared beside her. "He's here," she said in a low voice, her trademark gum-popping silent for once. Both women cast a glance to the backstage door. "Just thought you might want to know," she added, giving Annika's arm a gentle squeeze before walking away.

Turning in his direction, her pulse raced as it usually did at the sight of him, impeccably dressed in his dark suit, his violin case slung casually over his left shoulder. He spoke to a few musicians as he made his way past them, then went to a vacant corner to tune his violin. Though she wanted to approach him, she didn't dare. Words were futile at this point. She'd already proved incapable of voicing her feelings effectively. There was only one way to tell him how much she loved him.

Moments later she and the other orchestra members sat in their seats, waiting for the curtain to rise and for Josef to enter the stage. When he did, he bowed slightly to the applauding audience, then moved to his chair, keeping his eyes averted from Annika's. She ignored the slight slash of pain she felt at his rebuff, shaking it off as she watched for Simon to give the downbeat.

The concert went by swiftly, yet Annika didn't remember any of it. Her focus was on the end. For this last performance their duet would be the finale. When the time came she closed her eyes, once again offering a short but heartfelt prayer to God. Her eyelids fluttered open, and upon seeing Josef's outstretched hand, she slipped her trembling one into it.

He led her to the front of the stage like he'd done numerous times during the tour. Standing a few feet apart, their violins at the ready, she locked onto his eyes. She had never let them stray from his during a performance, always feeling the need to visually hold on to him as if he were her anchor.

*"Perfect love expels all fear."* The Scripture verse seeped into her consciousness. Her love for Josef would never be perfect, but Christ's love for both of them was. He would give her the strength she needed. When Simon gave the downbeat, she shut her eyes and let go.

Stripped of her pride, pouring all her love for Josef into the notes that flowed from her fingertips, her instrument transformed in her hands and became an extension of her heart. She forgot about the rest of the orchestra and the audience of thousands listening and watching the performance. As tears burned beneath her eyelids, she focused solely on Josef, his image so clear in her mind, consumed by the intense mixture of longing and joy that coursed through her body.

Applause filled her ears as she stroked the last note. She lowered her instrument, vaguely aware that she was crying and not caring enough to stop. Shouts and cheers reverberated through the concert hall, not only from the audience members but from the orchestra too. Then the noise faded as she saw Josef move toward her.

Within seconds he drew her into his embrace, and she was stunned when his warm lips lightly touched hers. Her heart thudded madly in her chest as he kissed her tentatively at first, then with one arm pulled her closer against him, deepening the kiss until she felt the floor spin beneath her feet. When they parted, she searched his face, smiling at the look of love she found there.

"I have always played for you, Annika," he said, his words slightly breathless and his face more than a little flushed. "But tonight, you played only for me." He gazed deeply into her eyes. "Can you forgive me for being such a *Dummkopf?*"

"If that means *jerk,* then yes, I forgive you," she answered dizzily.

He grinned. "Jerk is close enough."

Shouts of "Encore! Encore!" echoed around them, penetrating through her dazed mind. Reluctantly she tore her gaze from Josef's and glanced at the orchestra members who had joined in the chanting.

"It seems they want an encore," she said, unable to keep from smiling again.

Tightening his arm around her waist, Josef lowered his head and whispered against her lips, "Then by all means, my love, we must give them one."

# CHAPTER NINE

"WHERE do you keep the cheese?"

"What?" Annika turned around and peered over the back of her sofa at Stephanie, whose head had disappeared inside the refrigerator.

"Cheese," she repeated, then stepped back and faced Annika. "Gus will want a sandwich when he gets here, and all I've managed to find so far is ham."

"Bottom drawer on the right," Annika directed, then returned her attention to the magazine she'd been trying to read for the last hour. She hadn't read further than the table of contents and doubted she ever would.

*Where is he?* The question had plagued her for the past four days. Since she'd left Vienna, rarely a day passed that she didn't hear from Josef. Letters, an occasional surprise flower arrangement, but mostly phone calls—calls that she dearly anticipated and sorely missed when she didn't get them.

She hadn't heard from him since Tuesday, and it was now Friday. Her concern had been so great she'd broken down yesterday and called Franz Schneider, who'd assured her that Josef was fine and surely he would call her within the next few hours.

But he hadn't, and Annika had moved past worry to anger. It was hard enough to be separated these past five months. The night of their last concert in Vienna, she had balked at his suggestion that she return to Illinois and he remain in Austria until she finished her last semester of school. She needed to graduate, and he needed the time to sort out his career. Eventually she had to admit he was right, but it hadn't made their parting any easier.

"Know this, Annika," he'd whispered fiercely in her ear at the airport before she boarded. "I love you. That will never change. This separation is only temporary. Soon we will be together, and I promise it will be forever."

She smiled at the memory of his words. *Together forever*. When she'd fallen in love with Josef, she'd had no idea what a romantic he was.

"Mustard?"

Stephanie's query abruptly drew her from her pleasant memories. Tossing the magazine down on the floor in disgust, she jumped off the couch and went to the kitchen to make Gus's sandwich herself.

"If you would organize your fridge in a way that made sense I could have found everything I needed," Stephanie said defensively. "You've got stuff in there that's so old I'm tempted to call the biohazard department."

"Ha-ha. Here's the mustard." Annika thrust it at her friend, her eye catching the glittering square-cut diamond that rested on Stephanie's left hand. "I still can't believe Gus actually proposed," she commented with a sigh.

Stephanie twisted the ring with her thumb. "Me

either. What a late birthday present! Or an early Christmas present—take your pick." She grinned and spread a thin layer of mustard on a slice of wheat bread. "We decided on a June wedding. You'll be the maid of honor, of course. Or maybe by that time you'll be the *matron* of honor."

"Don't hold your breath. Josef's gone MIA this week."

"You're kidding," Stephanie said, genuine shock registering on her face. She quickly blanked her features and commented in a reassuring tone, "I'm sure he'll call any minute. Maybe he got caught up with work or something."

"But he's not working! At least, he wasn't last time I talked to him." She did remember that he'd hinted about something important that might happen in the near future, but he'd been so vague about it, she'd dismissed what he'd said.

The doorbell rang, but Annika didn't move. Although it was her apartment, she knew who was at the door. "You get it, Steph. I'm sure Gus would rather be greeted by his fiancée than her lonely best friend who has to spend Friday night all by herself."

"My, aren't we throwing a marvelous pity party tonight," Stephanie remarked as she went to the door.

"Humph," Annika replied, going to the fridge and searching for a diet pop. *I can indulge in some self-pity if I want to. I've earned it. I graduate next week, Christmas is in two weeks, and I still have no idea when I'll see Josef again. Ooh, Steph's right.* Carefully sliding aside a plastic bag that had at one time held something edible, she noticed it now resembled a pile of green-and-brown goo. She also detected a slightly putrid odor coming from the meat bin. *I'll deal with you later when I have my rubber gloves on.*

Eventually she located a lone can of pop on the bottom shelf at the very back. She bent a little farther and reached for the drink. As her hand curled around the cold metal can she suddenly felt a pair of hands grip both sides of her waist and squeeze. Startled, she straightened immediately but neglected to pull out her arm, which banged up against the shelf above it. The shelf broke with a deafening crash, and all of the contents spilled to the bottom of the refrigerator and out on the floor.

"Stephanie!" she shrieked, staring down at the sticky mess that coated her fridge and floor. Two dozen eggs had been sitting on that shelf. Now the sunny yellow yolks were smeared all over the white sweat socks that covered her feet. "I'm going to *kill* you. That wasn't funny."

Hearing a low chuckle behind her, she whirled around to see Josef, red faced from trying to hold in his laughter. "Sorry," he sputtered, before succumbing to his hysteria and doubling over.

Annika didn't know which surprised her more, that Josef was standing a few inches from her in her kitchen or that he was the reason for the disaster that used to be her refrigerator. "Josef . . . arrghh!" She let out a cry of frustration, angry with him for making her worry, thrilled that he was finally here, distracted by the seeping egg yolk saturating her socks.

He stepped toward her and caught her around the waist. "You are happy to see me, *ja?*" he asked, his grin lighting up his handsome face like a fireworks show.

*"Ja,"* she said softly, her anger gone the instant his lips met hers. *"Ja!"* she repeated breathlessly when he broke the kiss.

Stephanie joined them in the kitchen, accompanied by Gus, who had arrived just in time to see the show. They were both shaking their heads. "Well, at least you don't have egg on your face," Stephanie quipped, staring at Annika's feet.

Annika groaned. "That one was really bad, Steph."

Shrugging, Stephanie gingerly stepped around the mess. "I try." She reached for some kitchen towels. "Get out of here and change your socks," she ordered. "And enjoy your boyfriend while you're at it. Gus and I will clean this up."

One glance at Gus told Annika he wasn't too happy about this particular task, but he complied anyway. Stepping away from them, she bent over and slipped off her socks, depositing them in the kitchen sink. "Give me just a minute," she said to Josef, then suddenly felt unexpectedly awkward. "Um, you can have a seat right there on the sofa," she told him.

"Okay," he said. "But before you go . . . " He bent over and kissed her again, longer and stronger than before, bringing a heated flush to her face.

Later, after Stephanie and Gus left, they sat on the couch and talked. Josef told her what had been happening in Vienna since they'd last talked, then said he had a surprise for her.

Her heart skipped in triple time as he reached into the pocket of his coat, which had been carelessly tossed over the back of the couch. *He's going to propose!* Subconsciously she rubbed the ring finger of her left hand. Then her jaw dropped as he pulled out a folded blue-backed paper.

"That looks like a contract," she said, swallowing her disappointment.

Josef smiled. "It is. A recording contract actually."

"That's wonderful," she said flatly. He'd recorded several classical CDs before, so the news of a new contract wasn't exactly out of the ordinary.

He furrowed his brows. "You are disappointed," he discerned, brushing her cheek with his fingertip. "Were you expecting something else?"

"No, no. And I'm not disappointed. I'm very happy for you."

"Not for me. For *us*."

Confused, she stared at him. "Us?"

"Annika, I have never been at such peace as I am right now. Part of it is due to you," he said, kissing her temple, "but I have finally restored my relationship with God, and I now know what he wants me to do."

Excited, Annika sat up straight. "Tell me."

"Remember Cotteridge Home? There are children's homes like it all over Europe and the United States. I believe the Lord wants me to go to these places, to play for these children and give my testimony."

"Fantastic!" she responded and clasped her hands together, truly happy for him now. "You'll bring the gift of music to so many young ones."

"God's gift of music," he corrected gently. "And the message of Christ's love. Of course, to do this will cost money for travel and living expenses and such. I do not want the homes to have to pay. I have quite a bit of money saved up, but that will run out eventually. I wondered where I would find the income, and naturally the Lord provided the answer. This recording contract will bring in enough to last a couple of years so we will not have to touch our savings."

That he'd switched from *me* to *we* didn't go unnoticed by Annika. "Where do I fit in all this?"

Reaching for her hand, he entwined his fingers with hers. "Will you join me, Annika? Will you record with me, tour with me?"

Bemused, she pulled her hand away. She should be ecstatic that he offered her a recording career, along with the opportunity to return to Europe. Never in her wildest dreams had she thought those things would ever happen to her. But the one thing that had consumed her imagination since that night onstage in Vienna still eluded her, tainting everything else.

"Josef, I can't believe you'd ask this of me."

"Why?" He frowned. "I thought this would make you happy."

"It would," she said wistfully, shifting her gaze. *Just say it. Since he won't do it, I should ask him to marry me.* Yet she held back. *Call me old-fashioned, but I don't want to be the one doing the asking. If he wants me for his wife, then he'll have to tell me.*

Rising from the sofa, she went to the window. Gazing at the fluffy snowflakes that floated down against the nighttime sky, she folded her arms over her chest. She felt Josef slip his arms around her waist from behind, and she leaned against him as he rested his chin on her head. They stood in silence for a few moments, seemingly at an impasse.

Then he grasped her left hand, and she gasped as he slid the ring over her finger. He turned her around in his arms, a mischievous glint sparkling in his blue eyes.

"You, my dear Josef, have a cruel streak," she said, trying to sound angry but unable to. She stared at her hand, marveling at the pear-shaped diamond that not only fit her finger perfectly, but was the style and shape she'd always wanted. *How did he know?*

Chuckling, he ran his hand through her hair, making her glad she'd worn it loose tonight. He brushed his palm across her cheek and cupped her chin. "Can you forgive me?"

"You're asking for forgiveness again? I believe this is becoming a habit with you. I'll have to think about it."

"Then think about this too—I love you, and I want to marry you. I want you to be my wife and my ministry partner."

"Is that all?"

"Well," he murmured, bending down to nuzzle her neck, "when the time is right, I want you to be the mother of my children."

"Hmm," she said dreamily, "you've given me a lot to think about."

Lifting his lips from her skin, he stared deeply into her eyes, his formerly devilish look replaced with one of absolute seriousness.

"What is it?" she asked, searching his gaze.

"I remember clearly the first day I met you," he said.

"Because you were dazzled by my beauty?" she teased.

He shook his head. "No, because you almost sat on my Stradivarius."

Her eyes grew wide, and she flushed at the memory. "I thought you were just another conceited violinist."

"And I thought you were beautiful." His mouth lightly touched hers. "I was thinking about a June wedding."

Throwing her arms around his neck, she hugged him tight, speaking low in his ear. "Make it May, and you've got a deal."

# A NOTE FROM THE AUTHOR

*Dear Friend,*

*I hope you enjoyed reading "Encore, Encore" as much as I enjoyed writing it. This novella contains a few of my favorite things: music, traveling, and of course romance. Although I don't play the violin, I have great respect and admiration for those who have been blessed with musical talent. When I considered the idea of two musicians falling in love while touring some of the most romantic cities in Europe, I couldn't wait to write their story.*

*However, I also wanted to explore something I'm not so fond of—the emotion of fear. Fear can pierce holes in our self-esteem, as in Annika's case; at times it can also paralyze us into inaction, as it nearly did to Josef. I found myself easily indentifying with both of their plights.*

*To paraphrase 2 Timothy 2:7, God has not given us a spirit of fear, but one of power and love. Through our relationship with Christ, we can face any obstacle with complete confidence, even if the circumstances seem overwhelming or impossible. He is our anchor, a calming influence when we find ourselves adrift on a sea of fear and anxiety. We can take comfort in the fact that our Lord will see us through each and every trial. How fortunate we are to have such a source of strength, one that is so easily accessible. All we have to do is step out in faith and lean on him.*

*May the Lord fill your life with his abundant blessings.*

*Kathleen Fuller*

## ABOUT THE AUTHOR

Kathleen Fuller was born in New Orleans, raised in Arkansas, and now lives near Cleveland, Ohio. Her short stories have appeared in several on-line publications, including *lovewords, Short Story Magazine,* and *Short Story Writer's Showcase*. A former special education teacher, she and her husband, James, homeschool their three young children.

Kathleen welcomes letters written to her in care of Tyndale House Author Relations, P.O. Box 80, Wheaton, IL 60189-0080.

# Measure of a Man

Susan M. Warren

*To Andrew,*
*the guy in the candy-wrapper hat, for being my real-life hero,*
*and to David, Sarah, Peter, and Noah,*
*four munchkins who bring sunshine to each day.*

*To Vonnie. Thank you for helping dream up this story,*
*and for the courage with which you inspire me.*

*To my parents, my family, and our supporters,*
*for your limitless encouragement.*

*And most of all, to my Lord and Savior, for sending*
*me to Russia and teaching me that you are sufficient*
*and able to do abundantly more than I can imagine.*
*Give me a willing heart, O Lord!*

# CHAPTER ONE

PETER Samuelson leaned his forehead against the elevator doors, peered through the crack, and prayed for a savior.

"Hello?" he called, his hoarse voice pitching higher than the last time. No reply from the shadowed, dusty hallway of the Russian Intourist Hotel in the village of Georgivka.

The dim light slanting through the one-inch opening did nothing to dent the pitch darkness in the cold elevator. A draft, some leftover whisper of Siberian wind, hissed inside and down his T-shirt. He shivered, wishing he'd had the foresight to throw on his leather jacket before leaving his room. But how was he supposed to know a trip to get a midnight soda would turn into a two-hour wrestling match with a rickety hotel elevator? For some reason the lift had simply stopped, doused all light, and refused to budge another inch.

Peter gritted his teeth and slid down into a crouch against the wall, his arms dangling over his knees. He heard his soda bottle, now empty, careen across the floor and hit the wall. The musty odors of the ancient box clenched his stomach. Sinking his head into his hands, he lifted another prayer. *I know I'm not necessarily your favorite person, God, but I'd really appreciate some help about now.*

He fought to silence his drumming heartbeat, hoping to hear footsteps. He'd already tried to rouse Tomas, sleeping in the room adjoining his, but he had no idea if the lift had halted on the fifth floor, where their rooms were located. Besides, his partner was probably sleeping off his last round of toasts. He grimaced, wishing his father had chosen a different man than Tomas to accompany him to Russia. Peter couldn't shake the urge to hold on to his billfold whenever he saw him and his slick smile heading his direction.

Their translator, however, obviously entertained very different feelings about his coworker. Dina glowed like a Christmas bulb when Tomas walked into the room. Peter shook his head. Tomas attracted women like a magnet, but Peter hated to see Dina fall into the trap, even if she did seem a perfect fit for the smooth-talking American. Her sharp, black eyes never missed a detail, her translations flowed like syrup. She made the village women look like hobos with her sleek black suits and flawlessly prepared face. It was no wonder Tomas had selected her from the pool of translators in Moscow, totally ignoring Peter's request for a male interpreter.

There was probably a good reason why Dina hadn't heard his cries for help either. He didn't want to think about it and threaded his hands behind his neck.

Two o'clock in the morning and not a soul prowling the corridors. He would be stuck in the lift until dawn, when the desk clerk would resume her post. His throat thickened with the taste of despair. The way things had been running since he hit town two weeks ago, he might even spend the next week trapped in a box the size of a phone booth that looked like it hadn't been repaired since World War II.

It wasn't that he hadn't done his homework. He knew everything there was to know about this backwoods Siberian village, Georgivka. He'd spent the three months before this trip memorizing Russian names, terms, and culture until he was saying *Zdrastvootyeh* in his sleep. He'd filled his suitcase with enough chocolate to feed a small army and had outfitted thirty Russian kids in Chicago Bulls T-shirts. Even Dina had been impressed when he remembered to toast the mayor, although he'd done it with mineral water.

But despite his smiles, chocolate, and T-shirts, the Russian government officials continued to wring their hands over knitting forces with Samuelson Timber & Steel. A two-million-dollar logging contract for the Amursk Region hung in the balance, and if Peter didn't kick the charm into overdrive, twenty million acres of pristine pine, just waiting to be harvested, would go to a burly man named Hedstrom.

Tomorrow Peter would pull out his trump card—a gift of three brand-new Feller Buncher machines that could fell and pre-pile the timber. He could almost hear the clicking of the abacuses as the Russian number crunchers calculated the proceeds their joint venture with STS would bring to their village and others in the region.

It felt good to bring capitalism and prosperity to a struggling Siberia. Good, if not peaceful. That ought to count for something in God's great tally book. Peter needed the points, especially after he'd turned his back on God's voice. He'd been trying to make amends ever since—

amends that wouldn't actually require him to revisit the commitment he'd made under the influence of youthful emotionalism. God's request was simply unthinkable . . . even eight years later.

Peter stood up and shoved his fingers into the tiny crack between the doors. Wedging his foot against the wall, he threw his weight into the door and pulled. Nothing. His efforts erupted into a frustrated roar. The lift shuddered as he slapped his open palm on the door. "C'mon! Isn't anyone out there?"

Where were the desk clerks or the beggar children that followed him like ducklings around the village?

"Hello, is someone in there?"

Peter's pulse leaped. "Yes! Yes! I'm in here!" He pressed his eye between the doors, searching for a face. A dark blur streaked by. "Don't leave!" he called, jolted at the panic in his voice.

"You speak English," came the voice. Sweet and feminine, with a harmonic lilt, as if the owner had done time in the South.

"So do you! Can you help me?" He squinted into the gap and spied a strip of parka.

"I don't know. The lobby is empty. I had to take the stairs up. I think the electricity is out."

"What floor am I on?"

"Third. Wait here."

His chest constricted. "Don't leave!"

Silence. *Please, God, bring her back.* The cold had long since seeped through his slippers to his toes, turning them to bricks. He rubbed his hands together, praying. *Please, please come back!*

"Try this."

Peter stepped back as a long metal rod shot through the crack. He grabbed it. "Where did you get this?"

"It was under the bed in my room. Looks like a broken table leg. See if you can wedge the door open."

Peter braced his foot against the wall and pushed on the rod, grunting. Pain streamed into his palms, up his forearms. The doors cracked another half inch. "Arrgh!"

"Try again," the voice urged.

Peter pulled this time, rowing back as if the rod was an oar. The sound of metal rubbing against metal screeched down the corridor and set his teeth on edge. "No good."

He heard his would-be rescuer sigh. "I don't know what to do. The front desk is closed and there's not a person in sight."

Peter massaged the tense muscle pinching his neck. "I can't believe they don't have a backup generator."

A slight chuckle. "Russia isn't known for its conveniences."

He had to return the chuckle. After having his plane delayed six hours in Moscow upon his arrival, his baggage routed to Novosibirsk before it found him two days later, and his hotel room dirty when he checked in, he had to agree.

"Can I get you anything?" That honeyed voice reached through the crack and wrapped around his heart.

He swallowed the lump in his throat. "A blanket and pillow?"

Her laughter balmed his frustration. "Hand me back that table leg. I'll see what I can rustle up."

After a while the table leg again came through the doors, this time dragging with it a white cotton sheet. "That's the best I could do. I didn't think the wool blanket would fit. And as for the pillow . . . well . . ."

Peter yanked in the sheet and wrapped it around himself. "You're a lifesaver."

"I wish."

He heard a thump. "What are you doing?"

"Camping out."

If he could have, he would have hugged her. "Thanks," he said hoarsely, "but you can't spend the night out there."

"Sure I can. I have a burning curiosity to know all about the mysterious English speaker imprisoned in a Russian elevator."

He imagined her, from her voice, as a redhead with misty blue eyes and a lively smile. Leaning against the wall, he slid down to a crouch, not willing to sit on the grimy floor again, and pulled the sheet tight, hoping it would trap warmth. He could barely see his hand before his face, and if it wasn't for the milky shaft of light, he would easily believe he was knee-deep in a nightmare.

Her voice reached out and reminded him he wasn't sleeping . . . and he wasn't alone. "So, who are you and what are you doing here?"

Peter tried to keep the gratitude for her companionship from denting his voice. "I'm a lawyer."

"Someone commit a crime?"

"Other than the elevator maintenance man?"

Her laughter warmed him to the bone. "I'm a corporate lawyer. The company I work for is hoping to create a partnership with a Russian firm."

"In Georgivka? There's no company bigger than the bread factory in town. Are you going to teach them to make bagels?"

"No," he chortled. The sheet was beginning to gather heat, and sandbags weighed on his eyes. His legs, however, screamed, forcing sleep into the recesses of tomorrow.

"I haven't had a bagel in years," the sweet voice continued. "Oh, how I miss them."

"What kind?"

"Honey-wheat. I would hike to the next country for a honey-wheat bagel. I love them with honey, but I'd even settle for one with butter."

He'd have to remember that. "Sorry, no bagels. My company utilizes natural resources. We're looking at the timber in this area. The Russians have twenty million acres of forest just waiting to be harvested."

"Scalped, you mean."

He bristled at the chill in her voice. "No, I mean harvested. Russia has been plagued with sweeping forest fires. Responsible forestry management can clean the forests out, replant, and create a natural firebreak. Russian forests can actually be improved if we do it right."

"And do you plan on using Russian labor?"

"Of course."

He heard her harrumph and he stiffened, his brow knitting. "So, what are you doing here?" he asked, hoping he hadn't inadvertently sent her packing. "A pretty lady in the middle of Siberia?"

"How do you know I'm pretty?"

"You're sitting here in the middle of the night in a cold, dark hallway, keeping a stranger from sinking into despair. You're breathtaking."

He hoped the silence meant she was smiling.

"I'm a missionary."

An eight-year-old ache revived and hit him hard in the chest. "Really?" He sounded like he had a cold and winced. Of course God had to send him a missionary to save him. Just to shove all his past mistakes into his face.

"I work in a camp for kids of loggers about thirty kilometers north of here," she continued. "Out-of-work loggers."

He heard the indictment in her words, and it confused him. "This contract would put those loggers to work. And rebuild Russia's forests wisely."

"I'll believe it when I see it."

He rubbed his forehead with the back of his hand. "We're not enemies here. I want to help Russia rebuild, get back on her feet."

The thick silence made him wonder if she'd left him to ward off the chill alone.

"It's a nice thought," she finally admitted. "But Russians need more than a leg up. They need hope."

"And you're passing that out?" He instantly regretted the cynicism that surfaced in his voice.

"Absolutely. That's my commodity. God's hope through Christ."

"One soul at a time, huh?"

"If God allows."

He rubbed his chest where it burned. "Good for you. I knew a lady once who wanted to be a missionary. I hope she made it."

"You don't know?"

He shook his head in the darkness. "Where do you hail from?"

"I was born in New York State, but my family lived all over. You?"

"Where did you get that accent?"

She laughed and bumped up the drawl in her words. "That's my No'th Caroleena trainin' comin' at ya."

He suddenly longed for home, for the comfort of a five-star hotel, room service, and the power of his Gold Card. "How long have you been here?"

"Four years."

"That's a long time."

"And two years of language training in Moscow before that. It's been ages since I had a Whopper and a milk shake."

"If I get out of here, I'll make you one myself."

Her musical laugh made him believe all was forgiven. He dared to ask the question bouncing through his mind. "Are you here by yourself?"

He heard the staccato of cracking knuckles and a long sigh. "Yes."

He licked his parched lips. "Me too."

Her voice softened. "Not anymore."

How could a woman creep inside his heart so quickly? He stifled a moan, wishing he could invite her to stay. But no one could take Calli's place. Her presence still lingered nearly a decade after he'd forced her from his life. He'd been such a fool. Such an arrogant, stubborn fool. No matter whom he'd dated since then, it had always ended in a fiasco. He'd never again find the treasure he'd found in Calli—a woman who had known him well and hadn't flinched. A woman who had loved him despite his family and their materialistic expectations. A woman who was sold out to obeying God, regardless of the cost.

He hadn't deserved her.

"Thanks," he rasped.

Calli wrapped her ski jacket around her and leaned her head against the cement wall. Cold streaked down her back and she shivered. Pulling a blanket over her knees, she shot a glance at the elevator, wondering if there was a way she could tuck the blanket through the crack. The man had to be freezing.

It was clear that God's providence had kept her until the wee hours at Dmitri's mother's house, planning the camp activities. They had only three days to pin down the menu, order food, and collect supplies for their three-month summer camp nestled along the Amur River.

As usual God was providing the camp's every need. Calli's fourth summer as co-program director of Shamara Camp would be the best one ever. Peace swept through her, warming her despite the chilly, late hour. She was right in God's hand, safe in the center of his will. Her missionary experience in the remote Russian village had been the best four years of her life. Besides learning another language, she'd learned to trust in God for all things and had seen his amazing handiwork in everything from the provision of camp supplies to the joy of salvation written in the twinkling brown eyes of Russia's children. God had even preplanned this evening and allowed her to encourage some stranger—an English-speaking stranger at that. The providence of the Almighty never ceased to amaze her.

"So how long are you in town?" she asked, wondering if the man was still awake.

She'd heard the despair lining his voice, and her heart wrung for him. She herself had lived through a few unfortunate scrapes with Russian elevators and knew how easily gloom seeped into the bones. Especially at three in the morning on a nippy Siberian night. Calli shoved her hands into her pockets to pump some heat back into her fingers. May in Siberia still meant an occasional snowfall and average temperatures in the mid-forties. She hoped it would warm by the time the first load of campers arrived within a week.

"As soon as I can wrap up this deal, I'm out of here."

She couldn't help frowning at the disgust in his tone. "Have you ever been to Russia before? St. Petersburg is beautiful. You should stick around and see the sights."

"No, thanks. Kudos to you for braving it for six years."

"That's frustration talking. There has to be something about Russia you like so far."

Perhaps the silence meant he was pondering her words.

"Okay, I get the picture," she said. She rubbed her hands over her face, feeling sleep washing over her like a wave.

"Wait, I can think of something," he announced.

From his deep voice, she imagined him tall, with hair the color of coffee and honey brown eyes. But then again, every man she imagined came out looking like Peter Samuelson. Nearly eight years later, he still haunted her dreams. Thankfully, she'd been able to drive him from her daily thoughts. Someday, perhaps, he would also fade from her subconscious wanderings. His memory and the pain from his rejection were still vivid enough to keep other men at arm's length. Besides, the man who loved her would also have to love God—enough to surrender his plans to God's plans. Enough to follow her into missions. For, until God changed her course, she was committed to bringing the Good News to this tiny corner of Siberia.

She tucked her hair behind her ears and sat up straight against the wall. "Well, what do you like about Russia? Borscht? Pirozhki? Maybe it's the terrific hotel service." She stifled a giggle and heard him snort. She hoped he was smiling.

"No . . . it's you."

The heat of her blush started at her toes and rushed up to her ears. Her mouth turned dry. She quickly attributed it to the surreal rush of emotions at hearing her mother tongue spoken after such a long time. "S-so, what made you want to be a lawyer?" she stuttered.

Silence. Then tightly, "My father."

Was it her imagination, or did bitterness edge his tone?

"He wanted me to follow in his footsteps and take over the family business."

Resentment definitely lined his voice. She eyed the

elevator doors, wishing she could see his face. She was attacked by the outlandish impulse to run her hand down the side of his cheek and caress away any tightness in his jaw. "And you didn't want to?"

"No, not really. I like it now, but for a while I thought about being something different. Really different."

Curiosity arched her eyebrows. "What?"

He cleared his throat, as if the truth had a hard time coming out. For some reason, it sent gooseflesh up her arms.

"A missionary."

Calli couldn't have managed words even if she had any. She drew the wool blanket up to her chin, fighting a stinging sensation over her entire body. Her eyes burned.

"You still there?"

She nodded, still unable to find words and warring with the silly emotions that crested over her. So what? He wanted to be a missionary. It didn't mean she had to dredge up all the unwanted memories, all the hopes and dreams birthed one emotional night eight years ago at the foot of an altar. The missions conference had moved her heart and changed her life forever. She'd thought it had changed Peter as well. As they'd knelt together and pledged to follow God's call into missions, she'd believed he'd meant every word and that the tears in his eyes were a genuine reaction to Christ's work in his life.

Two weeks later reality had hit her hard when Peter began avoiding her like a leper, acting as if a college campus of ten thousand was too small for both of them. It soon became painfully clear that she and his promise to God had never existed.

She drew up her knees and rested her forehead on them. Her eyes filled.

"Hello?"

The worry in his voice brought her head up and made her press her fingertips to her eyes. "Yes, I'm sorry. I heard you. Why didn't you become a missionary?" She cringed at the tremor in her voice . . . but maybe, if this stranger could tell her his reasons, then she'd finally understand. . . .

"My father." A resigned tone. "He wasn't interested in his only son traipsing off to the far reaches of the planet."

Calli laid a hand on her chest, felt her racing heart. "Do you regret it?"

She heard his sigh and felt his answer, but before he had a chance to respond, the grimy overhead light flickered on, bathing the hall in blinding fluorescence. The elevator clicked, hummed, and suddenly the doors lurched open.

"I'm free!"

Calli climbed to her feet, bracing a hand on the wall just as the prisoner stumbled out of the lift. She caught a glimpse of him, and shock rooted her to the spot. The stranger was indeed tall, with coffee brown hair and warm honeyed eyes. He looked down at her, blinking, a crooked smile creasing his face.

Calli's heart dropped to her toes. Her knees turned to rubber. She barely noticed the outstretched hand he extended. But she plainly heard his voice, emerging from all her dreams to materialize as a nightmare before her eyes.

"My name is Peter Samuelson. And you are my heroine, I presume?"

Calli whirled and raced for her room.

# CHAPTER TWO

PETER'S heart lodged in his throat as he stared after the retreating redhead. He blinked rapidly, dropped his outstretched hand, and gathered his wits. No, it couldn't be . . .

He sprinted after her. "Miss?"

She never turned. Skidding to a halt at her door, she flung it open and dived inside, slamming it behind her.

A second later he reached the door. "Are you all right?" What had he done to make her run from him like a scared rabbit? Peter hesitated, wondering if he should just leave. He breathed hard and scrubbed a hand through his hair. When he heard a muffled sob, his heart fell an inch. He cleared his throat. "Miss, are you okay? I'm very sorry if I offended you."

"You didn't. Please, go away." Her voice shook, and he knit his brow.

His chest constricted as an odd feeling swept through him. "I'd like to thank you."

"You're welcome." Her voice choked as another sob erupted.

Peter braced two hands on the doorframe, frustrated. She'd been so kind. And he'd sent her running for cover. Why?

"I'm not going to hurt you. I'd just like to know the name of the lady who rescued me."

"I hardly rescued you."

"You rescued my spirit. Please, what's your name?"

Silence.

Peter tried the door handle. Locked. "Are you okay?"

"Peter, don't you recognize me?"

Her wretched voice nearly knocked him to his knees. Something heavy spread through his chest, and he tasted the acrid steel of shame. "Calli?" Her name emerged as a rasp of disbelief, building as astonishment turned to joy. "Calli, is that you?"

"Yes, it's me, Peter. Go away."

He cringed, feeling like a clod. He should have recognized her voice. Only Callidora Deane could wheedle her way into his heart in the matter of an hour. Because she'd never truly left.

"Go away, please."

Her tone ripped him into a thousand pieces. Go away? He winced. He'd hurt her worse than he'd thought. "Please, Calli, open the door."

"I'm just as shocked to see you. But I'm not opening the door. Ever. Go away."

He bowed his head. His heart thumped painfully, and he pressed his chest to calm it. "I understand; I truly do. I don't blame you for not wanting to see me. But don't you think it's a little odd that we'd meet again in the same town in the same hotel in the middle of Siberia?"

A pause told him she agreed. "No. I'm not thinking about it."

"C'mon, honey. Let me talk to you."

"Don't call me honey. We're way past that. Walk away, Peter. I don't want to see you." The sob at the end of her words laid open his heart.

"You can't forgive me?" Why did his voice always have to betray his emotions?

"I forgave you eight years ago."

Oh, how he wanted to open the door and gather her into his arms, bury his face in her hair, and inhale the fragrance that he could never seem to forget. He leaned his forehead against the cool wood grain of the door. "Then open the door."

"It's over. I don't want to relive the past."

He swallowed hard as memory crested over him. Her red, tortured eyes, the scream in his heart as he walked by her on campus and saw her struggle to keep her chin up. His fingernails dug into his palms. It wasn't supposed to be this way.

"Okay, Calli. You win. I won't bust your door down. Not tonight. But please let me thank you for keeping me company."

"You're welcome."

"I want to buy you breakfast."

Silence.

He shoved a hand through his hair again, feeling the stress of the night building in his shoulders. "Please, Calli. I can't undo the pain I caused you, but please let me see you and thank you for your kindness. I'll be downstairs in the morning around eight, waiting. Please, please be there." Not wanting to hear an argument, he whirled, strode down the hall to the stairwell, and sprinted up to his fifth-floor room.

Peter hadn't even recognized her. So her hair was shorter now, and she'd dropped thirty pounds. She'd identified him the instant he stumbled from the lift. Betrayal felt fresh and raw.

Calli slumped against the door, listening to his feet thump down the hall, away from her, out of her life again. But not out of her heart. Never. If she had known it was Peter Samuelson trapped in the elevator . . . well, she still would have tried to help. Despite the scars he'd left on her heart, she would have reached out to him.

But now he was safe, free and able to march right out of her life.

Just like he had eight years ago. She gulped back the wild impulse of hope that he would indeed break the door down. The old Peter would have. He wouldn't have let a flimsy wall of wood stand between him and the woman he said he loved. The old Peter would have beat down the gates of the underworld to gather her in his arms. But that was before he denied everything he said he believed in.

Memory cut a swath through her and she gasped. Swallowing deep breaths, she climbed to her feet and trudged to the bathroom. She rinsed her face with cold water, blotted away the tears, and stared into the grimy mirror. Freckles still splattered her face, her mousy red hair still refused to cooperate—she wasn't much changed.

Time had been kind to Peter Samuelson, however. He probably had an eager and lonely fiancée or wife waiting back home, someone who could garnish his life with poise and beauty—a perfect mate for a corporate lawyer. She draped her coat over an armchair, then kicked off her jeans. Pulling on her flannel pajamas, she fell into bed, tucked the covers up to her chin, and curled into a ball. His words replayed in her ears: *"I was going to be a missionary."*

"Ha!" she exclaimed into the night, then tasted the salt of tears. He was forgetting he'd had his chance . . . and blown it. *"My father didn't want his son traipsing to the far reaches of the planet."* Then what was he doing here? Peter would have been more accurate if he'd said, "My father didn't want his son traipsing to the far reaches of the planet with *you.*"

Bitterness burned a hole in her chest. *Help me, Lord,* she begged. *I can't take letting Peter into my life again.* He may not have recalled their two-year college romance, but she remembered everything down to his masculine scent and the feel of his hand in hers. She still ached to hear his laughter and his rich voice outlining his dreams.

Obviously, Peter had meant more to her than she had to him. Meeting him for breakfast was the last thing she would do, no matter how much her heart longed to. She put the pillow over her head and sobbed.

Peter fiddled with his watch, glancing at it now and again. Eight-thirty. He should take Calli's not-so-subtle hint. His eyes burned; his brain was foggy from lack of sleep. Memories of Calli—her soft skin, her fragrance, her laughter like a spring breeze—had pushed sleep into the folds of eternity. She'd reawakened all the dormant feelings he'd been running from far too long. If she didn't show up for breakfast . . . well, he'd acquired enough contacts in town to track her to the far reaches of the territory.

"Miss?" He raised a finger to a passing waitress. Her gray eyes latched onto him with annoyance. He thought by now the plump woman in the tiny restaurant café would be used to him. He tried a smile. "More coffee, please?"

"Coffee," she repeated and filled his cup without smiling.

Despite the thick smell of grease and an unnerving layer of dirt on the cement floor, he'd learned that the café turned out a decent breakfast, after he'd outlawed liver and instructed them to actually cook the bacon. His stomach growled. He hoped Calli would show up soon. His perch facing the door left no room for escape. She'd have to walk through the lobby and past the café to leave the hotel. He was prepared for a camp-out.

He'd replayed every word of last night's conversation in his head, clinging to her tender, encouraging words as if they were meant for him and not some stranger in an elevator. At least now maybe she'd finally believe that he hadn't lied to her eight years ago. Still, he ached to tell her the full truth about why he'd backed out on his promise. It was time, and maybe God had finally granted him the chance.

"Peter! How many cups of coffee have you had?" Dina glided up, looking crisp in a black leather skirt, black hose, and a frilly white poet's blouse. Not a strand of ebony hair escaped from the clip at the nape of her neck, and her dark eyes raked over him with the finesse of an art collector.

"Did our preacher have a rough night?" Tomas sidled up behind her as Peter climbed to his feet. Tomas had been calling him preacher since he'd turned down the vodka toast for mineral water. Dina smirked.

Peter extended a hand to his partner, then quelled the urge to clean his hands on his pants after the handshake. "I was stuck in the lift for the better part of three hours last night."

Dina's red lips parted in a perfect O. Tomas shook his head. "You have the worst luck, pal."

Peter chose not to tell him he considered it divine Providence. "I don't know when I'll be in the office. I have something to take care of."

Dina and Tomas exchanged a look. "Don't be too long," Tomas said, touching Dina's elbow. "We have a deal to close."

A streak of red flashed by the door, nabbing Peter's gaze. "Right," he answered. He flicked them a glance. "I'll be in soon." Whirling, he threw fifty rubles on the table and speed-walked toward the entrance.

"Calli!" He accelerated into a jog, noticing she was walking as fast as she could without breaking into a run. He caught up and snagged her elbow. She turned reluctantly. The strain on her face sent his resolve reeling. Fatigue streaked her eyes red and paled her face to the color of the moon.

"Please, Peter, I—"

"I just want to say thanks and see how you're doing. I promise, I'm not going to upset your life. Just breakfast." He didn't know why it was so important to be with her, but the need pulsed in his heart.

She shook her head. "I need to do some shopping."

"You aren't going to eat?"

She smiled ruefully, and pain edged her eyes.

With a groan, he remembered. She never ate breakfast. She drank a diet Coke and sometimes managed a bagel—a honey-wheat bagel. He grimaced and rubbed his forehead with his palm, feeling like a buffoon. "I don't suppose you can get diet Coke around here?"

"Only in my dreams." She zipped up her jacket and adjusted the black satchel she'd slung over her shoulder.

He was caught momentarily by the way her hair curled in ringlets around her face. Her new bob accentuated her high cheekbones and tickled her jaw in a way that made him want to twirl a finger through a curl. He clenched his fists and drew in a calming breath. "How about I tag along?"

Her eyes met his, searching them. He swallowed hard at the sadness swimming through them. *Calli, I'm sorry.*

Then she tore her gaze away and stared past him. Her eyes glistened. "I don't think so."

He didn't have the words to express his disappointment. He just stood there, feeling himself shatter, trying to scrape up composure.

"It was good seeing you again, Peter. May God bless your efforts here. I really hope it turns out for good." She curled a white hand around her satchel strap and strode out of his life.

The echo of her steps hurt him to the bone.

"Who was that?"

Peter couldn't look at Tomas. He shoved his hands in his pockets and watched Calli exit the hotel. "A friend."

Tomas said nothing, but Peter could feel the man's eyes on him. Peter manufactured a smile. "Let's go to work."

Samuelson Timber & Steel was camped out for the duration of their business stay in a room donated by the local administration. The cement-walled office smelled like it had been vacant for a decade, and only the crispy brown geranium on the windowsill evidenced previous life. Dina opened the orange-fringed curtains, letting in the crystalline rays of morning.

Peter pulled up a rickety brown chair to his matching desk and turned on his laptop. At least the phone system worked. He downloaded his messages, two from the office and one from his mother, and scanned them.

Dina slid a hip on the desk across from him, leaning over Tomas as he read his mail. Her perfume drenched the room, driving away the stale smell but wrinkling Peter's nose.

"I think we need to add an amendment to the contract." Peter drummed his fingers on the desk and studied Tomas's reaction.

As a junior vice president, Tomas was one notch below Peter and climbing fast. Peter had no doubt his father would make Tomas a senior partner if the man proved he could jockey the merger as well as Peter. And then there would be two vying for the vice president's position.

As the son of the president, Peter should have had a few extra advantages. But that wasn't his father's way: *"Earn your way, every step."* Just like Roland Samuelson had. He knew his father had taken Samuelson Timber & Steel and turned it into a conglomerate in the natural-resource industry. But Peter wasn't sure that was what Grandfather Alton had had in mind when he started his iron-ore shipping company in northern Minnesota back in the thirties.

Roland had made it clear that he expected his son to add on to the Samuelson empire, and if he couldn't, he'd find someone who could. Peter hadn't crammed his way through law school to be one-upped by a smooth-talking Bostoner who didn't know his way around a pine forest. Still, he couldn't help but feel Tomas had been sent along to watchdog him for the master.

Tomas frowned. "What kind of amendment?"

"A guarantee that we'll use only Russian labor. It came to me last night. I think that could be our ace over Hedstrom."

"Why? It's assumed."

Peter laid his hands flat on the desk. "Maybe, but I think we should let them know in writing that our intentions are honorable."

Tomas exchanged a look with Dina. "But the contract is already written, translated, and approved by Roland. It's a mess we don't need to bother with."

Peter shrugged. "It's just an amendment. Dina can add it this morning before our meeting. I'm sure my father will approve." Why did Tomas keep glancing at Dina, as if it inconvenienced her? She was, after all, hired to be their interpreter. "She can use my computer. We can send the amendment to the office for his approval. If we do it right away, he'll get it before STS closes for the day."

Dina pasted on a white smile. "*Nyet* problem."

Was that a glare from Tomas? Peter frowned at him as he surrendered his seat to Dina. He cleared his throat, breaking the crisp silence. "I'm going to the market to find a diet Coke."

Calli sat on the stone-laid wall overlooking the river and nursed her apple juice. The spring wind teased her hair, and she knew it was quickly turning into a wild mop. Siberia had given way to spring, and the last chunks of ice were surrendering to the current, bobbing toward the Pacific. The thick scent of pine layered the air. Calli inhaled long and deep, trying to balm her aching heart.

She'd faced Peter and said good-bye. Now, somehow, she'd have to drive from her memory those twinkling honey brown eyes, that rapscallion smile that turned her to mush, and the longing to be wrapped inside his strong arms. It didn't help that his arms filled out his cranberry dress shirt, or that the color lifted every scarlet highlight from his curly brown hair. And he'd sounded so genuine, pleading even. It had tugged at her emotions and nearly shattered all reason. *Why, O God?* Calli's eyes burned, and she blinked furiously. It would do her good to remember that Peter couldn't even recall her breakfast habits.

"Would you like a pirozhki?" Dmitri Dobran held out a fried-liver sandwich in a grease-dotted strip of paper.

Calli made a face and shook her head.

"So, what is left on the camp list?" Dmitri bit hungrily into the sandwich.

"We have to sign the contract with the bread factory, and I need to find baseballs."

Dmitri laughed, his baritone melody singing in the wind. "Good luck, dreamer. This is Russia. We don't play American baseball here."

"God will provide, Dmitri. Haven't you learned that yet?" She gave him a sly smile. "Baseball teaches teamwork and patience. It's good for the soul. If God wants it, every kid in the territory will hit a homer."

Dmitri nodded his head approvingly and fixed his dark chocolate-colored eyes on hers. "Promise you'll come back after furlough?"

Calli shrugged. After last night, she didn't know what other curveballs God was going to throw into her life. If she didn't believe God had all things knit together and that nothing happened outside his will, she'd chalk up meeting her one true love, the man who'd broken her heart forever, to chance. She bit her bottom lip and tried not to think about her theology. "Lord willing. It's up to God, but I hope he'll send me back here."

Dmitri fell silent. A magpie cried out, the caw snagged by the breeze and skipping away across the river.

"I think we need to split up," Calli suggested. "You go to the factory, and I'll see about the baseball equipment."

*"Da,"* Dmitri agreed.

Calli watched him walk away, reluctantly comparing him to Peter. He wasn't as tall, broad shouldered, or striking. But his gentle brown eyes always found the soft spot in her heart, and he outmeasured Peter in character. At least he wasn't afraid to surrender his future to God's control. Dmitri had thrown his life into youth work, seeking a lost generation for Christ, and although he couldn't make her weak in the knees, his steadiness and commitment to the Lord had earned him a place of respect, if not love, in her heart.

Tossing her bottle in a nearby can, Calli crossed the boulevard toward the market.

As the smell of charbroiled pork, mangy dogs, and truck exhaust invaded his nose in the outdoor market, Peter's esteem for Calli grew. He dropped some coins into the outstretched hand of an elderly woman. She bowed and mumbled something in Russian. Calli spoke Russian. That thought amazed him.

He glanced behind him. He'd picked up a fan club. A gang of bedraggled, probably homeless, kids followed him, not very unobtrusively. They'd become braver as the hour wore long, lurking ten feet away, peering out from between kiosks or pretending to peruse fruits or vegetables.

Peter paused at the stall of a younger woman dressed in a grimy brown parka. Deep lines in her face aged her a decade. She smiled and he noticed gaps between her teeth.

"Do you have diet Coke?" He pointed to a row of bottles, all of them unfamiliar. "Di-et Co-ke?" he enunciated slowly, louder.

She continued to smile and nodded.

He waited.

She nodded.

"No diet Coke, right?"

She nodded, still smiling.

Peter returned the smile. "Thanks."

Poor Calli. The woman had bought diet Coke by the case in the States. It was becoming painfully clear that she'd taken their pledge very seriously. Too seriously. His chest burned with the thought. At least she had the courage to keep her word. He shooed away a mangy dog that sniffed his leg. He was trying, but he never quite felt he hit God's mark after turning down the Almighty's first job offer.

One of the beggar children edged closer, and Peter caught a whiff of vodka. He groaned, hoping it wasn't coming from the ten-year-old with a year's layer of dirt on her face. Moving away, he spied a bigger kid in a tattered canvas jacket and misshapen moon boots following him with dark eyes. Peter hustled his pace. Surely someone in the market had a diet Coke. He'd spotted a Sprite earlier and suddenly wished he'd purchased it. At least then he'd have something to show for his efforts when he returned to the office.

He passed a woman selling flowers. Her pots were full of roses, red and white, and wildflowers. On impulse Peter pointed at a white rose. The woman worked it from the bunch and wrapped it in newspaper. He handed her a fifty-ruble note, not sure if he should expect change. She pocketed it and grinned.

Peter moved into the crowd, wondering if he'd just been had. A blur of dark green caught his eye, and he whirled, expecting the scruffy teen. He nearly plowed into an elderly man in an army uniform. With an apologetic smile, Peter backed away and found cover next to a potato vender. Gathering his wits, he watched foot traffic stream by. The sound of street traffic, foreign dickering, and the clink of weights on scales set his teeth on edge. Never had he felt so far from home.

An elderly woman with a cane bought five potatoes from the vendor, struggling to carry them under the stoop of her wide, aged body. Peter nearly offered to help, but the language barrier rendered him helpless. He was as fluent as a toddler.

He seemed to have lost his little shadows, however. Feeling like a pardoned man, he fell in step behind a sharply dressed brunette prancing through the market on spike heels. Veering through an alley of kiosks, he spotted his office building rising from the tangle of vendors and made a beeline toward it. Enough with the market. He'd have the diet Coke sent in. At least he had the rose to offer Calli when he asked her to reconsider.

An explosion at the base of his neck sent him to his knees. Peter's hands scraped the ground, ripping flesh as they met pavement. Another screaming blow to the back of his head drove his chin to the earth. His breath whooshed out in a violent gust when a final punch between his shoulder blades pressed him flat into the dirt.

"Leave me alone!" Panic took possession of his voice and body. He thrashed his arms, hoping for purchase, and hit air. His pulse roared as two gloved hands pushed his head into the cold pavement, crushing his cheek. A knee in his shoulder shot pain into his neck. As he clawed blindly, each frenzied jerk brought a fresh spasm of agony. He lay like a tied calf while hands ran over him, pulling at his clothes. *Help, oh, God!*

Then vodka breath washed over him. "I love Ammeerika," the voice hissed.

Peter swallowed hard, regretting every wrong turn he'd taken and wishing he'd had the chance to tell Calli how he really felt.

# CHAPTER THREE

CALLI stood at the edge of the market, letting the delicious smells wash over her. The smell of grilling shashlik, Russian shish kebabs, reached out and beckoned to her empty stomach, warring only with the enticing aroma of deep-fried cabbage sandwiches. The market never failed to buoy Calli's spirits—treasures abounded in the long aisles of kiosks. Baseballs were first on her list, then maybe a fresh baked roll and a shashlik.

Calli moved in behind a fast-walking man in a leather coat. She kept her hand on her satchel, pulled in close, and scanned the crowd for the neighborhood gang that worked the market with uncanny efficiency. She knew more than one person who'd had her purse slit open while buying potatoes.

She stopped in front of a kiosk where a large soccer ball hung from a net. Gesturing to it, she asked the woman if she had similar balls, only smaller.

"Get off me!"

The English pricked her ears, as did the panicked tone. She turned, searching.

"Get away!"

Behind the kiosk. Her heart drummed in her throat as she darted through a skinny gap between two metal booths. When she saw Peter, her breath left her. A thug in a ripped green jacket straddled his back. One of the attacker's knees was shoved into Peter's spine, and two hands forced Peter's face into the dirt. Three others rummaged through his pockets.

*"Oohaadee!"* she screamed and ran toward them, swinging her satchel. *"Otstan!"*

They stared at her, eyes wide, and for a split second she wondered what she'd do if they didn't leave. Then they scattered like pigeons, picking up speed as they fled.

She knelt beside Peter. "Are you okay?"

Peter got to his knees, his breath heaving in great gusts. She winced at an ugly scrape on his chin. His clenched jaw betrayed his fury as he watched the thieves escape.

Calli rested a hand on his shoulder and felt his rock-hard muscles pulsing beneath his tweed suit jacket. "Are you hurt?"

His eyes fixed on hers and he blinked, as if just realizing he'd been rescued. "Calli."

She brushed off a layer of pebbles from his reddened cheek. Her hand trembled. He caught it in his and held it to his face. "You saved me again."

The expression on his face tore through her heart. She gulped a breath and looked away.

He cupped her chin in his hand and directed her face back to his. "Thank you."

She bit her lip and yanked her hand from his, feeling

like jelly. Managing a shaky smile, she said, "No problem. I was in the neighborhood. Did they get your wallet?"

He patted his jacket. "Nope, just my pride." His smile shook at the edges.

"Muggings happen every day at the market. Just be careful." Peter didn't need any lectures about security, and the way he was looking at her told her to escape—and fast.

He climbed to his feet and offered Calli a hand. She reluctantly took it. "Now you have to let me buy you lunch. Please. I couldn't live with myself if I didn't."

Oh, why did he have to produce that crooked grin that always melted her heart? *Heavenly Father, this isn't what I had in mind when I said don't let Peter in my life again!* Calli felt a quiver of fear—and hope—shoot through her. She looked away and rubbed her arms, scrambling for a way to turn him down.

Peter picked up a crumpled roll of paper off the ground. He held it out to her and grimaced. "I meant to leave this at your door."

Calli frowned and took the bundle. Her mouth went dry at the damaged white rose. Despite the ripped petals, its fragrance still reached out and embraced her heart. She swallowed the lump in her throat and felt her resolve disintegrate. "You win. Buy me lunch."

She had to admit, the look on his face made her warm down to her toes.

"You look like you're really enjoying that thing."

Calli layered another chunk of meat with a healthy dab of chili sauce. "I love shashlik. I can't come to the market without buying one. Thanks for treating."

"My pleasure, my gallant heroine." Peter liked the way she still blushed at his compliments.

They wandered down the middle of a greening boulevard, the wind tickling the balsam and playing with her curly bob. He had to shove his hands into his pockets to keep from tucking the strands behind her ear. Red was her color. Her ski jacket illuminated all the copper highlights in her hair and made her face glow. She looked genuinely happy, walking along, talking about her camp.

"This is the fourth summer. We had two hundred campers last year, and eighty kids accepted Christ." Her voice could always lighten his step, but now it sounded like a melody, with the southern lilt she'd added since their college years. "Dmitri has a real heart for the kids. I've never seen anyone who can talk straight to them and still know how to be gentle."

"Sounds like a great guy," Peter said slowly.

"Oh, he is. He's really the one in charge. I just play camp nurse, counsel the girls, and teach everyone American games."

"American games?"

"Capture the flag, blindman's bluff, baseball." She wiped her fingers on the napkin and tossed the shashlik skewer into a nearby receptacle. "I'm supposed to be searching for baseballs right now."

She had a bit of chili sauce on the corner of her mouth. Peter chuckled, pulled out his clean handkerchief, and moved close to dab it away. She stopped, watching his movements with wide eyes. As he wiped away the stain, her face paled.

"What's wrong?" He withdrew his hand.

"I-I need to go," she stuttered.

Peter stepped back, wondering what he'd said wrong. "Calli, I'm sorry. I didn't mean to offend you."

She shook her head, eyes on the ground. "No, I just have to get these baseballs, see, and I need to get going. . . ."

Something chilly had definitely breezed into their conversation, and he was scrambling to figure out what it was. "I'll help you," he stammered over the sick taste of panic. "I've got some time before my meeting."

She looked up at him and his heart wrenched. Were those tears glistening in her eyes? He moved toward her.

She stepped away. "Watch yourself around town, okay?" She smiled, blinking quickly. "I can't be everywhere, you know."

He smiled at her attempt at humor, knowing she wanted him to. But he wanted to scream. Calli was running from him again, like a rabbit from a wolf. He could almost smell her fear. It killed him to see it and not know why.

She turned away, and he grabbed her jacket, wincing when she stiffened. He let go but came close. "Calli, let me take you out for dinner tonight."

She shook her head again.

He groaned and rubbed his forehead. "Why?" he blurted. "Why are you afraid of me?"

Her jaw tightened as she spun around to face him. His chest constricted at the pain in her eyes. "I'm not the one who is afraid," she said tightly.

Then she turned on her heel and strode down the boulevard.

෴

Dina's manicured fingernails were clicking on the keyboard when Peter walked in.

Tomas looked up, raised his eyebrows, and took his feet off the desk. "What happened to you?" He got up from his chair and walked over to Peter, scrutinizing his face with a frown.

Peter's hand instinctively touched the throbbing scrape on his chin. "I fell."

Dina stopped typing. "You fell?" She rose, and her perfume led the way as she came close to examine his wound. Her fingers brushed his chin, light as a whisper, and his skin prickled.

He stepped back, nodding. "In the market." He had no desire to rehash his mugging at the hands of children. The last thing he needed was sympathy or an inept police investigation to lengthen his stay in this primitive village.

Tomas shook his head. "You're an accident waiting to happen, pal."

Peter smiled ruefully. "How are you doing on that amendment, Dina?"

"All done." She propped herself on his desk.

"Approved and translated?" Peter scanned his gaze from Tomas to Dina.

Dina held out her hands. "*Nyet* problem."

Everything was "*nyet* problem" with Dina. Why couldn't it be that way with Calli? "Great. Thanks."

Tomas eyed him up and down. "You'd better change into some clean clothes before the meeting."

Peter surveyed his suit and grimaced when he saw the ragged tear in the knee of his pants. "I'll meet you in the hotel lobby in an hour."

Peter found Dina giggling and perched on the arm of Tomas's armchair. Freshly coiffed, she made the lobby look that much more dingy. Next to her, Tomas was equally dapper in his black silk suit. Peter smoothed his tie and buttoned his wool suit coat, thankful he'd packed for Siberia, even though it was warmer than he'd expected.

A quick shower had done wonders for his appearance and self-esteem. He felt ready to charm his way into Georgivka's commerce.

"Remember," Tomas said, bouncing to his feet, "don't offer the Feller Buncher machines unless they start to balk."

Peter held the door open for Dina and Tomas, falling into step behind them. "Tomas, don't forget who butters your bread. I know what I'm doing."

Tomas faltered in his step as Peter stalked past him. Peter felt the man's eyes burning his skull, but Peter brandished a smile as he opened the taxi door, turned, and faced Tomas.

Dina slid into the car, but Tomas halted near Peter, his face taut. "I'm not here to take notes, Peter. There is twenty million dollars' worth of lumber out there, and your father wants to make sure we get it."

If Peter had questioned his father's motives in sending Tomas to Siberia, they became crystal clear as Tomas slipped in beside Dina. The old man didn't trust him.

Peter clenched his jaw and climbed in the passenger seat in front.

◎

Calli ducked into the hotel lobby, hid next to a wilting hibiscus plant, and searched the lobby for Peter. Good, no sign of him. Taking a cleansing breath, she ran for the stairwell and scampered up the three flights to her room. If God were merciful, she'd get her things packed and check out before Peter knew she was gone. Then she would have only the memory of his smile, the touch of his hand over hers to remind herself of her stupidity. For a second she actually thought . . .

She jammed her key into her door and opened it. Slamming it behind her, she leaned against it, scraping up her composure. They'd been laughing, he'd been genuinely interested in the camp . . . and then she had to go and smear food across her face. He'd gallantly wiped it off, but she'd shriveled in embarrassment. Sure, she was thirty pounds lighter than her college days, but she'd never shed her inherent clumsiness, and her wild red hair always made her feel unkempt. No wonder Roland Samuelson had never approved of her.

Calli massaged her temples. She had to leave before Peter turned her heart inside out and she was left gasping. Racing through the room, she threw her clothes into her duffel. Hopefully Dmitri's parents would let her bunk on their sofa for the duration of her stay in Georgivka.

She flicked on the bathroom light, avoided glancing in the mirror, and grabbed her toothbrush. She never wore makeup—it couldn't soften the smattering of freckles on her face anyway. She tossed the toothbrush into the bag, zipped it up, and sank onto the bed.

*I don't know why you brought Peter back into my life, God. But I can't do this again. Please, help him understand.* A verse in Proverbs flickered through her mind: *"Trust in the Lord with all your heart; do not depend on your own understanding."* Well, she didn't pretend to know the mind of the Almighty and she did trust God with her life. She just knew she wasn't ready to have Peter Samuelson walk back into her heart. Ever.

The next verse nagged her, however, as she threw the satchel over her shoulder, left the room, and locked the door. *"Seek his will in all you do, and he will direct your paths."* She winced. She hadn't really asked God what he wanted her to do about Peter, hadn't wanted to consider that perhaps God had meant for them to meet again.

Peter's words from the night before echoed through her memory: *"Don't you think it's a little odd that we'd meet again in the same town in the same hotel in the middle of Siberia?"*

The thought stopped her cold. Standing with one hand on the stair rail, she closed her eyes. *Okay, I admit, it's odd.* She blew out a shaky breath. *It could even be you, Lord, I suppose.*

Slowly, she descended the stairs. *Is it you?* She turned over the thought, and as she did, a spine-tingling peace swept through her. Her knees turned weak. *Okay, it feels like you. But I don't want my heart to tell me something you're not.* Standing on the bottom step, she stared into the lobby. *So, if you don't want me to check out of this hotel and Peter Samuelson's life forever, please show me.*

On rubber legs, she walked to the checkout desk. Her duffel burned into her shoulder; her hands shook. She cast a glance over her shoulder. No Peter.

"Can I help you?" a slender young clerk in a brown uniform asked in Russian.

"I'd like to check out." Calli's tentative reply, in Russian, quivered. She swallowed the lump in her throat and repeated herself, setting her room key on the counter.

The clerk picked up the key and searched her desk for Calli's registration. After calculating the bill, she handed it to Calli. As she paid the young woman in large bills, Calli's heart felt oddly deflated.

The woman counted the rubles, then shook her head. "I don't have change."

Calli arched her brows. "What?"

"You'll have to wait while I go to the bank and get change."

Calli cringed, wondering if she should surrender the four hundred rubles in change. She decided against it and nodded.

"Please, have a seat," the clerk suggested.

That was the last thing Calli wanted to do. Setting her bag on a chair, she rubbed her arms and rocked from side to side. The setting sun had turned the dingy lobby to a gloomy gray. A ripped orange vinyl sofa and two scuffed end tables spoke of happier days and added to her mood.

She sneaked a peek at the desk. Empty. Glancing at the gift shop, she hauled up her duffel bag and strolled inside. She bought a Snickers bar and a pack of Wrigley's, her eyes returning to the front desk. To her dismay, the clerk still wasn't back. Biting her lip, she perused a shelf of Matryoshka dolls.

"Where are you going?"

Calli groaned and raised her eyes heavenward.

"You look packed." His voice fell. "You going somewhere?"

Slowly she turned and met Peter's pensive gaze. They stared at one another, and an array of emotions swept through his eyes.

She licked her lips and dredged up a brave smile. "Not anymore."

Peter grinned like a rogue schoolboy as he tied his tie. God must have decided to smile on him . . . the contract was all but signed, and Calli had agreed to have dinner with him.

He not only looked like a schoolboy, he felt like one. He was running full speed ahead, without a care where tomorrow would lead. All he knew was that God had finally seen his heart, had seen him trying to make amends, and had decided to reward him. Eight years ago he'd made the mistake of letting Calli go. He wasn't going to let it happen again. Even if he had to drag her back to

America. She may have toughed it out here for four years and done a great job, but the backwoods of Siberia was no place for Callidora Deane. She belonged beside him. Now he knew why he had to see her. She filled up his heart like a refreshing spring wind. With her, he felt peace.

Peter braced his hands on the sink and hung his head. *Lord, I know I haven't been on your good side for a while, but I want to thank you for bringing Calli back to me.* He paused and a flint of acid rose in his stomach, tasting like regret. *I know I blew it with her, Lord. Help me win her heart again.* He knew it was a selfish prayer, but he couldn't stop himself. Seeing her had clawed open all the old wounds, and there was only one cure.

Grabbing his suit coat, he nearly skipped down the hall. He skidded to a stop at Dina's door and knocked.

*"Shto?"* Dina asked as she cracked it open. She gave him a syrupy, red-lipped smile.

"Did you talk to the chef?"

"*Nyet* problem. You're all set." She stepped out of the room, reached up, and straightened his tie. "Don't stay out too late."

"Thanks, Dina." Maybe the lady did have some good points . . . like helping him not appear a total fool in front of Calli. He wanted to be able to take his date to dinner without sounding like a kindergartner.

Calli stood in the lobby rubbing her arms, and Peter took in her every movement as he stole up behind her. When she absently tugged a lock and began twirling it, memory nearly took his breath away. She'd changed significantly over the years, and time had been generous. Before, he'd loved her for her sweet spirit, her wise words, her purity of character. Now he also loved her for her simple beauty, the way her hair fell in ringlets around her face, the curve of her jaw, that delicious smattering of freckles across her nose. He wondered if her feelings for him had changed also. He certainly hadn't given her any precious nuggets of memory to cherish.

Swallowing hard, he fisted his hands in his pockets. "Calli?"

She turned, smiling, and he thought his knees would buckle. "Good evening."

She was heart-stopping in a simple black sweater over an azure dress that made her blue eyes glow. He scrambled for composure and helped her into her red parka. When she took his offered elbow, ripples streaked up his spine.

"Where are you taking me?" she asked. "I know this town like the back of my hand, and there are no restaurants within a hundred kilometers."

Somehow he dredged up his voice. "Trust me." He cupped her hand on his arm and steered her out the front door, down the sidewalk, and around the hotel to a cracked, dried patio.

"Here?" Calli asked.

Peter stayed silent, led her across the patio and down another flight of stairs, which ended at an overgrown trail that had been freshly cut. Holding her elbow, he guided her over the trail until it opened onto another patio . . . and a panoramic view of the Amur River. A robin sang over the hum of the river, and the wind gently nuzzled the trees.

"Your table, milady," he said, sweeping his arm toward a plastic table, cleverly concealed by a bright blue tablecloth. Dina had done well. The table, complete with china and two crystal glasses, was set like one in a five-star restaurant. Calli's delighted gasp filled his heart.

"How did you do this?" Her eyes shone approval when she turned to look at him.

He shrugged. "I've made a few friends while I've been here."

She arched her brows but said nothing. He pulled out her chair and she sat down.

Sitting across from her, he took her outstretched hand. "Calli, I haven't been able to get you out of my mind. I've missed you so much, and I can't help but believe God brought you back to me."

Her chin trembled, and she quickly tightened her jaw. Her eyes fixed on his. "What have you missed about me?"

"Everything. Your laughter. Your genuineness. Your faith. My heart is full when I'm with you."

She shook her head. Her expression clouded. "It's not me, Peter. I'm just a reminder of what you're really missing." She pulled her hand away.

Peter exhaled a frustrated breath and reached for the bottle of Sprite he'd unearthed in the gift shop. He filled her glass, then his. Running his finger down the side of the glass, he watched her. She stared at the river, her eyes dry, her face chiseled with an unfamiliar, determined look that unsettled him. Calli had indeed blossomed into a beauty, but there was something inherently striking about her he hadn't noticed before. Something that made him feel scruffy next to her. The question that had haunted him all afternoon burst from his chest, "What am I afraid of?"

Her gaze snapped back to his; etched in her eyes was an unmistakable pity. "You're afraid of being the man God wants you to be."

Peter flinched. A quick gulp of Sprite soothed his suddenly parched throat. "I'm trying to be that man, Calli."

Her expression softened, and when she touched his hand, the warmth coursed up his arm. "I'm sure you are. But you're missing so much."

He gaped at her. "What, this? Life in the backwoods? I can do so much more for God by being a successful businessman." He folded his hands on the table. "I support missions and our local church well above the average member. I even support a missionary in Mongolia!"

"That's great. But I'm not talking about what you can do for God. I'm talking about what God wants to do for you." Her eyes stared hard into his.

He met them. "Come home with me. Marry me."

Calli paled. She blinked, swallowed, and her eyes filled. "My future is here, Peter, for as long as God wants. This is where I belong."

He shook his head. "You belong with me. Our meeting here proves it."

"No, it just proves that God isn't finished with you yet. He's giving you another chance to keep the pledge you made to him eight years ago." Calli stood up, the color quickly returning to her face. "You denied it then and you're denying it now. That's why you think you need me . . . to find peace." Her misty blue eyes turned dark sapphire. "But you'll never find peace until you obey God."

Panic tensed Peter's voice. "Please sit down." His evening was unraveling. He held out his hands, as if pleading. "Dinner is just about to be served."

As if on cue, the crabby waitress from the café made her entrance, carrying two plates of food. Ribbons of steam curled into the air from the pork chops and fried potatoes he'd ordered for them. Calli glanced at the meal and closed her eyes. Time drew out as he watched her wrestle, with what he had no idea. *Please, God, make her stay.*

Calli sat down. The waitress clunked the plates down in front of them, sent Peter a glower, and headed back up the steps.

"I hope it's not poisoned," Calli said, watching the waitress leave. Then she turned and smiled.

Relief poured out of him. "Thanks."

God wasn't done with him. As Calli watched Peter fiddle with his cup of coffee and stare at the sunset, she knew that was why they had met. There would be no tomorrows for her and Peter. God simply wanted to remind him that he wanted Peter's heart—the one he'd pledged to the Lord at a missions conference years ago. The one that said he'd serve God wherever God led. Maybe it was with Samuelson Timber & Steel, but Calli couldn't dodge the uncanny feeling that there was more waiting for Peter Samuelson. Unfortunately, it had nothing to do with her.

"You didn't eat your chops," Peter said, squinting at her.

Calli twisted her napkin on her lap. "The fries were great. I just wasn't very hungry."

Peter hummed in reply. He blew on his coffee. "I love sunsets."

"I know."

Peter turned, his eyes roaming over her face. Calli's stomach flipped, and she stared at her hands knitted together in her lap. It simply wasn't fair that he could unravel her with a look. She bit her quivering lip.

He was suddenly standing next to her, holding out his hand. "Walk with me?"

Calli slid her hand into his, not relishing the confusion that made her want to snuggle into his side and at the same time run away at the speed of sound. But as his touch seeped through her, she was overwhelmed with the moment and clung to it, opting to enjoy it, even if it would perish with the setting of the sun.

They walked down the steps, onto the beach. A strip of orange sizzled along the far horizon, and the sun lit a fiery path across the inky river. The wind lifted the hair from her neck and played with Peter's short brown locks. She quelled the sudden desire to run her fingers through his hair, to see if it was as soft and silky as she remembered. She cleared her throat and focused on the wreckage of a fishing boat rotting in the distance.

Peter's hand embraced hers, and she couldn't stop the heady rush of nostalgia. How many times had they walked across campus, hand in hand? She always felt so safe beside him. Always felt like he respected her, needed her, that there was no other woman for him . . . until . . .

"Peter, why did you walk away from us?"

Even in the dim light, she could see the pain on his face. "My father. I wasn't lying in the elevator, Cal. My father needs me. I'm his only son, and he has expectations for me. I knew I couldn't leave him to run STS by himself."

Baloney. She stiffened, unable to believe her ears. "But he knew you didn't want to be a part of the business. You told him when you became a Christian that you were going to spend your life serving God as a missionary."

"No, I didn't."

Calli stopped cold. She tugged on her hand, and he let it drop.

He turned away from her, staring out past the river. "I couldn't."

Calli looked at her empty hands. Tears pricked her eyes. God wanted so much more for this man if he would only have the courage to say yes. Even if God did want him at the helm of STS, at least Peter could do it with a heart fully dedicated to God instead of trying to appease him with tithes and offerings. God wanted Peter's obedience. His whole heart. She tasted salt on her trembling lips.

"Are those tears for me?"

She hadn't heard him turn, but suddenly his warm hand cupped her chin, gently raising her eyes to his. She tried to fight it, knowing she could drown and be lost forever in his warm gaze. But he searched for her eyes and found them. "I don't want to lose you again. I need you more than air."

Calli's mouth parted in amazement. Peter's eyes caressed her face; then he lowered his lips to hers. She closed her eyes, losing herself in the never forgotten wonder of his gentle kiss. His thumb traced her jaw, sending ripples to her toes. "I've missed you so much," he murmured against her lips.

Before she could reply, he groaned loudly and stepped away, clutching his stomach.

"Peter, are you okay?"

He moaned again and fell to his knees on the shore. His face contorted, and pain streaked through his eyes.

"What's wrong?"

He braced a hand on the ground as he hauled in shallow, pained breaths. "If I didn't know better, I'd think someone was trying to get rid of me."

# CHAPTER FOUR

"CAN I get you anything?" Calli grimaced as Peter's face paled and his eyes glazed in pain. "I think we need to call a doctor." Worry strummed in her voice.

Peter shook his head. "I think it's something I ate." Easing himself onto his bed, he gingerly settled back on the pillows. He cringed when he looked her direction. "Some date, huh?"

Calli managed a wry smile. "It wasn't all bad." The memory of his hand on her face, the taste of his kiss. "There were some good parts."

Their eyes locked, and she went weak at the hunger in his gaze. "I meant what I said. I need you, Calli." His face screwed up on the last word.

Calli sat on a nearby chair. "What you need is a doctor."

"You're trying to kill me, aren't you?" Peter reached up and caught one of her curls, twirling it around his finger. Calli's heartbeat quickened at the intimate gesture. She shook her head.

"I'll be fine." His voice broke on the last word, and his eyes grew wide. "But I think maybe I should just call you in the morning."

"If you're still alive." Calli ran her fingers along his face. He leaned into her caress.

"If I don't knock on your door by nine, stop by and pick up my dead body."

Calli whacked him on the shoulder. He made an exaggerated cry. "You *are* trying to kill me!"

"Just get better; then we'll talk about the future."

His jaw dropped. "You mean it?"

Calli bit her lip, not even sure what she meant. "Tomorrow, okay?"

He cupped his hand around the back of her neck, drawing her close. "Tomorrow," he whispered, before kissing her.

She started sinking into his arms but caught herself before she tumbled completely from her senses. Palming his chest, she pushed away. "See you in the morning, tough guy."

He was groaning when she shut the door. No amount of reassurances could keep worry from wrapping its tentacles around her heart and squeezing. Poor Peter. Russia was not his country.

She paced her room for fifteen minutes, her fingernails digging into her palms, before dropping to her knees. *Please, God, heal Peter.*

She buried her head in her hands, not daring to ask for more. *"I need you more than air."* She shook Peter's voice from her head. *No, Peter, you think you do, but I'm just a substitute for the One who can give you real peace.* Still, Peter had been convincing.

A tremor shot through her. Could there be a place for her in Peter's life? she wondered. Refined, cultured Peter, who turned heads in his wake, who could reduce a woman to mush with his honeyed eyes and sultry baritone. She certainly didn't fit her image of Peter's wife. He needed someone who could accentuate his polished life, not a backwoods missionary who was better at tromping through the woods than steering a course through a social gathering. She didn't even own a dress coat. When he'd helped her into her neon red parka, she'd just about died. She felt like a ragamuffin next to him in his sleek tweed sport jacket. *Help me to focus, oh, God. Please help me know what you want me to do.*

As she crawled into bed, a flame of hope flickered in her heart. *"I need you more than air."* She went to sleep spelling Peter's name on her pillow and feeling like a giddy teenager.

The sunrise trumpeted into her room in the form of a rosy glow as Calli stepped out of the bathroom. Her hair hanging in wet ringlets, she flopped down on the bed and propped open her Bible. *What do you have for me today, Lord?*

She read 1 Samuel 16:7: "The Lord said to Samuel, 'Don't judge by his appearance or height, for I have rejected him. The Lord doesn't make decisions the way you do! People judge by outward appearance, but the Lord looks at a person's thoughts and intentions.' "

Calli buried her head in her arms and trembled before an awesome God who knew her heart. *Please make me the woman you want me to be, God. I know I'm not much on the outside, but I hope to be yours on the inside.* Tears edged her eyes. It hurt to admit it, even to her loving God. But he promised to know her and love her, and she clung to that. *Thank you for this day. Please guide and direct me.*

The hallway was quiet when Calli opened her door. Padding down the hall, a smile crested her face. She hoped Peter was feeling better. She couldn't wait to see him, offer him the same hope that ignited her heart. Maybe God did have a future for them. She had a year's furlough scheduled in three months—a year for Peter to step back onto God's path. Certainly, when he said he needed her, he meant he would serve with her, wherever God wanted them. It meant he was finally saying yes to God's call on his life. Joy buoyed her steps. Nearly skipping by the time she reached Peter's door on the fifth floor, she knocked, biting back a grin.

Movement inside had her wrapping her arms around herself, holding back the bubble of delight that threatened to possess her and fling her into Peter's arms the minute he opened the door.

*"Da?"* The door opened, and a trim beauty with piercing dark eyes and waist-long ebony hair, looking way too elegant in a man's wrinkled shirt and tight leggings, stood in the open doorway.

The air left Calli. Licking her lips, she wrestled out her voice. "I'm looking for Peter Samuelson?"

The beauty frowned, and for a split second Calli thought she'd knocked on the wrong room on the wrong floor. Then the woman opened the door wider. Peter was sprawled in the middle of the bed, the bedclothes across his bare chest, his eyes closed.

Calli hung on to the doorframe with a white hand. Her gaze ranged from Peter to the brunette, who stared back with a curious tilt to her mouth. Her eyes blinked innocently. "He's still asleep. Can I tell him who stopped by?"

Calli's mouth opened, but no words emerged. Her

stare settled on Peter, and with each passing second, her heart splintered further. Peter's clothes were hung neatly over a chair. He certainly didn't look ill! Somehow she shook her head and moved away. The brunette slowly closed the door.

Calli braced a hand on the wall, closed her eyes, and felt her heart shatter.

⑨

Perfume filtered into his nose, thick and sweet, and Peter knew Dina was in the room before he opened his eyes. Still, shock paralyzed him as he stared at his translator. Her hair was loose and her dark eyes ran over him, a closed smile decorating her face.

*"Dobra Ootra,* Peter. Feeling better?"

A chill prickled Peter's bare chest. He pulled the blanket up to his chin and scanned the room. "Is Tomas here?"

Dina frowned and shook her head.

"What are you doing here?"

She smiled, reached over, and rubbed his cheek. He stiffened and pulled away. She pouted slightly. "You were sick. I came to help."

Peter squinted at her. "How did you know I was sick?"

Her wide eyes betrayed confusion. "I stopped by to ask about your date. Don't you remember? Your door was open, and I got worried."

He shook his head, sorting through his memories. After Calli left, he'd taken a shower, drunk an Alka-Seltzer, and climbed back into bed. He had no recollection of Dina entering his room. "Have you been here all night?"

"You sleep very soundly." Her eyes darted to the other pillow. "That's too bad."

He followed her gaze and groaned at the mussed pillow and sheets. His heart turned to lead as he thought about the rickety door. It must not have latched when Calli closed it last night, another casualty of bunking in a century-old hotel. Regardless of Dina's concern, real or otherwise, the last thing he needed was false accusations mucking up his relationship with Tomas or casting shadows on STS's reputation. "Dina, you need to leave—right now."

She looked hurt. "If you're worried about your girlfriend, she already knows."

Peter winced as if he'd been slugged in the gut. "What?"

Dina rose and pulled her hair back into a ponytail. "She stopped by. Didn't leave a message." Malice—or was it envy?—flickered in Dina's dark eyes.

Peter bristled, his breath burning in his chest. "Please tell me you're lying." Just when he'd started to convince Calli he still loved her . . . he pushed himself to a sitting position. The blanket fell to his waist. "Leave. Now."

Dina slammed the door behind her.

Peter climbed out of bed. His stomach flopped, empty and weak from the night before. Hobbling over to his suitcase, he unearthed a pair of jeans and a sweatshirt, threw them on, then ran out of his room barefoot, a hand pressed against his throbbing stomach. *Please, Calli, still be there.*

He pounded on her door five minutes before he braved the elevator to the first floor. At the front desk, the clerk shrugged her petite shoulders. Peter laid his forehead on the cool wood of the desk.

Calli had checked out of the hotel—and his life.

Calli walked stiffly to Dmitri's parents' apartment, her duffel bag cutting into her shoulder, tears chapping her cheeks. Fool! To believe Peter's plea. To think he could look past her unrefined exterior to the lady within. Roland Samuelson had won. Her chin up, she flicked another rebellious tear from her cheek and climbed the stairs to the apartment. She would simply bury the horrid experience, relegate it to the Peter Samuelson file of memories, never to be opened again.

When she knocked, Dmitri opened the door, took one look at her, and pulled her into an embrace.

౷

The sunshine filtered through the birch and pine forest like the rays of heaven, dappling the ground with fragments of light as if the loam were sprayed with particles of glass. Calli marked off thirty more steps, then tied a red plastic ribbon around a towering ghost white birch tree.

*"Gatov!"* she hollered in Russian to Dmitri, who waited at their last orienteering point.

He bushwhacked toward her. "You sure no one will get lost this year?" He screwed up his face in mock terror.

Calli swatted him with her topographical map. "A little fear is good for a kid."

"But not for the camp director," he retorted.

"These markers will help. They'll keep the kids pointed in a straight line as long as they look for the ribbons."

Dmitri flashed her a dubious look before aligning his compass and setting out for a distant pine.

As they tracked toward the camp from a logging road, Calli couldn't help but remember Peter's assertion that responsible logging would make Russia's forests safer.

Two years ago, a forest fire on the opposite side of the river had drenched the air in soot and smoke for a month. September rains had doused it, but not before the blaze incinerated five remote villages and left nearly a thousand people homeless. Still, Calli had been to the end of the logging road and seen what clear cutting did to the pristine woodland. Giant acres mowed out of a lush pine forest. Her stomach churned at the thought. She could perhaps justify the attack on the wilderness if the locals were benefiting from the industry. She saw, however, the people who manned the trucks and lived in the camp at the end of the road. Peter's promise to use Russians was probably as reliable as his breathless lies about his love for her.

Irritation strummed her nerves, thinking of the two-timing weasel. She hadn't seen him for eight years, and suddenly a chance encounter had him possessing her every thought rampaging through her mind. Why had she let him kiss her? Calli stumbled over a hidden root, bit her tongue, and grimaced.

A woodpecker drilled a nearby poplar, and the fresh spring air drenched the forest in a heady floral perfume. The soft thump of her hiking boots ministered to her sagging spirit. *This is where I belong, Lord. Not in a silk dress, eating caviar at a corporate function.* The thought wrinkled her nose. No, God had a different woman for Peter.

*"Gatov!"* Dmitri yelled, and Calli set out in the direction of his voice, amazed at how off route she had drifted. She focused on her partner and found him sitting on a downed, mossy log, eating a piece of sausage. "Want some?"

Calli accepted a piece and sat next to him.

"No baseballs?" Dmitri had refrained from commenting on her sudden appearance on his doorstep two days prior. Even now he seemed to be going out of his way to keep her thoughts from touching on the heart-wrenching chance encounter from her past.

"Not a one in all of Georgivka," Calli answered. "We'll have to use soccer balls and play kickball."

"Still a fun game."

Calli twirled the piece of sausage between her fingers. "It's not the all-American pastime, but it will have to do for this year. I'll pick up some baseball equipment for next summer while I'm home on furlough."

"You're coming back?"

Calli glanced at her friend, and the expression in his eyes made her heart stumble. "Absolutely."

His soft brown eyes roamed over her face, then steadied on her eyes. "Come back as my wife."

She nearly choked. His gaze was soft and probing, and the love in it made her eyes smart. She licked her dry lips but couldn't tear her eyes away from his. Her hands grew slick. Her voice abandoned her.

"Please?"

The wind had tangled his chestnut hair, and beneath his green flannel shirt and muscled chest beat a shepherd's heart. He'd make any woman a fine husband.

"Can I think about it?" she whispered.

He nodded before ducking his head. She noticed a blush stream up his face. Pitching the sausage into the weeds, she pushed to her feet. Her legs barely held her.

Dmitri mimicked her movements. "Let's go home. Your turn to lead."

Numbly, Calli set a course and headed toward camp.

"Tell me again why this budget doesn't seem to balance." Peter blew out a breath and dropped the report onto his desk with a slap. "How can we budget less for labor than the going Russian wage?"

Tomas looked up from his computer. "You must have

calculated wrong. Those numbers are accurate." He rolled his eyes at Dina, who smirked.

Peter gritted his teeth. "I know how to add, Tomas."

Tomas's eyes flashed. "What you don't know how to do is focus on your work. I'm the accountant; you're the legal eagle. You make sure we have all our i's dotted, our t's crossed, and I'll make sure we make money."

Peter pinched his lips. "I'm taking the contract to my room. To read over. Again." He scooped up the file.

"It won't do any good. You checked out of this deal the minute your girlfriend left town." Tomas's voice carried a sharp edge.

Peter whirled. "And whose fault is that?" He shot daggers at Dina, whose smirk faded. She stared blankly back, tapping her pen on a pad of paper.

Peter closed his eyes and cupped the back of his neck. "It's been a long week." He sighed, calming his racing heart. "I'm going to see if I can make heads or tails of this budget."

"It's correct. STS is going to make a bundle, and your father is going to make you president."

The words pinged in Peter's hollow heart. "Great."

His hotel room had been cleaned, the bed linen changed, the floor swept. Peter set a carton of lukewarm apple juice on the round table and sank into a fraying armchair. Tomas was right. His focus had blurred the minute Calli exited his life. The budget was probably correct. He tossed the file onto the table. STS would make a fortune, Roland would promote him, and Peter would return to Minneapolis with a wad of cash in his pocket.

He hung his head in his hands. Success never hurt before. Seeing Calli only made his emptiness ache like an ulcer. He dug his hands into his scalp, unsuccessfully fighting back a swelling headache. It brought with it the memories. . . .

*Where was his father? The auditorium was filling. Peter held his graduation cap in his hands as he watched his mother work her way through the crowd. The gold valedictorian tassels swayed as he flipped the seat down for her. She patted him on the cheek with manicured fingers. "He'll be here."*

*Peter had to walk by Calli on his way to his seat among the other graduates. Samuelsons after Deanes, alphabetical, heedless of prestige or wealth. Her eyes no longer followed him, but he watched to make sure. Peter sat tall through the speeches, eyes glued on the empty seat beside his mother until he noticed Roland walk in, commanding and austere in a black three-piece suit. Overdressed as usual. His dark eyes found Peter, without a smile. Peter looked away but edged up his chin.*

*They called Calli before him, of course. The spring in her step had died, but her smile could still light up a stadium. His heart stopped when her blue eyes settled on him, then swept past. He swallowed a lump and watched her return to her seat. When he received his diploma, he glanced at his mother and waved it.*

*He had no taste for the cake, the punch, the nuts. His father clumped near the president and others on the board. Peter watched Calli laugh, regretting every moment of the last three months.*

*"Congratulations, Son." Roland swaggered up and clapped him on the shoulder. Peter forced a smile. Roland's faded as he followed Peter's gaze. "Isn't that the girl you were dating?"*

*Peter's fists whitened and he nodded slowly.*

*"What is she going to do?"*

*Starkly, "She's going into missions."*

*Roland watched her an eternal minute. Peter gathered his courage, swallowed twice, and tried to find a voice to accompany his thoughts.*

*"She looks the part."*

*Peter winced. "How's that?"*

*"Missionaries are those who can't make it in the real world." Roland squeezed his son's shoulder, sending arrows of pain down Peter's arm. "Look at her. She's . . . well, not your type. You did a good thing dropping her, Son. She has nothing to offer you."*

Peter's throat burned now, hearing his father's words anew, feeling their bite and the accompanying death of promises with them. He clenched his jaw. *Maybe you aren't done with me yet, God. I hope not. Please forgive me. I was wrong to think I could please you with tithes and offerings when I really owed you my life. Calli was right, Lord. I've missed you. I want to be the man you want me to be.* He reined in his emotions and took a cleansing breath.

If God wasn't done with him yet, then perhaps God wasn't done with Calli yet either.

And neither was he.

# CHAPTER FIVE

A SLATE gray sky spit rain on Calli's parka as she dashed for the lodge. Standing on the covered porch, Dmitri rang the dinner bell, then opened the door for her to scuttle inside. "So much for capture the flag," he commented wryly.

Calli scowled and pulled off her parka. Rain ran in rivulets down her face. "I guess I'll have to pull a trick out of my magic hat." She sent him a sly grin and he groaned. Last time it rained, she had the campers create a concoction for Dmitri to drink. He'd ended up downing a milk shake with cottage cheese, green peppers, Tabasco sauce, honey, and sour milk.

"I'm not thirsty," he said in warning.

Three campers ran past, knocking him in the knees. He stumbled and braced a wide hand on the door.

"Slow down!" Calli called as three more scurried in.

Thirty campers lined up to three long tables, their adolescent faces eyeing the mashed potatoes and gravy like beggars. Well, Calli thought, some of them were beggars. Part of their camping program was about gathering all the kids in the region and filling them with healthy food for two weeks. It was probably the best eating they had all year.

Calli led them in a song of prayer; then an eerie silence swooped down as the campers sat and shoveled in their dinner. Calli pinched back tears as she watched a scrubby girl of ten with dull stringy hair and wide eyes pile three rolls on her plate.

The rain pinged on the metal roof. Calli picked apart her roll while digging through her mental files for an inside activity. The David and Goliath story would go over well, with Dmitri acting it out. She supposed she'd have to be Goliath. A box of goodies from her home church—balloons and a case of shaving cream—tucked in the supply shack might offer some hints. The night had promise if she could find a willing victim.

Headlights streamed past the lodge windows, luring the diners from their seats. Calli stood, commanded everyone to sit, and strode toward the door. Probably a confused logger who'd headed up the wrong road.

She stepped out of the lodge and folded her arms across her chest, watching a pickup truck turn around in the muddy drive. Just before it pulled out, she heard a door slam. Then, spitting up mud, the pickup drove away.

A man in a gray wool coat, turned-up collar, and grime up to his knees stared at her. She couldn't mistake the build or the honeyed eyes. Calli's mouth opened as Peter sprinted through the mud and up the lodge steps. He stopped and the expression on his face said more than she could believe. "I found you."

All thoughts left save one. Calli balled her fist and fired.

Peter dodged her blow and caught her hand. Horrified surprise instantly replaced the anger on her face. "Oh!" She brought her other hand to her mouth.

He wished she'd connected. A blow to his gut would have been easier to cope with than the pain in her eyes. He watched miserably as she yanked her hand away, whirled, and stalked toward the lodge door.

"Calli!" He grabbed her arm. She stiffened and didn't turn.

"Let me explain. There was something wrong with my door. It was open, and Dina saw it and came in to check on me. Please, believe me. Nothing happened between us."

"She's perfect for you."

"What?" He turned her, but she kept her eyes down. "What are you talking about?"

"She's pretty and elegant and just your type."

Peter frowned. Calli was his type. Someone whose beauty emanated from the inside out. "She's not you."

"Exactly my point."

He winced. "I don't want her." He heard her sharp intake of breath and continued. "You're the one I can't stop thinking about."

Her tone wrenched his heart. "My life is a world away from yours, Peter. I don't belong. I'd just be in the way."

Surrender entered his voice. "You're right; you already are."

Her eyes blazed when she met his probing gaze. "Well, let me make a fast exit. Go away. I should have listened to my instincts when I said it the first time. I'm not going to make the same mistake again."

His feet moved of their own accord, and he closed the gap between them. He cupped her face in his hands, and by the widening of her eyes, he guessed she was too stunned to move away. He counted his blessings and searched her face. Her eyes blinked back a flood of raw emotions; his heart jumped when he read in them what he wanted. What he'd hitchhiked through the rain for twelve hours to find out.

"It's not a mistake," he whispered as he lowered his lips to hers. She trembled beneath his touch, and he felt her fear.

"I love you, Calli," he murmured against her hesitance.

She stiffened, then suddenly mouthed his name and surrendered. Her kiss tasted of forgiveness, acceptance, trust; the enormity of her love rendered him weak. When he drew away, he held on to her, burying his face in her hair until he gathered his control.

"How did you find me?" Her voice shook.

He kept his hands on her shoulders and studied her sweet freckled face; he longed to kiss each freckle and be lost forever in her blue eyes, now shimmering with unshed emotion. Thickly, he replied, "Divine Providence."

Her melodic laughter scattered any doubts. Calli was his.

She eyed him with a sly glint. "Divine Providence is right."

Calli didn't know who looked more uncomfortable—Dmitri, arms akimbo, standing against the wall or Peter sitting in the middle of the room, a sheet draped over his shoulders.

Dmitri's face had betrayed his skepticism when she'd introduced Peter to her friend. Loyal to the bone, Dmitri all but glared at Peter when he shook his hand, and a chill had rattled up Calli's spine. These two men who loved her were worlds apart, and she was suddenly profoundly thankful they couldn't communicate beyond gestures. But perhaps the white-fisted handshake said enough. They'd retreated into their separate corners, and Calli had been trying to shrug off guilt all evening. While Peter's appearance swept her off her feet, she couldn't deny how out of place he looked—his pressed, albeit grimy khaki pants, a white oxford shirt under his tweed suit coat. He didn't belong here.

"Calli, did I mention how sorry I was?" Peter's voice lifted above the giggling campers, and she hid a smile at the urgency in his tone.

"Repentance has its price," she sang as she sauntered up to him. She pulled the sheet around his neck and fastened it with a clothespin. "Don't worry; we'll be gentle."

His eyes widened, and she patted him on the cheek, unable to contain her mirth. He smiled, cockeyed, and his eyes twinkled. "Promise?"

She shrugged. His smile dipped.

Turning, she held her hands above her head. The campers quieted. "Form ranks."

They gathered into five lines.

"Everyone armed?"

The captains of each team held up their cans of shaving cream.

"Okay, each team gets to decorate a part of Peter's head. Add a beard, mustache, hat, whatever. We'll judge you on creativity. Team one—go!"

Five giggling campers clustered around Peter. Calli met his eyes briefly and enjoyed the fear in them. She waved. "Keep your mouth closed, Peter."

"Revenge is so sweet," Dmitri said over her shoulder.

She nodded, then noticed he wasn't smiling.

"What does this mean for us, Calli?"

Calli curled her arms around her waist and watched Peter. He had his eyes closed, which was wise because team two had decided to give him bushy eyebrows. Poor Peter. If only he knew how unkempt he looked with shaving cream piled on his head like a dunce cap.

The rain had stopped, driven away by a nasty Siberian wind. The trees hissed outside the lodge, but inside a warm fire and waves of children's laughter drove the chill from the room. Still, Calli shivered. What *did* Peter's appearance mean? Did she hold on to his words or cast them into the realm of his other broken promises? She slanted a look at Dmitri, whose gaze roamed over her face. "I don't know," she answered honestly.

Team three stepped up to Peter and added a gnome's beard. Peter dared to open his eyes and cast a look at Calli. His brown eyes twinkled and sent warmth shooting to her toes.

Team four added ear tufts, filling poor Peter's ears with foam until his eyes widened. Calli cupped a hand over her mouth to throttle her laughter. He was taking his punishment like a trooper, and behind his smirk and sparkling eyes, she glimpsed a remnant of the Peter she once knew breaking to the surface.

The old Peter roared to life when the last team, a group of five bedraggled girls, stepped up to add nose hair. With a howl that shook the room, Peter pounced to his feet, grabbed the can of shaving cream, and attacked. Double-fisting the can, he sprayed the girls in rapid fire, then turned and lathered two burly youths who had rushed in for a rescue.

Bedlam broke loose, and suddenly it was every camper for himself. Three boys jumped on Peter, wrestling the can from his hands, while others began dousing their teammates with white foam. Calli stood paralyzed, mouth agape, until Peter rose from a mound of giggling campers, a can of shaving cream in each hand. His gaze found her, and her heart stopped at the focused look in his eye.

Thirty heads swiveled in her direction.

Calli jumped a bench, heading for the door, but a gaggle of ten-year-olds blocked the way. Mischief glinted in their eyes. Calli stuck out her tongue at them, whirled, and climbed on a table. The kids clumped around her, pulling at her jean cuffs. Her eyes glued on Peter as he shook off like a wet dog, shaving cream flying from his hair, ears, chin, and jacket. Then, looking like Santa with a bad shave, he stalked toward her. The delight in his eyes turned her weak. She swallowed hard, dashing her gaze around for an escape.

He leaped onto the table. "Divine Providence, huh?"

Calli held out her hands and shrugged, biting back a nervous giggle.

Peter approached, a rapscallion smile garnishing his face. He was so positively outside his sleek element, so roguish and unrefined . . . her heart swelled with joy.

"What are you going to do to me?" she asked, her chin jutted, but fighting a grin.

The kids began to beat on the table, chanting, "Cal-li, Cal-li."

She held her breath as Peter reached out and drew her to his cream-layered chest. His arms went around her. Her heart shuddered to a halt.

Icy shaving cream streaked down her back.

"You do this all summer long?" Peter traced his steps carefully. His loafers were no match for the muddy trails. Beside him, Calli illuminated their path with a tiny flashlight. Heavy drops from the soggy trees thudded in the black underbrush on each side of the skinny beam. The moist air crept inside his soggy coat. He tucked his hands in his pockets, feeling like a misfit. Calli, prepared as usual, marched along in sturdy hiking boots and her warm parka.

"Yep," she answered. "From June until August, two weeks each camp." She suddenly stopped and opened the squeaky door to a small log cabin. She called out in Russian, and he heard a chorus of girls' voices in reply.

"You amaze me," he said. "How did you learn Russian?"

He couldn't see her face, but her smell, a soft mixture of jasmine and lilac, drifted his way. He breathed deeply and let it engulf him.

"Lots of studying and mistakes." Her steps were sure, and her hiking boots gripped the ground as they continued walking. "You could do it too if you set your mind to it."

"I don't know, Cal. You have to have a significant amount of guts to learn another language. There's always the risk of sounding like a fool."

"Absolutely. But we're supposed to be fools for God."

They walked out into the yard in front of the lodge, and Peter stopped. The sky had cleared, and a few brave stars winked at them. A dusty moon hung like a thumbnail.

"I don't think your friend Dmitri likes me." Peter studied her face as he said it, hoping he wouldn't see anything more than affection written there. He didn't miss the way the camp director had watched her all evening; the look in the man's eyes told him more than he wanted to know. He supposed he had revealed a matching expression that would keep Dmitri awake through the night as well.

"He's just being protective. Doesn't want me to get hurt."

Peter winced as the past opened its ugly jaws and roared to life.

Calli didn't look at him; instead she stared at the stars. "You said you never told your father about your call to be a missionary. Why?"

The question tightened his jaw. Tones of voice, comments from years ago flickered through his mind: *"Missionary work is for the poor and rejects of society, Son. You can do better."*

He sighed, wanting to turn away. But he owed her a part of the truth at least; he had to give her some reason why he'd sacrificed their future before the great Roland Samuelson.

"I wasn't sure, Calli. I'd spent four years preparing to go to law school, and I wasn't sure one emotional night before an altar was enough to change that."

"You pledged before God with me." Her voice was as soft as the breeze, but it pricked his skin.

"I know."

"I don't believe you're a coward, Peter. I know you have it in you to be a missionary, if God wants you to be."

Her words made his eyes burn. He turned away from her. "Thanks. I wish that was true."

He felt her hand on his arm but didn't surrender.

"The thing is, if God calls you to be a missionary, he'll help you be what he asks. Even if he wants you to be a corporate lawyer, he'll equip you for that."

"Maybe that's what I was supposed to be."

"Maybe. But I was there that night, and I saw your heart."

Her words lodged a lump in his throat. He grasped her hand and turned. The moonlight bathed her face in streams of pale light, and her misty blue eyes sent a quiver through him. He swallowed and summoned his voice. "It's been eight years. Maybe I've changed."

"You say your love for me hasn't changed." It sounded more like a question.

He caressed her face, pushed a lock of hair behind her ear. Softly he said, "No, it hasn't changed. I still love you."

She nodded, and her expression hardened. "Then your heart hasn't changed either. Inside that pressed . . . well . . . sort-of-pressed veneer—" a smile edged up her face—"is a man who wants to serve God with his whole heart."

He closed his eyes and drew her close, longing to know his own heart like Calli did. She wrapped her arms around his waist and held him. He wove one hand into the soft ringlets of her curls and the other around her back. Here, in her arms, inside her trust, he could live forever.

"Missionaries struggle with the same things you struggle with, Peter," she said against his shirt. "You don't have to be perfect to be a missionary. You just have to be willing."

He flinched, then slowly let her go. She stepped away and raised her gaze to his. He couldn't meet it.

"I'm leaving tomorrow," he said starkly. "I have a deal to close."

A cloud shifted across the moon, and her face darkened. With her eyes masked, he couldn't see them, but he sensed her feelings in the hurt that entered her voice. "You can sleep on the sofa in the lodge."

He stood there, watching her walk away toward the girls' cabin. Her footsteps were muffled by the soggy ground, but he shuddered at the emptiness echoing in his heart.

Calli tossed the night away on her canvas cot, praying, dreaming, wishing, aching at the distraught look on Peter's face. She'd been wrong when she told Peter he wasn't a coward. He *was* afraid. But not of Roland Samuelson, as she had suspected all these years. Of himself. Of giving in to God's call and failing. It was his fear that kept him from saying yes to God.

Tears ran into her ears. Dynamic Peter, who could talk a group of students into emptying the teachers' lounge of furniture and moving it onto the roof. Peter, who had waged an editorial war in the school paper with a professor over the sovereignty of God in the face of tragedy. Where had this un-Peter-like cowardice sprouted from?

And why had she allowed him to kiss her—again! She was some kind of glutton for heartache. A fool that melted in the face of gentle brown eyes and the touch of a strong hand weaving through her hair. Her lips still tingled.

She watched dawn sneak through the cabin windows, bathing the room in rose gold. Her fifteen girls, stacked in slumber on rows of bunk beds, wouldn't rise for another hour, but Calli's back screamed, her neck ached, and her heart wanted answers. She set her feet on the floor, pulled on her jeans and a sweatshirt. Grabbing her toothbrush and a towel, she jogged down to the ladies' washhouse and splashed herself awake. Having buffeted the onslaught of weariness, she started back up the trail to her cabin.

Peter was leaving today. Perhaps forever, despite his gallant words. If he couldn't get a grip on who God wanted him to be, he was no use to her, as much as it stung to admit it.

Her feet found their way to the lodge. She halted momentarily at the door, peering inside. Only a folded blanket lay on the tattered sofa. Frowning, Calli stepped inside. Peter's coat hung over a chair. She spied a stapled sheaf of papers lying on the seat. Calli picked it up and discovered it was the translated contract between STS and Georgivka for logging rights. She flicked her thumb on the paper, indictment streaming through her. She had no business reading it.

Abruptly, she turned and headed for the kitchen. Irina, the cook, had already started water boiling. Calli grabbed a mug and ladled in a spoonful of instant coffee. Pouring in the hot water, she stirred it to a dark mahogany, then found a spot at one of the long tables with the contract to discover what Peter was really up to.

Peter dipped his feet into the icy water. Jolts of pain shot up his legs, but he kept them in until they acclimated. Soon they were numb and matched his heart.

*"You don't have to be perfect to be a missionary. You just have to be willing."*

He palmed his chest, where the muscles clenched, and watched an eagle lift and soar across the surface of the river. Its wings dipped into the water as it scanned for breakfast. In a second, it had nabbed a fish and was again airborne, a lonely streak against the backdrop of the rose-and-lavender sky. If it weren't for the language, he'd think he was perched somewhere in northern Minnesota. Memory swept him back to a similar day eight years ago, before life crested over him, carrying him away to today. . . .

> *"This blanket taken?" He'd been watching the redhead for an hour.*
>
> *Sprawled tummy down on a stadium blanket, she was reading a textbook, highlighting passages like she was coloring. She looked up at him when he spoke, and he nearly drowned in the depths of her blue eyes. "I beg your pardon?"*

*He forced words through his dry mouth. "I said, can I sit by you?"*

*She narrowed her eyes, but a smile creased her face. "I've seen you on campus, haven't I?"*

*He crouched beside her and held out his hand. "Peter Samuelson, senior class president."*

*She cringed and shook his hand. "Calli Deane. Have a seat, Mr. President." He laughed, delighted in her honest embarrassment. She righted herself, sat crossed-legged, and flicked her hair back. The wind skimming off Lake Harriet gently teased it, fascinating him.*

*"Are you stalking me?" Her eyes glinted playfully.*

*A crimson maple leaf drifted onto the blanket. He picked it up and twirled it between two fingers. "Sort of. I sit two rows behind you in sociology, and I wanted to know what you're doing your term paper on."*

*She spiked an eyebrow. "Why?"*

*"Because the topic has me stumped. What's the most important issue threatening our culture today? There're too many."*

*"Pride."*

*Her eyes fixed on his, and he couldn't deny the ripples that coursed through him. "Pride?" he echoed weakly.*

*She pushed a pen up over her ear and drew a tiny blue line across her cheek, matching two others. He bit back a smile. "People can't admit they need God's help. They want to live life in their own strength, and they're more concerned about how they look than who they are."*

*"But that's how we make our mark on the world. We change it by the people we become."*

*"I couldn't agree more. But our mark shouldn't be made from our outward appearance, but our inner one."*

*He frowned and freed the leaf to the wind. "Our actions and life are a reflection of our inner person."*

*"I know; isn't that sad?" She tucked a chunk of hair behind her ear. The wind dislodged it. "If people would just surrender their pride and let God do the molding, he could change them from the inside out, and then they could change the world as they bless people's lives."*

*"One soul at a time, huh?"*

*"If God allows."*

Pride. Peter stared at his reflection streaming out over the water, watched it stretch and move with the ripples. Calli's words of wisdom echoed from the past and mingled with her statement under last night's heavenly gaze. Was he afraid, or was it his pride that refused to surrender to God's call? The glaring result of either meant that joining Calli in the vocation of missions was about as likely as his jumping from the Empire State Building. Both ideas generated the same amount of fear. No, his life had set its course and so had Calli's. Blowing out a labored breath, he climbed to his feet.

The lodge was quiet, but a stream of smoke curled from the chimney. Someone had stoked the fire. He'd enjoyed listening to it crackle through the night. It took his mind off the burning in his heart.

Calli sat at the long table. Her curly auburn hair hung over her face. She had a towel flung around her neck and rested her elbow on her drawn-up knee.

"Hey, there," he called cheerily, his spirit buoyed by her presence.

She looked up, and the anger on her face rocked him. He stumbled to a halt and put a steadying hand on the table. "What's the matter?"

Shaking her head, she pounced to her feet. Her eyes sizzled, and the set of her jaw made his chest constrict. "You lied. Again."

She stalked toward the door with white fists clenched, as if fleeing from the urge to belt him. He made to move after her, but suddenly she stopped and whirled. "Go home, Peter. I never want to see you again."

# CHAPTER SIX

"CALLI! Stop!" She could really motor when she wanted to. Peter leaped off the porch and scrambled to catch up to her. "Please, tell me what you're talking about." He grabbed her arm.

"You know." She stopped but didn't look at him, her posture rigid, her jaw stiff.

"No, I have no idea. How did I lie?"

"Your contract. You lied to me."

It physically hurt looking at her face and seeing the pain written there. He drew a deep breath and scraped his hand through his hair. "Back up. You read the contract?"

Her eyes nearly spit fire when she looked at him. "I know I shouldn't have, but I'm glad I did. Now at least I know your true intentions." She balled her hands at her sides. "Don't think for a second you're going to get away with it."

"Listen to me when I tell you I have no idea what you're talking about." He tried a pleading look.

Her stance relaxed . . . slightly. "Didn't you read the contract?"

"Of course."

She threw her hands in the air and looked heavenward.

Peter put his hands on her shoulders. She shrugged them off. "What don't I know here?" Frustration ignited his every nerve.

She narrowed her eyes and stared at him hard, as if peeling off layers to find his soul. "You better be telling the truth, Peter." Whirling, she stalked toward the lodge. He fell in step behind. Suspicion fueled him. What was in the contract that he didn't know about, and why did he sense Tomas's fingerprints on it?

Calli burst into the lodge, strode to the table, and picked up the papers. Flipping to the last page, she scanned until she found the right section. Then, pointing to it she read, " 'All existing labor will be utilized prior to seeking outside resources.' "

He blinked at her. She rolled the contract into a tube and handed it to him. "Follow me." Grabbing keys from a hook on the wall, she hollered something in Russian to the woman in the kitchen.

"Where are we going?" he said, melting into her long strides. It bothered him that she could be so beautiful when she was angry. Eyes a dark blue, hair tousled by the wind, she looked as if she could wrestle a grizzly.

"To the top of the world."

Calli tried not to slam the gas pedal into the floorboards, but Peter was such a fool! The tires kicked up mud behind them. The sun had burned away the clouds, leaving only the faintest streaking of cirrus under a turquoise sky. The logging road had taken serious hits during the recent storm, and Calli fought the wheel as the truck jarred into potholes.

"Slow down!" Peter had a hand braced on the dash and the other on the ceiling. He'd jammed his foot into the floorboards. "Where did you learn to drive?"

"Upstate New York. Hang on." She floored it, and they skimmed through a deep puddle, water flying over the top of the cab.

"Whatever you want to show me . . . you can just tell me. I can take it."

She harrumphed and leaned over the wheel.

The road dipped and curved through a spectacular pine forest, one Calli dearly loved to hike through. The grade grew steeper as they drove farther from the river. Calli shifted into low. "This is Bald Mountain. It's the highest point in the area." Her voice tightened. "And the base of logging ops in the area."

As they topped the hill, Calli's chest constricted to see it again. Beside her, Peter stiffened, gazing out over the swath of forest felled by broad-cut forestry. She stopped the pickup. They sat there in silence as Peter took in the miles and miles of acreage, cleaned out, regardless of age or size of tree.

He looked over at her, and she caught the pain on his face. "STS doesn't do this kind of rape of the wilderness," he said.

She leaned across him, opened the glove box, and pulled out binoculars. Wordlessly she handed them to him.

He frowned as he took them. Peering into the vast wilderness, she pointed at the operating machinery to the south.

He focused on it, and she knew he saw what she had intended when his mouth slacked. "Chinese?"

"North Korean. They ship them in by the hordes and keep them under lock and key. Maybe they're prisoners. I don't know what they pay them, but regardless, it's money the Russians don't earn."

Peter lowered the binoculars. His eyes darkened, and his voice turned solemn. "They don't pay them much, I can tell you that."

The look on his face ignited a delicious flow of memory. This was the old Peter. On fire, principled.

"Can I borrow this truck to get back to town?"

"Will you return it?"

He reached out to her, cupped his hand on her face, and rubbed a thumb along her cheekbone. The tender touch matched his expression. Oh, he could still turn her to slush with a look. She leaned into his hand and wanted to believe him when he replied, "As soon as I can."

๑

The little Lada pickup had guts, and Peter spent the first ten kilometers bumping against the speed limit. He gripped the steering wheel with white fists. His heartbeat had slowed to a steady, thunderous thump, but fury frayed his nerves. He recited reason in his head. Tomas had just made a mistake. Of course he wouldn't have known that the current operation utilized North Korean workers. Doubt nagged Peter, however, and tensed the muscles in his neck.

Peter cut his speed as he rolled into town, searching landmarks until he finally found the hotel. Sitting in the cab, he gulped a string of calming breaths. *I don't know what you are doing in my life, God, but make me wise and rational.*

He strode through the lobby and stopped himself from taking the steps two at a time. By the time he'd reached the fifth floor, a fine layer of perspiration dotted his forehead.

Dina's unmistakable laughter filtered through Tomas's door. Peter paused a moment before knocking, dearly hoping he wasn't interrupting anything he didn't want to know about.

Dina opened the door, and her smile faded. Dressed in a short leather skirt and a bright red cashmere sweater, she hooked one hand on her hip and ran her piercing gaze over him. "The boss returns. Have a good trip?"

"I need to talk to you both."

She opened the door wider and he stepped in. Tomas sat at the round table, shirtsleeves rolled up, an array of papers before him. "Hi, Peter. What can I do for you?" His face cracked a smile that didn't reach his eyes.

Peter scanned the papers littering the table. "I'm trying to give you both the benefit of the doubt here."

Tomas's fake smile dimmed and his face darkened. Dina glided up and gripped the back of Tomas's chair. Her trim eyebrows arched.

"The amendment you added to the last page of the contract was rather vague." Peter took off his coat and draped it over a straight-back chair. "Did you know the current labor force was North Korean?"

Dina and Tomas exchanged a look of surprise. Peter narrowed his eyes. Not enough surprise. "That's why the budget didn't balance, right, Tomas? You were planning on using the existing labor force, which just happens to be North Korean, not Russian."

Tomas wiped all pretenses from his face. He rolled a

pen between two fingers as he met Peter's eyes. "We're here to make a profit, not to save Russia."

"STS is not about scalping Russia." Peter braced a hand on the table, leaning into Tomas's glare. "I would like to see this country get back on its feet, and I want to start here in Georgivka."

"Since when did you turn into a philanthropist?"

Peter's jaw slacked. "I've never been shy about my goals here. Yes, I'd like to see STS grow, but not at the expense of Russians."

Tomas shot another glance at Dina, who shook her head and rolled her eyes.

Anger flared and bunched Peter's neck muscles. "I'd like to see this village pull itself out of poverty, but it needs our help. That's why we're here."

Tomas snorted. "You're such a fool! Russians are so used to handouts, they'll never be able to compete in the world market."

"I don't believe that."

Dina laughed. "Do you really think bringing more employment to Georgivka is going to help these people?"

Peter pinched his lips, fury eating his words.

Dina continued. "Even if they could afford better homes, better food, better clothes, it wouldn't change their character. More money just means more vodka on the table. Who do you think you are, preacher?"

Her words hit him like a slap. He reeled, blinking as he realized a portion of Dina's statement was right. She knew her countrymen, and while he couldn't embrace her cynicism, there was only one thing that could change the Russian soul from despair to hope.

Salvation. Jesus Christ. People like Calli bringing the Good News.

The thought made him wince. He tore his eyes away

from Dina and met Tomas's furious expression. The room still crackled with the sting of her words. Finally, Peter tapped the papers and in a shaky voice said, "Fix it. I want the amendment to specifically outline that we will use Russian labor."

Tomas shook his head.

Peter sent him a crippling look.

"Fine, but we're going to lose money."

Peter grabbed his coat. "There's more to life than making money."

"Not according to your father."

Peter slammed the door behind him.

Peter paced his room. Dina's laughter rang in his ears. He winced at his foolishness, the accuracy of her taunt. Yes, the intent he had in his heart was good—to help Russians. But it hit so far off the mark. So far off the pledge he made years ago at the foot of an altar. His own words streamed from the past and filled his ears: *"I will go where you want me to go, God, do what you want me to do."*

Calli had been on her knees beside him, sobbing. The moment of their surrender had bonded them—and that bond had never been broken. For eight years God had been tugging at his heart and had to bring him to Siberia to finally break his stubborn will. Peter had been deceiving himself to dismiss the call, to relegate it to the emotion of the moment, a response to the eloquent plea of the speaker.

God wanted his whole heart. And he wasn't going to stop dogging Peter until he surrendered. Thankfully. Peter cupped a hand over the back of his neck, kneading the taut muscle.

A rap at the door made him jump. He stalked over to it and flung it open.

Dina walked past him into the room.

Peter kept the door open. "Can I help you?"

She put a hand on the knob and closed it. "Maybe I can help you." She moved toward him. "I sense you're rather tense. I thought you might want to talk." She fingered his collar.

Peter's eyes widened. "I don't think so, Dina."

She pouted. And moved closer. Her perfume washed over him. Every nerve bristled.

"We can work this out, Peter. Don't be so idealistic." She touched his face. He clenched his jaw. "STS is helping people. Georgivka will have more shipping, and they are receiving a payout for the logging rights. I shouldn't have been so hard on you." She traced her manicured finger down to the hollow of his neck.

He grabbed her hand and pushed it away. "No, you were right. Russia needs to change from the inside out. They need hope. That's what I want to give them."

Her ruby lips curled into a sardonic smile. "How are you going to do that?"

"I'm not sure. Maybe by telling them about Jesus Christ."

She laughed. "You? Who is going to listen to you?" She shook her head. "Tomas may call you preacher, but I think I can persuade you that you're a man just like every other." She trailed a finger down his arm.

Peter moved toward the door, his mouth dry. All he could do was open it and glower at her.

Hurt crested in her eyes. "I don't understand you, Peter." She shook her head again and marched out.

Peter closed the door and sagged against it. Burying his hands in his hair, he slid down to the floor and groaned. He didn't understand himself either. What made him think he could make a difference? A few years ago, he might have reacted to Dina's suggestion, and the realization made him shudder. He was no man of God, no preacher. He'd made too many mistakes, veered too far off the path to be of any use to God now. He'd blown his chance, and all the good intentions in the world would never make him worthy to share the gospel.

Peter was surprised to feel tears cooling on his cheeks. He closed his eyes. *I know you've forgiven me for my mistakes, my rejection. But I've changed too much, God. How could you ever use someone like me?*

His heart chilled as he climbed to his feet. Dina was right. Who would ever listen to him? He'd close the deal and leave Calli to do the work of the righteous.

"Are you going to sit or pace?" Dmitri watched Calli's catlike movements, and she felt the pressure of a blush move up her face.

She sank into a chair across from him in the lodge office and hung her head in her hands. "I can't dodge the feeling he needs me."

The revelation made Dmitri sigh.

She felt his disappointment to her bones. "I'm sorry, Dmitri."

Dmitri tapped a pen against his knee, not looking at her. "I saw your eyes, your face. You didn't touch the ground once when he was here."

She gulped the lump in her throat.

"Ride the bus into town tomorrow," he suggested.

Tears edged her eyes.

"He's a good man, Calli. And I watched him with you. He loves you."

Calli pushed her fingers into the corners of her eyes. Tears flowed over them. She heard movement, and suddenly Dmitri was on his knees before her. He took her hands in his. "God's not finished yet," he said solemnly.

# CHAPTER SEVEN

PETER smoothed his tie down and buttoned his coat. His insides were coiled rattler tight, and Tomas's pacing wasn't helping in the least.

"Hedstrom's upping his offer right now," Tomas growled under his breath, but loud enough to rankle Peter, "and if he gets the logging rights, he'll actually make money!"

Peter clenched his jaw. "We stand to make a tidy profit as well, Tomas, even with the labor clause."

Tomas angled him a dark look and shoved his hands into his pockets. "Roland isn't going to be pleased."

Peter bit back a retort. He'd paced his room for half the night mulling over that reality. Perhaps it was time, however, for his father to smack face first into the Christian principles he touted at church. If STS wasn't willing to extend a hand to the underdog, then it shouldn't have a Christian at the helm. The conviction steeled Peter's resolve.

The door cracked. A petite brunette dressed in a black suit stepped out and indicated for them to enter. Peter filed in behind Dina and Tomas. Dina had sent a cold front in his direction since he walked into the office this morning, and now she straightened her shoulders, lifted her chin, and quickened her leggy stride.

Peter shook the hand of the mayor and sat down at the table. Mayor Shubin folded fat hands in front of him and stared at Peter with a solemn face and his pudgy lips drawn into a flat line. He cleared his throat and spoke in Russian.

Dina translated, monotone. "Mr. Hedstrom has laid a new offer on the table. His offer tops yours by one percent."

Peter palmed the black leather folder in front of him.

"And Mr. Hedstrom's offer includes a larger land package. It means more revenue for the workers, a longer contract."

"Can I see Mr. Hedstrom's proposal?" Peter asked. Dina translated like a robot.

Mayor Shubin shrugged and handed over a sheaf of papers. Peter took it and felt all eyes on him as he flipped through the offering. Turning to the final page, he stared at the tract of land Hedstrom was asking for. His breath lodged in his chest, and he struggled to keep emotion from coloring his face.

"Tell Mayor Shubin that we'll match Mr. Hedstrom's offer, without including the extra land."

"What?" Tomas hissed.

Peter held up a hand while Dina translated. Her voice shook slightly.

"Are you nuts, Peter? Your father will skin you alive."

Peter shot him a warning look.

Mayor Shubin addressed Dina, who translated, "Why don't you want the land?"

Peter looked at the contract. "I do want it. I want them to deed it to Dmitri Dobran for a camp." A smile lit inside, but he kept it from his expression.

Blood drained from Dina's face.

"Translate, please," Peter reminded her.

Stiffly, Dina translated. The mayor eyed him suspiciously. He leaned over and conferred with the panel, who were also scanning Peter with obvious skepticism.

"Tell them I want it for a children's camp . . . for the territory."

He saw the smile poke at Dina's lips and a glimmer of something unfamiliar in her eyes. She turned his statement into Russian.

Next to him, Tomas seethed. Peter could almost feel his coworker's burning stare peeling his skin. Peter drummed his fingers on the notebook.

Suddenly, the mayor took to his feet. He extended a hand to Peter.

As Peter took it, an unfamiliar satisfaction engulfed him. He pumped the mayor's hand, riding a current of joy stronger than the euphoria of success. "Tell him we'll draw up the contract by the end of the day."

Dina rose also. When she turned to Peter, he saw tears shimmering in her eyes.

He frowned.

"Maybe I misjudged you," she whispered before following Tomas out of the room.

"You are a fool!" Tomas prowled the room, his hands on his hips. Peter leaned a hip on the edge of his desk, watching the junior vice president unravel. "You have the business sense of a goat!"

Peter clenched his jaw. "You may be right, Tomas. But for some reason I think I am here to save that little bit of land."

"For what reason? To give it to a bunch of kids?" Tomas threw his hands in the air. "Besides, that's not your money to spend. That's STS cash you just committed. Your father could have you jailed."

Peter drew a deep breath. "You forget I'm the president's son. STS not only has the cash, but I am authorized to spend it. Besides, this is a good move for the company. We've endeared ourselves to the community, and we've done a good thing for the kids here. They need this camp."

"I couldn't agree more." Dina came over and sat beside Peter. "That was a good thing you did, Peter. Maybe you are the preacher Tomas says."

Tomas snorted.

Peter blinked at her, started to protest, then squinted at her in confusion. "Thanks," he rasped. He stood on wobbly knees. "I need some air. Can you type up the new contract while I'm out?"

Dina smiled. "With pleasure, boss."

The sun glinted between portly gray-white clouds, and the wind carried the fresh aroma of spring. Peter turned up his collar and headed down the boulevard toward the market. The smell of a charcoal grill reached out and reeled him in. Suddenly his stomach growled, craving one of Calli's shish kebabs. Setting a course for the meat stand, he kept his head down and tried not to let the memory of his last visit to the market rattle him. He found the food vendor and bought a stick of fat, juicy meat.

Dina's words ricocheted through his mind: *"Maybe I misjudged you."*

No, she hadn't misjudged him. They'd both misjudged God. For the first time in his life, Peter felt used of God. The feeling swelled through his soul and nearly turned him inside out. He'd saved Calli's camp. He couldn't wait to tell her.

Calli. She wasn't going to leave her camp. His heart fell. She loved her work. Joy shimmered on her face when kids surrounded her. Watching her as she moved among them, speaking to each one in a different language, he knew he couldn't ask her to give it up. His chest clenched.

He walked through the hotel parking lot, around the building, and down the trail to the spot where he and Calli had eaten dinner. Sitting on the stone wall overlooking the river, he ate his shish kebab slowly, listening to a woodpecker drill a far-off tree. The sun had moved to the western side of the sky and was turning a deep crimson. Calli had crimson highlights in her hair. He swallowed his last bite of meat, appreciating Calli's taste in food.

Perhaps he could come to enjoy this land she now called home. Perhaps, just as God had used him to save Calli's camp, God could use him to deliver eternity to the souls of the lost. Hadn't God done that with another Peter ages ago . . . a rough fisherman who had to do nothing but obey? "Do you love me?" Jesus had asked that Peter.

Peter recalled the Scripture as if it had been spoken aloud. Gooseflesh raised on his arm. He flicked a gaze heavenward. "Feed my sheep," Jesus had instructed the fisherman. Laying the kebab stick on the stone wall, Peter wiped his fingers on a napkin and swallowed a forming lump.

A sudden blow to the back of his neck knocked him off the wall. Pain spiked into his head and down his arms as dirt embedded his palms. He gasped in a ragged breath. Another shot to his kidneys pushed the air from him. He dragged a gaze up toward his attacker but was blinded by a crushing blow to his shoulder. Agony exploded down his arm, and his face hit the ground. The last thing he felt was intense heat searing through his head and plunging him into darkness.

Calli stepped off the bus in Georgivka. The sun, hidden behind the Intourist Hotel, sent long shadows streaking across the parking lot. Calli spied the camp pickup in the lot, and a wave of anticipation started at her toes and crested through her. She barely maintained a walk as she headed toward the lobby.

A half hour later, settled into a room and freshly showered, she pulled on a pair of black jeans and a red sweater. Adding a dab of perfume to her wrists and neck, she laughed at her silliness. Still, she couldn't help wanting Peter to find her beautiful, overwhelming. She was, after all, a woman, even if she had spent the better part of the last four years tromping about the forest.

Pausing at the window, she stared out toward the river at the sun sinking quickly into the far horizon. The sky had darkened to a deep magenta, and the sun had surrendered feebly, scuttling under the horizon under a cover of slate gray clouds. The wind had shifted, streaming from the north, stirring the river current into white-caps.

Calli rubbed her arms, bracing herself for a storm. Her skin prickled, the foreboding doom that had blanketed her journey into town hovering like a guillotine. She drove it away with the thought of Peter's warm honeyed eyes, his muscled arms around her, laughter she could cocoon herself inside for eternity. Closing her eyes, she bit her trembling lip. *Lord, I give you this relationship. Please help me to trust you, no matter what happens.*

She took the stairs slowly, willing herself not to skip. Peter's floor was silent, and as she rapped on his door, she heard no movement. Her heart fell, but she headed back to her room. He was probably still at his meeting. The expression on his face when he'd left told her the forest and the Russians were in good hands. She lifted a prayer for him, praying his contract negotiations had gone as he hoped.

Calli sat in her room, reading her Bible. Twilight turned to pitch, and somewhere in the black expanse, angry clouds began to spit on her windows. Calli checked Peter's room twice more without an answer. Worry strummed her nerves despite her attempts to stay calm.

Surrendering to hunger, she padded down to the lobby. A stream of welcoming fluorescence flowed from the gift shop. Calli browsed, killing time, then bought a Snickers bar and a bottle of apple juice.

Turning, she nearly mowed down the dark-haired beauty she'd met in Peter's room. "Excuse me!" Calli stammered.

The woman's eyes glistened. "Have you seen Peter?"

Something hard landed in Calli's chest. She shook her head.

The woman took her elbow, drawing her out of the gift shop. Her voice was low. "He never came back to the office." She glanced around the lobby. "I think something happened to him."

Calli swallowed the dread lumping her throat. "Why?"

The woman's voice broke. "Tomas was very, very

angry. He thought Shubin would take Hedstrom's offer for sure. But Peter outmaneuvered him."

Calli scowled.

"Tomas set Peter up. He knew the mayor would see through the clause about the laborers. That was one of the biggest reasons they broke their contract with Thompson Timber, the company who held the previous logging rights. As they negotiated, Peter kept offering them more and more, finally adding the amendment about using Russian labor. Still, Tomas thought Hedstrom had the contract until Peter changed the deal and offered the camp. She swallowed and Calli felt her fear through the grip on her elbow. "Tomas scares me."

Calli struggled to focus. "Do you think Tomas would hurt Peter?"

The expression on the woman's face sent a chill up Calli's spine. Summoning her composure, Calli gripped her hand. It was icy. "Don't worry; God isn't finished yet."

She nodded. "My name is Dina, by the way."

"Calli."

A sheepish smile flickered on Dina's flawless face. "Tomas told me to go to Peter's room that night. Nothing happened."

Calli's jaw opened. She immediately clamped it shut and nodded. "Thank you." Dina's eyes filmed with tears, and Calli's heart washed with pity. She gathered the woman into her arms.

"I'm sorry," Dina said on a wisp of breath.

Calli nodded again. "Listen, you go call the police. I'll see if I can find Peter."

Dina swerved her gaze outside, at the pitch darkness and hammer of rain on the window.

Calli squeezed her hand and dashed toward the door.

*Please, oh please, Lord.* Calli flicked on her flashlight, pushing back a one-meter block of darkness. Rain fell in thick sheets, slicing through the light like needles, then disappearing into blackness before pelting the ground. Calli called again as she headed back from the market. Water ran rivers down her face and into her collar. She'd zipped her parka to her nose, but the coat had surrendered to the downpour only moments after Calli dashed out into the rain and feebly tried to ward off a vicious chill. Calli started to run, eyes on the ground. Her feet were blocks of ice, her nose numb. *Please, God, help me find him!*

Earlier, the hotel security had opened Peter's door, and Dina and Calli exchanged hollow looks at Peter's barren, tidied room. Calli had left her new friend wringing her hands in the lobby while she dashed out into the rain.

Returning to the hotel, she saw three militia cars pulled up to the drive. Hope lit a warm fire inside her and she sprinted the last few meters, sliding into the foyer like a gale.

Dina stood in the middle of the group, her hair in strings over her drawn face. Two officers stood beside her, questioning her. She had a manicured nail to her mouth, chewing it.

Calli strode over and put a reassuring grip on her elbow. "Nothing yet?"

Dina met her gaze with red-rimmed eyes. "They can't find Tomas. Or Hedstrom."

Calli groaned.

"Excuse me, do you speak Russian?"

Calli nodded at a young officer with a jacket two sizes too large and a sprout of hair over his upper lip.

"Is there any place your friend might go? Any special place?"

Then it hit her. Calli felt adrenaline rush to her legs. She whirled and ran toward the door. She fell twice racing down the path, but the pain in her knees and hands vanished the minute she saw Peter's dark form, crumpled by the wall of the riverside patio. She skidded to her knees beside him.

The rain had washed his wound clean, but she saw the gash on the side of his head and flinched. His face was as white as chalk, his lips purple. She worked a hand inside his coat and found a thready pulse.

Light flickered through the swill of the storm. "Over here!" she shrieked. Rocking slightly, she slid a hand under his face, between his cheek and the ground. It was as cold as her heart. "Please, Peter, don't die," she begged as tears blinded her and mingled with the spray of rain on her face.

# CHAPTER EIGHT

IODINE and starch. Bright lights piercing the depths to find him, claw at him, beckon him forward.

Peter frowned and slowly blinked his eyes open. Confusion knotted his chest and tightened his fists as he scanned the room. Green cement walls. A cart holding white porcelain pots painted with letters in bold red Cyrillic. A gray, dusty ceiling. Cotton sheets pulled up to his chest. Voices, unfamiliar, jumbled.

Peter winced from the pressure in his head, and a dull ache in his lower back made him shift. He couldn't move his left arm. Panic tensed every muscle until he crawled his fingers across his chest and felt a rough web of plaster encircling it. Breaths came, deep and labored.

"You're awake."

A familiar voice. Peter searched for it, and in a second his heart jolted to see Roland Samuelson staring over him.

Peter licked his parched lips, but no words formed. He frowned again.

"How do you feel?"

Peter rolled his eyes to the ceiling, assessing. "Broken," he rasped.

A smile split the man's chiseled face, creasing thick wrinkles around dark brown eyes that always reminded Peter of a hawk.

"Where am I?"

"The hospital. Someone beaned you good and left you in the rain."

Peter blew out a breath, letting those words sink in and scanning his memory.

"You've been out for three days. I'm sorry I couldn't get here earlier. I just arrived and was making arrangements to rescue you from this backwoods butcher shop."

"I remember the sunset."

His father laughed. "You would."

"And Calli."

"Who?"

Peter scowled. "Calli Deane. She's here. In Siberia."

Roland shrugged. "Sorry, Son, I haven't seen anyone." He sat on the opposite bed and made a face like he'd infected himself. "I signed the contract you made with Georgivka."

Peter's eyes widened. "Did they deed the camp—?"

"Good thinking. Dina says you're a bit of a local hero. Hedstrom's plan would have taken out the camp and sent Georgivka's economy into a downward spiral." He shook his head. "You're turning into quite the businessman."

"Hedstrom offered them more money."

"Hedstrom is a liar and a thief. He was going to use North Korean prisoners for labor and scalp the forest. You gave this community a fighting chance. And—" he smiled in a way Peter knew well—"you made STS a good bundle of money. I'm just sorry you had your shoulder dislocated in the process."

"How did it happen?"

"You don't know who hit you?"

Peter shook his head.

"Tomas. Hedstrom bribed him shortly after you all arrived in Georgivka. Tomas has been trying to sabotage you ever since."

Peter winced. "The attack in the market?"

"And Dina mentioned some sort of laxative in the gravy."

"Pork chops," Peter hissed through clenched teeth. "I am such an idiot!"

Roland held up his hands as if to stop him. "The Russian Security caught Tomas and Hedstrom boarding a plane in St. Petersburg."

Peter reached up and rubbed the back of his neck where his muscles were bunching in suppressed fury.

His father saw the gesture and knocked him lightly on his chest cast. "I'll see if I can get you out of here and back home today." He stood and his eyes raked over Peter. "I'm proud of you. You may not be as hard-nosed as your old man, but you've got business savvy. STS is going to have a good man at the helm someday."

Calli stood in the hallway. Her apple juice shook in her hand, and she felt a sick acid welling in her stomach. Peter was going home. To take over STS. She hung her head and chided herself for her foolish dreams. She should have known better than to trust him.

Her heart stuck somewhere around her knees; she turned and shuffled down the hall.

"No, it won't, sir." Peter arched up on one elbow as his father stopped in his tracks. "God has different plans for my life."

Roland turned, eyebrows pinched.

"I think God brought me here for a bigger reason than to make STS a great deal and help Georgivka. I think he also brought me here to continue a work he started in my life eight years ago. A work he isn't finished with yet."

Roland took a step toward him, dark eyes glinting.

"I'm going to be a missionary."

Peter saw anger flood his father's face. To Roland's credit, he contained it and kept his voice low. "Don't be a fool. Missionaries are weak and outcasts in society. You have everything. Money, looks, position. Don't waste your life."

Peter took in his father's pressed suit, his gleaming watch, his polished wing tips. "There's nothing wrong with those things—for you. But God wants something different for my life. Obedience. I think in God's economy, this is the best investment I could ever make. It's God who measures the worth of a man, not money, looks, or position. It's how I look in God's eyes that I care about."

"Of course." Roland's all-business tone took control. "But imagine all you can accomplish for God by heading STS. The money you could make for the church—and missions."

Peter shook his head. "It's not about what I can do for God. It's about what God wants to do for me. Maybe he could even make me into the man he wants me to be."

Roland's jaw pulsed. "Can't he do that at STS?"

"I'm sure he could. But I don't think that's his plan."

"You can't throw away everything your mother and I sacrificed for you! I didn't help you climb the STS ladder so that you could jump from the top."

Peter saw the years of schooling, the advantages he'd been given written on his father's furious expression. "I'm not ungrateful, sir. I appreciate everything you've done. But I can't ignore God any longer. Not without regretting it for the rest of my life."

"Do you honestly think people will listen to you?"

"You're the one that said I was the local hero," Peter reminded lightly, but the past roared up in his ears, taunting him. Peter fought it with hope. "It's not even about who I am, but rather who God is. Maybe he can take even a selfish corporate lawyer and use him for good. Maybe even eternal good."

Roland narrowed his eyes. "I hope you know what you're giving up." Then he stalked out the door.

"Calli, please come out of the tent. I promise, it doesn't look bad."

"Don't lie to me, Dmitri. I know I look like I have a runaway case of chicken pox." Calli angled the quarter-sized compact mirror and dabbed calamine lotion on the blisters creeping up her neck and jaw. "That is the last time I'm playing capture the flag in the woods."

Dmitri's laughter made her bristle. "Go away. I have twenty-four hours before the next batch of kids arrive, and I am going to pray this stuff away."

"I'll set your dinner outside your door, Poison Ivy Queen."

"Get!"

She heard him tromp away, glee lightening his step. Scowling into the mirror, she couldn't decide if she looked better with a red-and-white rash prickling her skin or with the marmalade orange lotion covering it. Snapping her compact shut, she flopped back on the cot and stared at the ceiling. A month later it still hurt to think of him, and it was in lonely moments like this that Peter's face roared up from its captive place in her heart to haunt her. She felt her eyes filling and quickly blinked. Tears would smear the allergic rash across her face.

Sitting up, she stuck her feet into her hiking boots. With the campers gone, only the rustle of a gentle wind through the trees broke the silence.

Calli stepped out of the tent. A magpie noticed and called out. The July sun winked from a nearly cloudless sky and jutted rays through the forest in shafts of light. Calli couldn't help but inhale deeply the smell of balsam, wildflowers, and feel the breath of peace. Walking toward the river, she veered a wide detour around the lodge and treaded down the path.

The sun dappled the tiny peaks of current in the river, and they glinted like fragments of glass. Calli sat on the dock and peered into the water, scanning for fish. The sun illuminated the depths and turned the stones at the bottom to jewels.

A shadow loomed over her, streaming out across the water, a dark swatch over the river. "Go away, Dmitri. Just because I emerged from my hideout doesn't mean I am accepting visitors."

"What a shame. I've come such a long way, and bearing presents as well."

The voice stopped her heart cold. Calli swallowed, horror fisting her chest in a death grip.

"Aren't you going to turn around and greet me?"

"No."

Silence. The dock creaked as Peter shifted his weight. Calli froze.

"I'm sorry it took so long for me to get back here. I had a dislocated shoulder and a few other rumples to smooth out."

"I didn't expect you."

"I told you I'd come back . . . as soon as I could."

Calli heard the hurt in his voice. She licked her parched lips, forcing words past the ball of memory lodged in her throat. "I heard you at the hospital. You're going to take over STS."

"I resigned."

Calli gripped the dock to keep from turning around. But the desire to fling herself into his arms engulfed her, pitching her voice high. "Why?"

"I'm not supposed to be there." His knees cracked as he knelt behind her. She felt his strong, wide hand on her shoulder and closed her eyes.

"I'm supposed to be here. With you. Eight years is a long time to veer off God's path. Will you help me find it again?"

Her eyes misted. "I think you found it just fine, Peter. You don't need me."

She fought the gentle pressure to turn. "Yes, I do. You're the one I long for, the one I need to spend my life serving God with."

Her voice caught and came out ragged. "I'm not beautiful."

He groaned. "You're not just beautiful, Calli. You're breathtaking. That's what God does to a woman who serves him. Turns her irresistible." The pressure on her shoulder increased. "Please turn around."

Cringing, she turned. She couldn't meet his eyes.

He laughed but gentled it by cupping his hand on her face. "You look great in orange. Matches your hair."

He nudged her chin upward, while searching for her eyes. She met his gaze and nearly melted at the warmth in it. "I love you, Calli. Will you marry me?"

Calli bit her lip. A tear crested and rolled down her cheek.

"I brought you something." Eyes twinkling, he reached inside his coat. Calli braced herself, not knowing what she'd say if he produced a ring. Could she say yes to a man who'd crushed her heart, not once, but three times?

He pulled out a bottle of diet Coke. Calli put a hand to her mouth. Then laughter bubbled through.

"Wait, I have another gift."

Her eyes widened as her heart thundered.

He tugged a crumpled white bag from his coat pocket. "I hope it's still fresh."

With trembling hands, she opened the offering. "A honey-wheat bagel! Peter, you rascal! I was expecting—"

"I have that too." Reaching into his inside pocket again, he pulled out a small velvet box. He flipped it open. The sunlight glinted off a simple solitaire diamond. "Be my wife, please. If you don't, God's going to flatten my tires or break my leg or something until you say yes."

Calli laughed. Peter's eyes roamed over her, falling on her hair, her eyes, her lips. He reached out and pushed an errant lock behind her ear, then sent ripples up her spine as he caressed her cheek with his thumb.

"Can I think about it?"

Peter nodded, a rapscallion smile tweaking the corner of his mouth. Then he lowered his face and kissed her. His touch, gentle and tentative on her lips, sent waves of warmth flowing through her veins. When he wrapped a hand around her neck and deepened his kiss, her insides danced with delight. Drawing back slightly, he leaned his forehead on hers. "You have all summer. I'm your new sports director."

Calli's jaw slacked. Peter kissed her forehead. "And it's going to take me that long to get rid of the poison ivy you just gave me."

Calli palmed his chest, pushed, and he fell back, laughing.

"Hey, Calli!" Dmitri stood on the lodge porch, waving. Calli cupped a hand over her eyes and waved back. He lifted a lumpy bag. "Guess what your friend brought!"

Calli glanced at Peter.

He shrugged, and oh my, did that blush look good on him. "Baseballs," he admitted.

She scooted toward him on her knees, reached for the collar of his shirt, and kissed him full on the lips. "Yes, my hapless American. I'll marry you."

# A NOTE FROM THE AUTHOR

*Dear Friend,*

*I've always wondered why God called me into missions. I never felt particularly gifted in evangelism or leading Bible studies, yet I knew, even as a child, that God had called me to be a missionary. It wasn't until I was on the mission field that I realized that my biggest qualification was a heart willing to follow where God led. More than that, I realized that being a missionary wasn't so much about what I could do for God, but rather how he was working in me.*

*Throughout the years, I've shared my struggles and joys about missionary life through our ministry newsletter and increasingly felt God's call to write Christian fiction that would touch lives. I've been writing since the first grade, when I won a book writing contest, and journalizing my prayers and walk with Christ since I was a teenager.*

*Calli and Peter's story is in many ways my own—the two faces in my mirror. I've even lived Peter's frustration, locked in an elevator on a frigid Siberian night, and I share Calli's longing for bagels and diet Coke. Perhaps what we share the most is the knowledge that, through the struggles and the joys of missionary life, God is always sufficient and able to do more than is expected or imagined for those with a willing heart.*

*I pray that Calli and Peter's story will bless you with the thought that God looks at our hearts, not our performance, and loves us dearly.*

*Susan Warren*

## ABOUT THE AUTHOR

Susan Warren is a career missionary with SEND International serving with her husband and four children in Khabarovsk, Far East Russia, where she divides her time between homeschooling, ministry, and writing. She holds a B.A. in mass communications from the University of Minnesota and has been published in numerous Christian magazines and devotional books. This is her first novella.

Susan invites you to visit her Web site at www.warren.khv.ru. She also welcomes letters written to her in care of Tyndale House Author Relations, P.O. Box 80, Wheaton, IL 60189-0080, or you can e-mail her at susanwarren@mail.com.

**CURRENT HEARTQUEST RELEASES**

- *Magnolia,* Ginny Aiken
- *Lark,* Ginny Aiken
- *Camellia,* Ginny Aiken
- *Letters of the Heart,* Lisa Tawn Bergren, Maureen Pratt, and Lyn Cote
- *Sweet Delights,* Terri Blackstock, Elizabeth White, and Ranee McCollum
- *Awakening Mercy,* Angela Benson
- *Abiding Hope,* Angela Benson
- *Ruth,* Lori Copeland
- *Roses Will Bloom Again,* Lori Copeland
- *Faith,* Lori Copeland
- *Hope,*Lori Copeland
- *June,* Lori Copeland
- *Glory,* Lori Copeland
- *Winter's Secret,* Lyn Cote
- *Autumn's Shadow,* Lyn Cote
- *Freedom's Promise,* Dianna Crawford
- *Freedom's Hope,* Dianna Crawford
- *Freedom's Belle,* Dianna Crawford
- *A Home in the Valley,* Dianna Crawford
- *Prairie Rose,* Catherine Palmer
- *Prairie Fire,* Catherine Palmer
- *Prairie Storm,* Catherine Palmer
- *Prairie Christmas,* Catherine Palmer, Elizabeth White, and Peggy Stoks
- *Finders Keepers,* Catherine Palmer
- *Hide & Seek,* Catherine Palmer
- *English Ivy,* Catherine Palmer
- *A Kiss of Adventure,* Catherine Palmer (original title: *The Treasure of Timbuktu*)
- *A Whisper of Danger,* Catherine Palmer (original title: *The Treasure of Zanzibar*)
- *A Touch of Betrayal,* Catherine Palmer
- *A Victorian Christmas Keepsake,* Catherine Palmer, Kristin Billerbeck, and Ginny Aiken
- *A Victorian Christmas Cottage,* Catherine Palmer, Debra White Smith, Jeri Odell, and Peggy Stoks
- *A Victorian Christmas Quilt,* Catherine Palmer, Peggy Stoks, Debra White Smith, and Ginny Aiken
- *A Victorian Christmas Tea,* Catherine Palmer, Dianna Crawford, Peggy Stoks, and Katherine Chute
- *A Victorian Christmas Collection,* Peggy Stoks
- *Olivia's Touch,* Peggy Stoks
- *Romy's Walk,* Peggy Stoks
- *Elena's Song,* Peggy Stoks
- *Chance Encounters of the Heart,* Elizabeth White, Kathleen Fuller, and Susan Warren

HEART
QUEST

## HEARTWARMING ANTHOLOGIES FROM HEARTQUEST

*A Victorian Christmas Collection*—Now available in one volume, four delightful Christmas novellas from beloved author Peggy Stoks: "Tea for Marie" (originally published in *A Victorian Christmas Tea*); "Crosses and Losses" (originally published in *A Victorian Christmas Quilt*); "The Beauty of the Season" (originally published in *A Victorian Christmas Cottage*); and "Wishful Thinking" (originally published in *Prairie Christmas*).

*Letters of the Heart*—What says romance more than a handwritten letter from the one you love? Open these historical treasures from beloved authors Lisa Tawn Bergren, Maureen Pratt, and Lyn Cote and discover the words of love that hold two hearts together.

*A Victorian Christmas Keepsake*—Return to a time when life was uncomplicated, faith was sincere . . . and love was a gift to be cherished forever. These three Christmas novellas will touch your heart and stir you to treasure your own keepsakes of life, love, and romance. Curl up next to the fire with this heartwarming, faith-filled collection of original love stories by beloved romance authors Catherine Palmer, Kristin Billerbeck, and Ginny Aiken.

*Sweet Delights*—Who would have thought chocolate could be so good for your heart? A cup of tea and a few quiet moments are all you need to enjoy these tasty, calorie-free morsels from beloved romance authors Terri Blackstock, Elizabeth White, and Ranee McCollum. Each story is followed by a letter from the author and her favorite chocolate recipe!

*Prairie Christmas*—In "The Christmas Bride," by Catherine Palmer, Rolf Rustemeyer can hardly wait for the arrival of his Christmas bride, all the way from Germany. You'll love this heartwarming Christmas visit with friends old and new from A Town Called Hope. Anthology also includes "Reforming Seneca Jones" by Elizabeth White and "Wishful Thinking" by Peggy Stoks.

*A Victorian Christmas Cottage*—Four novellas centering around hearth and home at Christmastime. Stories by Catherine Palmer, Debra White Smith, Jeri Odell, and Peggy Stoks.

*A Victorian Christmas Tea*—Four novellas about life and love at Christmastime. Stories by Catherine Palmer, Dianna Crawford, Peggy Stoks, and Katherine Chute.

*A Victorian Christmas Quilt*—A patchwork of four novellas about love and joy at Christmastime. Stories by Catherine Palmer, Peggy Stoks, Debra White Smith, and Ginny Aiken.

## OTHER GREAT TYNDALE HOUSE FICTION

- *Safely Home,* Randy Alcorn

- *Jenny's Story,* Judy Baer
- *Libby's Story,* Judy Baer
- *Tia's Story,* Judy Baer

- *Out of the Shadows,* Sigmund Brouwer
- *The Leper,* Sigmund Brouwer
- *Crown of Thorns,* Sigmund Brouwer

- *Looking for Cassandra Jane,* Melody Carlson

- *Child of Grace,* Lori Copeland

- *They Shall See God,* Athol Dickson

- *Ribbon of Years,* Robin Lee Hatcher
- *Firstborn,* Robin Lee Hatcher

- *The Touch,* Patricia Hickman

- *Redemption,* Gary Smalley and Karen Kingsbury

- *The Price,* Jim and Terri Kraus
- *The Treasure,* Jim and Terri Kraus
- *The Promise,* Jim and Terri Kraus
- *The Quest,* Jim and Terri Kraus

- *Winter Passing,* Cindy McCormick Martinusen
- *Blue Night,* Cindy McCormick Martinusen
- *North of Tomorrow,* Cindy McCormick Martinusen

- *Embrace the Dawn,* Kathleen Morgan

- *Lullaby,* Jane Orcutt

- *The Happy Room,* Catherine Palmer
- *A Dangerous Silence,* Catherine Palmer

- *Unveiled*, Francine Rivers
- *Unashamed*, Francine Rivers
- *Unshaken*, Francine Rivers
- *Unspoken,* Francine Rivers
- *Unafraid,* Francine Rivers
- *A Voice in the Wind,* Francine Rivers
- *An Echo in the Darkness,* Francine Rivers
- *As Sure As the Dawn,* Francine Rivers
- *Leota's Garden,* Francine Rivers

- *Shaiton's Fire,* Jake Thoene